AUNT BESSIE REMEMBERS

AN ISLE OF MAN COZY MYSTERY

DIANA XARISSA

✿ Created with Vellum

For David and Catherine.

AUTHOR'S NOTE

I seem to be getting through the alphabet rather quickly now. For those of you who are new to the series, this is book eighteen, and the series is best read in order, alphabetically by the last word in the title. Each book is a complete story, but the characters do change and develop as the series progresses.

Aunt Bessie first appeared in my romance *Island Inheritance.* Sadly, she'd just passed away in that book, so the cozy mysteries are set about fifteen years before the romance. (The first Bessie was set in April, 1998, and they have progressed monthly since then.)

Those of you who read my Isle of Man Ghostly Cozy series will be familiar with Mona Kelly, the ghost who shares the main character's apartment with her. I couldn't resist having Mona make an appearance here, giving you a chance to see her when she was alive and well. I hope you enjoy her as much as I do.

This is a work of fiction and the author has created all of the characters. Any resemblance that they may bear to real people, either living or dead, is entirely coincidental. The setting, the Isle of Man, is a real place, and the historical sites mentioned in this book are also real. The businesses within the story, however, are fictional and have been located where convenient for the story and not necessarily where any real businesses exist on the island. Any resemblance that they may bear to any real businesses is also coincidental.

As the setting is the crown dependency of the Isle of Man, I use British English (and Manx) for spellings and terms throughout the book. I include a short glossary at the back for anyone who is unfamiliar with any of them. As I've lived in the US for many years now, I'm sure many Americanisms have snuck into my writing. I try to correct them if they are pointed out to me.

I love hearing from readers. Please feel free to get in touch. All of my contact information is available at the back of the book.

CHAPTER 1

"You have to come and you have to convince John Rockwell to come as well," Elizabeth Quayle said in a determined voice. "The party won't be the same without you."

Bessie Cubbon frowned at the pretty blonde girl. "I don't have to do anything," she replied tartly, "and I have no intention of trying to make John do anything, either."

Elizabeth sighed dramatically. "I know you don't have to, but I'd be ever so grateful. I planned the whole thing around your being there, you know. And John is meant to be the star of the whole show. I really need him there."

Bessie counted slowly to ten before she said anything further. She'd known Elizabeth for long enough to know that the girl was spoiled, capricious, and impulsive. She was also sweet and kind, and Bessie knew she was trying hard to establish her party planning business on the island. She'd already tried three or four different universities and had dropped out of all of them. Bessie knew Elizabeth's mother, Mary, was really hoping that Elizabeth would actually stick to the new business and make a success of it. While Mary and her husband, George, had a great deal of money, they didn't plan to support Elizabeth financially forever.

"Start over," Bessie said eventually. "I don't really remember you even mentioning this party before today."

"I told you all about it last month," Elizabeth protested. "Well, maybe not all about it, but I'm sure I mentioned it."

Bessie was far less certain of that. She was fairly sure she would remember any party invitations that had come her way. "As I said, I don't recall discussing it. Tell me everything."

"The party is on Saturday," Elizabeth began.

"This Saturday? It's already Thursday," Bessie gasped.

"I know. That's why I came down to talk to you. I wanted to make sure you hadn't forgotten about the party."

"If we did discuss it, I don't believe you ever gave me a date for the event," Bessie replied. "I always put such things on the calendar in my kitchen and there's nothing on it for this weekend."

"Well, anyway, it's this Saturday," Elizabeth continued, unconcerned. "It's a murder mystery dinner party. The whole concept is simply huge in America, I understand. I thought it would be fun to try it here. I've arranged for someone from across to come over. She runs these events in London. Some of my friends have been to similar evenings and they've all raved about how much fun they are."

"A murder mystery dinner?" Bessie echoed.

"Yes, exactly. Everyone gets a part to play and it's meant to be really exciting. At some point during dinner, the lights all go out, and the person playing the murderer has to go and pretend to kill the victim. When the lights come back on, the detective is summoned and everyone is questioned. It's meant to be great fun."

"It doesn't sound fun at all," Bessie said flatly. "I've been involved in far too many real murder investigations to think that a pretend one would be enjoyable in any way."

"But that's just it. It's fun because it's all pretend. By the end of the evening, the murder is solved and the victim gets up and goes home. I've been tangled up in a real murder investigation, too, but this isn't really anything like that."

"I'm sorry, Elizabeth, but I don't think it's something I would enjoy," Bessie said firmly.

"Mum said you wouldn't want to come," Elizabeth replied sadly, "but I thought it would be so much more interesting with you there. After all of your experiences over the past eighteen months or so, I just know you'd solve our little pretend crime in no time at all."

Bessie almost smiled at the girl's obvious attempt at flattering her. She had been caught up in a great many murder cases recently, that much was true, but through no fault of her own. "I'm sorry, but I really don't think it's for me," she told Elizabeth.

"I shall have to cancel the whole thing, I imagine," Elizabeth sighed. "Everyone will be so disappointed. I've a dozen friends coming over from across, and Mum has invited several of her friends as well. She doesn't have many friends, so she was really looking forward to getting them all together."

And now she's trying to blackmail me into it, Bessie thought. "I can't see why you'd have to cancel just because I don't want to attend."

"As I said, it simply won't be the same without you," Elizabeth sighed.

This discussion had not been in Bessie's plans for this morning. She'd been woken at six by an internal alarm that was nearly always accurate. After a shower, she'd made her way out onto Laxey Beach, where the small cottage she'd purchased when she was eighteen was situated. For more years than she wanted to add up, Bessie had taken a walk on the beach every morning, and it was a habit she planned to continue for as long as she was able.

As it was August, the holiday cottages that stretched along the beach beyond Bessie's cottage were full to capacity. Luckily for Bessie, very few of the occupants were awake at half six in the morning. Bessie had had the beach to herself as she'd strolled past the cottages and then past the stairs to Thie yn Traie, the huge mansion perched on the cliff above the beach. She'd kept walking for several more minutes, enjoying the peace and solitude as she'd meandered along the water's edge.

Now that the cottages were busy with holidaymakers, Bessie often preferred to walk before breakfast, to give herself extra time while the beach was still empty. When her stomach had begun to protest that decision, Bessie had turned back towards home. She'd been approaching the stairs to Thie yn Traie when Elizabeth had appeared, racing down the steps in an unsafe fashion.

Now Bessie gave the girl a stern look. "You can't order, flatter, or bribe me into coming," she said firmly. "I'm sure it will be a lovely party, but it isn't the sort of thing in which I have any interest in taking part. I will mention it to John Rockwell, if you'd like, but I can't see him being interested either."

"Oh, but we have to have a proper police inspector," Elizabeth wailed. "It simply won't work without an inspector. I'll pay him, if you think that would help."

"I don't," Bessie said.

"I thought you wanted to help me with my business," Elizabeth said. "This is just the sort of thing I need to do to get it off the ground."

"I'm not sure I understand that," Bessie replied coolly. She felt as if she'd done quite a lot to support the girl's new business already, actually.

Elizabeth sighed and then shook her head. "I'm sorry. I'm being horrible. You've been incredibly helpful, and I wouldn't be as far as I am without everything you've done. I'm just frustrated. I was sure I'd talked to you about the mystery evening, but now I think I must have imagined the entire conversation."

"Really?"

"I do that a lot, actually," Elizabeth said sheepishly. "I plan everything I want to say to someone and mentally rehearse exactly how the conversation is going to go, and by the time I've done that a dozen times, I start to think that I've had the conversation, even when I haven't. I usually only do it with Mum, but sometimes I do it with other people as well."

Bessie hid a smile. "I am sorry that you didn't talk to me about this earlier. I could have told you that I wasn't interested in attending then, and saved you planning for my being there."

"The whole thing is just meant to be a trial event, anyway," Elizabeth told her. "I'm paying the woman from across to come and teach me how to run murder mystery evenings, you see. That's why it's all going to be my friends and my mother's friends at the event, rather than anyone else. I know my mother was really hoping you'd be there, though."

Bessie knew Mary well enough to know that Elizabeth was telling the truth about that, anyway. "I'm sorry, but I have been involved in too many real murders to want to spend an evening pretending to do the same. I suspect John will feel the same way. Murder is a sad and serious business; it isn't a game."

"But you enjoy reading about fictional murders," Elizabeth pointed out. "This is much the same thing. Instead of reading a book, you're simply in the middle of it, like a play where the audience is involved."

While she did enjoy reading mystery novels a great deal, the event Elizabeth was proposing didn't seem the same thing at all. "I'm sorry," Bessie repeated herself, "but I'm not coming."

She said the same thing to Mary a few hours later when Mary rang her. They were the first words out of Bessie's mouth when she recognised the other woman's voice.

Mary laughed. "I haven't actually invited you anywhere yet," she said.

Bessie sighed. "I'm sorry. I simply assumed that you were ringing about this party that Elizabeth is having, the murder mystery evening. I told Elizabeth that I wasn't coming, and I assumed she'd asked you to ring me and try to get me to change my mind."

"She did ask me to do just that," Mary replied, "but I told her I wouldn't. I think the whole thing is a ghastly idea, and I'd be much happier if she'd simply cancel it, but having been told that, now she's even more determined to make it happen."

"Oh, dear," Bessie sighed.

"I was hoping you might be willing to come over to Thie yn Traie on Saturday evening to keep me company," Mary continued. "I've told Elizabeth that I won't be taking part in her little game, but I suspect most of the guests I've invited will be happy to join in. I thought you might come over and sit with me in the study or something while the others are playing detective."

"I'm quite sure Elizabeth will try to persuade us both to participate."

"She won't," Mary assured her. "I've had a long talk with her and she understands why we don't want to take part. She's promised to be on her best behaviour and let us simply enjoy the food and drinks before slipping away when the game begins."

"I don't know," Bessie said slowly.

"Andy is doing the catering," Mary told her. "I'm sure the food will be amazing."

Bessie grinned. Mary had just said the one thing that actually tempted her to agree. Andy Caine was only on the island for a short while on a break from culinary school. He was already an excellent chef and his puddings were the best Bessie had ever tasted. He'd stayed with Bessie for a few days recently and she'd been quite spoiled by his cooking and baking. A chance to eat his food again might make a trip to Thie yn Traie worthwhile, as long as she wasn't expected to take part in Elizabeth's event. "That's tempting," she admitted to Mary.

"He's been helping out here, as our regular chef has had some medical issues. He and Elizabeth are, well, I'm not sure what they are, but they seem to like one another. Anyway, he's going to prepare a full sit-down dinner and an amazing pudding for Saturday night. He's going to be taking part in the mystery evening as well, I understand."

"I don't know," Bessie said after a moment. "I still feel uncomfortable with the whole idea."

"I know. I do as well, but Elizabeth is convinced that these sorts of parties are going to be very popular, and this is her chance to be the first on the island to offer them. Apparently, they can be used by corporations for team-building exercises and they're popular for stag and hen nights across, among other things. At least that's what Elizabeth has been telling me."

"I still think it's a very odd way to spend an evening, but I'll give some thought to coming, just to spend some time with you."

When she put down the phone, Bessie frowned at it. She'd promised Elizabeth that she'd ring John Rockwell on her behalf, but she'd been putting it off. There was no time like the present, she told herself as she picked the phone back up again.

"Laxey neighbourhood policing, this is Doona. How may I help you?" a familiar voice came down the line.

"It's Bessie. Is it possible that John is free?" Bessie asked her closest friend.

"You know you can ring him on his direct line," Doona replied.

"Yes, but I don't want to interrupt anything important." This way, there was a chance she might not be able to speak to him, and if she were really lucky, he might be tied up until some time on Sunday, when it would be far too late.

"He's doing paperwork. I'm sure he'll be grateful for the interruption," Doona laughed. She put Bessie on hold. John answered only a moment later.

"Good morning, Bessie. What can I do for you?" he asked in a cheerful voice.

"Good morning. How are you?"

"I'm doing well. The children and I had a wonderful time in Barcelona and now we're trying to work out somewhere else we could go for a few days before the summer is over. We're also trying to work out what's going to happen in September, but that's another story."

John and his wife, Sue, had recently divorced. Sue had moved back to Manchester with their two children, Thomas and Amy. When she'd remarried in July, she and her new husband, Harvey, had gone to Africa for an extended trip. Harvey was a doctor, and the trip was designed to give him a chance to help people in a developing country. While it wasn't the sort of honeymoon Bessie thought she'd fancy, it seemed a kind thing to do. While Sue and Harvey were away, John was looking after Thomas and Amy. Bessie was delighted that the children seemed to be enjoying the island and the time with their father. She knew that John had missed them terribly when they were in Manchester.

"When does Sue get back?"

"That's a good question," John sighed. "It was going to be late

September, but when she rang the kids the other night she said something about the first week of October. She doesn't seem to realise that the kids need to be settled into schools somewhere well before then. You didn't ring to hear me complain about my ex-wife, though. What can I do for you?"

"I promised Elizabeth Quayle that I would ask you about something, but I'm not trying to talk you into attending in any way," Bessie prefaced her remarks.

"That sounds interesting already," John laughed.

"She's having a sort of murder mystery evening," Bessie explained, "and she wants you to attend. Apparently, having a real police inspector there is desirable."

"When?"

"Saturday."

"Saturday, as in the day after tomorrow? I'm sorry, but even if I wanted to go, it's far too short notice. I'm actually working on Saturday morning and I'm on call for the evening. We're a little short on staff at the moment, you see."

"She meant to tell me about it earlier," Bessie replied, "and then I was meant to tell you about it earlier. It's a long story, but basically she forgot to tell me."

"I'm not sure a murder mystery evening is the sort of thing I'd want to attend anyway."

"It's not for me, that's for certain. I've already told her that I've no interest in taking part."

"I hope she isn't too upset with you, especially as you'll have to disappoint her about my attending as well."

"Mary is on my side," Bessie assured him. "I'm going to go over on Saturday and sit with her while Elizabeth's little game is taking place."

"I've a colleague across who went to one of those evenings," John said. "He was invited because he's a police inspector, but he wasn't very pleased with how it went. Many of the clues were red herrings and he ended up fingering the wrong suspect as the murderer while several guests selected the right one. By the end of the evening he felt as if he had been set up to fail and as if he'd damaged his reputation as an inspector."

"Oh, dear. That's simply dreadful," Bessie exclaimed. "I'm sure you'd be more than clever enough to work out the right solution, but it isn't worth the risk, is it?"

"No, it isn't. And now that I know that such things are going to be happening on the island, I think it's time for a chat with the chief constable about them. I suspect he'll want to issue some sort of guide-lines for members of the constabulary who are considering taking part."

"Elizabeth has no idea what she's started."

"No, and I doubt she's given it any thought, either. She's had so much given to her in life that she doesn't generally think things through enough."

Bessie couldn't argue with that. "I'll ring her and tell her that you're busy and also suggest that she give up on finding an inspector to take part."

"I hope she isn't too upset with you," John said.

"She won't be," Bessie replied. "I've already told her to expect you to say no. I think the entire thing is in poor taste."

"That's only because you've been involved in so many actual murder investigations," John said. "If you'd never been involved in a single one, this sort of thing might actually appeal to you."

Bessie put down the phone and thought about what John had said. He was probably right, she had to admit to herself. She loved reading murder mysteries, especially cosy ones set in country houses or grand estates. If she'd never found a dead body or been questioned by the police, an evening spent at Thie yn Traie analysing clues and matching wits with a pretend murderer might have sounded inter-esting to her. As she couldn't change the past, though, there was little point in worrying over it.

"May I speak to Elizabeth, please?" she said when the phone was answered at Thie yn Traie. "It's Elizabeth Cubbon."

"Oh, aye, Aunt Bessie. How are you?" a familiar voice replied.

"Jack Hooper, I'm fine, thank you. How are you?"

9

"Oh, I'm very good, thanks. I'm really enjoying working at Thie yn Traie, and Mrs. Quayle is a wonderful person for whom to work."

"I'm sure she is," Bessie said with a smile. Jack had been working as the butler at Thie yn Traie for a few months now and Bessie still hadn't managed to see him there. In her mind, he was still a small boy with ginger hair, freckles, and a skinned knee. It was hard for Bessie to picture him as a formally trained butler, but Mary had told her that he was one of the best they'd ever employed.

"I'll get Miss Elizabeth for you," he said.

"Oh, wait. Before you go, what do you know about this party that Elizabeth is having on Saturday?" Bessie asked.

"I don't talk about the family," Jack said in a formal voice. "At least not with anyone but you," he continued casually. "You mean this murder mystery thing? I don't know much, but I'm not looking forward to it."

"Why not?"

"Miss Elizabeth has five or six of her friends from across coming to stay, for a start. Her friends are always incredibly demanding. And then there's Ms. Susan Haymarket. She's the one who's running the actual murder mystery part. She's been ringing three or four times a day to add to her list of things she absolutely has to have to make the evening a success. About all she hasn't asked for at this point is a unicorn on a silver tray."

"My goodness."

"And then Mrs. Quayle has invited a few friends as well, which is lovely, because she has the nicest friends, but now she's told me that she isn't actually going to be going to the murder mystery part, and I've no idea where that leaves her share of the guests." He sighed deeply. "I can't believe I'm telling you all of this. I'd lose my job if you repeated any of it to Mrs. Quayle."

"You know I won't say anything," Bessie assured him. "I was just curious, as I've been invited, you see."

"Have you? Are you coming? It sounds a bit, well, tacky, if you ask me."

"I'm going to be coming over to spend some time with Mary. We won't be taking part in the actual murder mystery part of the evening."

"I don't blame you a bit if you're only coming for the food," Jack said. "Andy Caine is going to do incredible things, I'm sure. Miss Elizabeth doesn't properly appreciate that man."

Bessie laughed. "I am looking forward to the food. Do you have any other skeet to share before I talk to Elizabeth?"

"I don't think so, but I'll ring you back if I think of anything," the man laughed. "Let me go and get Miss Elizabeth for you."

"Hello, Aunt Bessie. I hope you have good news for me," the bubbly voice came down the line.

"I'm sorry, but John is working on Saturday and on call on Saturday evening. He can't attend."

"I didn't think he would, really," Elizabeth replied. "I'd be ever so upset, but I've just finished speaking to a police inspector from across who's willing to come and help out. The woman organising the event has used him before and she says he's simply fabulous."

"Oh, I'm so glad everything has worked out. I was afraid you'd be disappointed that John wasn't free."

"I am, a little bit, only because he'd so dreamy to look at," Elizabeth giggled. "I'm sure he'd be much more fun than the man I've booked, but I have to take what I can get, don't I? Anyway, this Inspector Rhodes has done these parties before, so he'll know what to expect more than I will. That should help."

"I'm glad you found someone to attend," Bessie told her. She made a note of the man's name. Maybe she should ring John and mention it to him, she thought as she put the phone down. Unable to decide whether or not to do so, she pottered around the kitchen and then curled up with a book. By the time she thought about ringing John again, the day was nearly over.

Friday was Bessie's regular day for grocery shopping. After her walk, which was happily uninterrupted this morning, she got ready for her usual car service to collect her. She'd been using the same service for a great many years, although it had changed hands some time back. Her favourite driver, Dave, turned up exactly on time.

"A full morning in Ramsey?" he asked as he drove.

"Yes, please," Bessie replied. "I want to spend some time looking at books, and then I need to get my food shopping done."

Dave left Bessie as close to the door of the bookshop as he possibly could. "I'll see you at ShopFast later, then," he said cheerfully as she climbed out of the car.

As ever, the bookshop had several books that Bessie wanted. She had an arrangement with them that had them shipping her new titles by her favourite authors whenever they came out, but that didn't stop Bessie from finding new potentially favourite authors when she actually was in the shop. She tried to restrict herself to paperbacks, to limit what she'd have to carry around ShopFast, but today she found a hardcover she couldn't resist.

"I can add it to your next shipment if you don't want to carry it," the shop assistant suggested as Bessie paid for her purchases.

"I suppose I can wait," Bessie said, touching the book gently. She really wanted to sit somewhere in the shop and read it from cover to cover right then, but she didn't have the time.

"We have an order coming in on Saturday with two or three titles for you," the girl said. "We'll be shipping them, and this, off to you by Tuesday at the latest."

"Okay, then, let's do that," Bessie said. She pushed the book away firmly, not letting herself look at the enticing cover again.

ShopFast was always busy in the summer months. Bessie reminded herself to be patient as summer visitors crowded the aisles, seemingly unable to find what they were looking for and for some reason determined to stand still and shout to one another about it. Dave was waiting outside when Bessie finally pushed her trolley out of the shop.

"I hope you haven't been waiting long," she said as he loaded her shopping into his boot.

"Not at all," he assured her. "Traffic is terrible. I was worried that I was going to be late."

Back at home, Bessie unpacked her shopping and then glanced at her answering machine. She didn't have any messages, but as she looked her eyes fell on the notepad next to the phone.

"You never did ring John," she exclaimed to herself as she reached for the phone.

"Inspector Rhodes," John repeated thoughtfully. "You didn't get a Christian name?"

"I didn't want to look nosy," Bessie replied, flushing.

"Did she say he was from London?"

"She didn't say that specifically, just that he'd gone to similar events in London," Bessie explained.

"I'll ring a few people and see what I can find out about Inspector Rhodes. I'm surprised he's able to drop everything and come over to the island for an evening. Perhaps he's retired from the police."

"He must be," Bessie agreed. "Did I give you the name of the woman who's organising the event?"

"No, do you have that?"

"Jack Hooper, the butler at Thie yn Traie, happened to mention it to me," Bessie explained. "She's called Susan Haymarket."

"I may make a few discreet inquiries into her as well. If she plans these sorts of parties on a regular basis, one of my contacts in London may well know her."

"You don't suspect her of doing anything wrong, do you?" Bessie asked.

"No, not at all, but if there have been any problems with any of her parties in the past, I'd like to know what to expect," John explained. "Elizabeth isn't always the best at selecting her friends and associates."

Bessie nodded. She knew that the police had had to speak to the girl on more than one occasion about the behaviour of some of her friends, usually when they were spending time at the small pub in Laxey. Heavy drinking on a weekend might be considered normal for young people in London, but it was frowned upon in Laxey Village.

"She is having friends over for the party tomorrow," Bessie warned him. "She didn't tell me who was coming, so I don't know if I've met any of them before."

"I'm sure it will all be fine," John replied, "but I do appreciate your passing along the names to me. I'm especially interested in the inspector who is willing to take part in Elizabeth's game."

Bessie found that she was intrigued by the man as well. John took police work very seriously. She couldn't imagine him agreeing to take part in something like what Elizabeth was planning. As Bessie fell asleep Friday evening, she was quite looking forward to meeting Inspector Rhodes the following evening.

CHAPTER 2

Saturday was dark and dreary. Bessie kept her morning walk short, turning back as soon as she'd reached the last holiday cottage. It was the only cottage that wasn't currently occupied, and Bessie was fairly certain that Thomas and Maggie Shimmin were planning to demolish it and build a new cottage to replace it. Bessie glanced at the cottage and shivered involuntarily. While the flashing neon sign that had illuminated the body on the bed was long gone, Bessie could still recall the eerie effect it had had on the beach the night the murdered man had been found.

A light rain began to fall as she made her way back to her own cottage. She patted the sign that read "Treoghe Bwaane" as she dashed inside. The words were Manx for "Widow's Cottage" and Bessie had thought them particularly apt when she'd bought her new home at the age of eighteen. While not technically a widow, she'd purchased the cottage with money left to her by the man she'd loved and lost. When she'd bought it, she'd imagined that it would be her home for a short while and that, given time, she'd meet someone else, marry, and have children. That was what women did in her day.

The reality had turned out somewhat differently, but Bessie had no regrets. She loved her little cottage by the sea and the life that she'd made for herself. Since she'd never had children, she'd been happy to act as an honourary aunt for most of the boys and girls who grew up in Laxey. Many unhappy teenagers had spent a night or two, or sometimes considerably longer, in Bessie's spare room. She was always wiling to listen to their problems, feed them cake, and share her thoughts on their concerns.

The day passed quickly for Bessie. She spent much of it lost in one of Jane Austen's books, which made a nice change from the mystery novels she usually read. For some reason those titles didn't appeal today, but Jane Austen was almost always pleasing. Once the heroine had safely made it through all of the little trials that came her way and found her way into the hero's arms, Bessie closed the book and was surprised to find that it was later than she'd realised.

She changed into a black dress and matching shoes and combed her short grey hair. The quick application of just a tiny bit of makeup finished her efforts. When she looked outside, she frowned. It was still dark and grey and a light rain was falling. She's planned on simply walking to Thie yn Traie, as it wasn't far, but she didn't want arrive at the party dripping wet, either. It seemed silly to ring for a taxi to take her such a short distance, but as the rain grew heavier, Bessie didn't feel as if she had much choice. She was reaching for the telephone when someone knocked on the door.

"Mrs. Quayle sent me to see if you'd like a ride to Thie yn Traie," the uniformed chauffeur at the door said when Bessie opened it.

"Oh, goodness, that would be wonderful," Bessie replied. She grabbed her handbag and locked her cottage door behind her. The driver held an umbrella over her head as she did so and then escorted her to the car. As he reached for the rear door, Bessie shook her head.

"Please, may I ride up front with you?" she asked. "I don't feel comfortable in the back of fancy cars."

The man grinned, and then quickly recomposed his face to a practiced neutrality. "Of course, madam," he said as he opened the passenger door for her.

Bessie slid into the car and settled back on the plush leather seat.

Nothing like arriving in style, she thought as the man drove away from her cottage.

Thie yn Traie looked enormous as the car drove through the front gates. Bessie was used to walking up from the back of the house and rarely saw the imposing front façade. The driver stopped the car at the front door, and a man in a black uniform descended the front steps to help Bessie from the car.

"Good evening, madam," he said as he escorted her to the front door.

"Good evening," Bessie replied, feeling intimidated by the formal atmosphere. Wishing she'd walked and come in through the kitchen, Bessie let the man lead her into the huge foyer at the front of the house.

Elizabeth dashed over to her a moment later. "I'm so glad you came," she exclaimed happily. "Mum was worried that you'd change your mind."

Bessie smiled at the girl. "I told your mother I would come, but only to keep her company. I won't be taking part in your game."

"That's fine," Elizabeth assured her. "I'm just glad Mum will have some company. She does have some other friends coming, but I'm expecting them to play along. I didn't want Mum just sitting by herself while everyone else is rushing about looking for clues."

Bessie nodded. "You look lovely tonight," she told the girl.

Elizabeth was wearing a bright red dress that showed off her slender figure without being too short or too tight. It made a nice change from some of the outfits Bessie had seen her wear in the past. The colour went nicely with the girl's blonde hair, as well. "Thanks. If we were doing this right, all of the guests would have been asked to come in fancy dress, but as this is just a test run, I thought it would be easier for people to just wear their normal clothes."

"I still think that was a mistake," a loud voice called across the room.

Bessie looked at the tall brunette who was striding towards her and Elizabeth. She was wearing a black jacket and matching skirt that Bessie thought were more suited for a boardroom than a party. Her

17

hair was pulled back in a tight bun and her brown eyes were partially hidden behind unattractive square glasses.

"Bessie, this is Susan, Susan Haymarket. She's one of London's most successful party planners. She's here to teach me everything I need to know about planning murder mystery evenings," Elizabeth said.

"It's very nice to meet you," Bessie told the woman. She held out a hand. Susan shook her hand firmly.

"It's nice to meet you, as well. Bessie, was it?"

"Sorry," Elizabeth giggled. "This is Elizabeth Cubbon, but everyone calls her Bessie. Some of us even call her Aunt Bessie. She lives just down the beach from here in a darling little cottage that's simply perfect for her. She and my mother are dear friends. She'll be keeping Mum company once the murder mystery part of the evening starts, as she's not interested in taking part, either."

Susan frowned. "It really is a fun evening," she told Bessie.

"I'm sure it is, for some people, but I've been involved in a number of actual murder investigations, and I'm not interested in being involved in a pretend one," Bessie told her.

"My goodness, what an exciting life you must have had. Were you with the police?" Susan asked.

"No, I've just been in the wrong place at the wrong time rather too often," Bessie replied.

Susan looked as if she wanted to ask more, but then she glanced at Elizabeth and frowned. "You should have had everyone dress appropriately," she told her. "It's much more fun if everyone is in fancy dress according to a theme."

"I know, but there simply wasn't time to arrange it properly," Elizabeth replied. "The island isn't like London. We don't have a dozen fancy dress shops where people can get period costumes on a moment's notice. We'll have to do the best we can for tonight, and I'll have to investigate what's actually available on the island going forward."

"I've done my best to rewrite the story as a modern murder mystery, rather than the period piece it's always been," Susan said, "but I'm not sure how successful I've been. Certain things may not hang together exactly right."

"How does it all work, then?" Bessie asked.

Susan raised an eyebrow. "The murder mystery, you mean?"

"Yes, how does it work?"

"You're more than welcome to observe it all," Elizabeth told her. "You can watch from the sidelines. I'd love your feedback when it's all over, actually. I'm sure there will be things that we'll need to improve."

"The basic story is fairly simple," Susan said. "The setting is an old country house. I usually suggest having the guests dress in late Victorian dress or twenties-era clothing and adjust the story accordingly. Each guest, as he or she arrives, is assigned a part in the story. Elizabeth, for example, is the daughter of the wealthy man who owns the country house."

"Typecasting," Elizabeth giggled.

"Along with character notes, one of the guests is also assigned the role of the murderer, and another is designated as the victim. When the lights go out, the murderer has to make his or her way to the victim and say a certain code word. That's the victim's cue to pretend to die. When the lights come back on, it's time for the guests and the detective to try to work out who the killer was," Susan explained.

"And there are clues?" Bessie asked.

"Yes, there are clues built into everyone's character descriptions for a start. Careful questioning of all of the guests is the first job for the detective. He does his questioning in front of everyone, so that everyone has an equal opportunity to solve the crime," Susan told her.

"I see," Bessie said, not sure that she did.

"Other clues are handed out as necessary," Susan continued. "There are dozens of red herrings, of course, as well. At the end of the evening everyone says who he or she thinks the murderer was, and then the actual killer is unmasked."

"How often do people work out the right solution?" Bessie wondered.

"Maybe half the time," Susan shrugged. "People seem to be happiest when they work out the right solution and the detective gets it wrong. That's one of the reasons why I like working with Inspector Rhodes. He's usually wrong."

Elizabeth laughed. "I can't wait to meet him," she said.

"He should be here soon," Susan replied. "Hopefully a good half hour before the rest of the guests."

Bessie frowned. "I thought the party started at six," she said.

"Oh, we had to move it back to seven because the inspector couldn't get an earlier flight," Elizabeth told her. "I had the car go and collect you early, though, because Mum was fussing."

"Where is your mother?" Bessie asked, suddenly concerned about her friend.

"I'm right here, and I was not fussing," Mary said from a doorway. "I simply said that I wasn't certain what I should do with myself while I was waiting for Bessie to arrive. My daughter took that to mean that she should send a car for you straight away. I didn't realise she'd done it, or I'd have been here to greet you properly," Mary explained as she crossed to Bessie.

Bessie gave her friend a hug. Mary was a tiny woman who was always impeccably dressed and perfectly made up. Tonight was no exception and as Bessie stood next to Mary, she couldn't help but feel as if she should have tried harder with both the outfit and her makeup.

"Come through and have something to eat while we wait for everyone else," Mary invited her. "Andy's already putting food out and there's plenty of wine as well."

Bessie followed Mary into the huge "great room" with its wall of windows that showcased the sea. A large rectangular table was set up in the middle of the room.

"We'll be having dinner in here," Mary explained, nodding at the table. "Susan wanted as much room as possible for the murder mystery, so everything will be happening in here."

"How many people are coming?" Bessie asked.

Mary shrugged. "Elizabeth has a group of friends here, and I've invited a few people as well. It's just a sort of test run of the whole concept, so the idea was to keep the numbers fairly small. I'm not sure that Susan agrees with that. I believe she's been encouraging Elizabeth to invite more people."

"Aunt Bessie, you look lovely," Andy Caine said as he walked into the room with a tray of food in each hand. He put them down on a large table near the wall and then walked over to give Bessie a hug.

"Andy, I'm only here because Mary said you were doing the food," Bessie said.

The man laughed. "I hope you won't be too disappointed. Elizabeth didn't want anything too fancy, really. The food is just to give everyone enough energy to solve the crime."

"I'm sure it will be delicious," Bessie replied. "And I'm not planning on taking part in the murder mystery part of the evening, so the food is important to me."

"Not taking part? I was counting on you to solve the case," Andy exclaimed.

"After everything I've been through lately, I really don't want to get involved," Bessie told him.

Andy nodded. "I can understand that. I'm just glad you came at all. I've made a special pudding based on your shortbread."

Bessie smiled. "Is it time for pudding yet?"

"You can have a few starters while you wait," Andy suggested. He waved a hand towards the table where he'd left the trays. It was full of trays of food, and everything looked delicious.

"I shall have to be careful not to eat too much," Bessie murmured as she and Mary approached the table. "I must save room for pudding."

The pair filled small plates while Andy headed back to the kitchen. A uniformed waiter was just pouring them each a glass of wine when another man rushed into the room.

"Aunt Bessie, my goodness, just look at you," he exclaimed as he pulled Bessie into a hug.

When he released her, Bessie stared at the new arrival. "Jack? Jack Hooper? I'm not sure I would have recognised you if I didn't know you were here," she exclaimed. His ginger hair had darkened considerably, although Bessie could still see a smattering of freckles across his nose. When he smiled at her, she noticed that the gap between his front teeth was also still there. But he looked much older than the boy in her memories, especially dressed in formal butler attire.

"You haven't changed a bit," Jack said. "But you really must call me Jonathan now, and I really must calm down and behave." He glanced over at Mary and then looked at the floor.

"Don't mind me," she said quickly. "I didn't even realise you knew Bessie."

"Oh, aye," the man replied. He cleared his throat and when he spoke again, it was in perfect Received Pronunciation rather than his Manx accent. "Miss Cubbon's cottage was one of my favourite places when I was a small child. I would spend hours on Laxey Beach in the summer, and she was often kind enough to offer my mother and myself a cup of tea and a biscuit at some point during the day."

Mary smiled. "How fun for you," she said.

"Yes, madam. Those are some of my favourite childhood memories," Jonathan said, "and now I must get back to the door to help Miss Elizabeth greet guests."

Bessie gave him another hug before he left, and then settled into a chair next to Mary with her plate of food. She'd only taken a single bite when Elizabeth strolled in, in the company of an older man. The man appeared to be in his late sixties. He was heavyset and was wearing a rumpled brown business suit and scuffed black leather shoes. What little hair he had was combed into something like a circle on the top of his head, and Bessie could only imagine that it had been dyed dark brown as she couldn't imagine the colour was natural.

"Mum, Aunt Bessie, this is Inspector Jerome Rhodes," she said. "Inspector Rhodes, this is my mother, Mary Quayle, and her friend, Elizabeth Cubbon."

"It's a pleasure to meet you both," the man said, nodding at them as his eyes scanned the room. "Oh, food," he exclaimed. Before anyone could reply, he'd crossed the room and begun to fill a plate from the starters on display.

"Wine, sir?" the uniformed waiter asked.

"Oh, yeah, whatever you have," the man replied, barely looking up from his plate.

"I'm going back to greet guests," Elizabeth said loudly before she turned and left the room.

Bessie settled back in her seat and amused herself by watching as the police inspector added more and more food to his plate. He seemed to be doing so methodically, carefully arranging things by shape to maximise what he could fit onto a single plate. She exchanged glances with Mary and then they both stared as the man added still more to his selections. Bessie was certain that something was going to fall off the plate as he made his way back to join her and Mary, but even with a glass of wine in his other hand, he managed to get his heaping pile of food safely across the room.

"So, Mrs. Quayle, this is quite a house. How long have you lived here?" he asked before shoving a canapé into his mouth.

"Not long," Mary replied. "We're still settling in. I'd very much like to redecorate this room, but we're having trouble working out what to do with it."

"It's too big," the man said around another mouthful. "It's rather similar to being in a bus garage."

Bessie gasped and then quickly took a sip of wine before she could reply to the man's rude comment.

Mary smiled graciously. "I'm sure we'll find a way to work with it, eventually," she said. "Have you ever been to the island before?"

"Nope," he said, pushing the food around on his plate. "Lived in London most of my life. I like big cities." As he took his next bite, Bessie and Mary exchanged glances.

"Isn't it nice that everyone is different," Mary said after a moment. "We lived in London for a while, but I never felt settled there. Are you staying on the island for long?"

"Going back in the morning," he replied. "Susan didn't reckon I could get a flight back tonight after the party, so she's found me a hotel near the airport. I'll be on a flight out at seven, and I don't plan to come back."

"Perhaps you should give the island more of a chance," Bessie suggested, choosing her words carefully. "It really is lovely."

"Too small. Nothing happening and nothing to do," the man said.

"There are a number of interesting historical sites," Mary told him.

"Not really interested in history. All those dates and dusty old documents? Not for me."

"What are you interested in?" Bessie had to ask.

The man shrugged. "I go to the pub a lot," he said. "There's one just down the road from my flat."

"Do you like to read?" was Bessie's next question.

"Nah, not much," was the not unexpected reply.

"It was kind of you to agree to come and help with the murder mystery evening," Mary said after a moment.

"Kind? Ha," the man said while chewing. "Susan is paying me for my time, you know. It isn't a bad way to make some extra dosh really. I ask a few questions and pretend I don't know who the killer is and the guests all leave happy. I could do this every night of the week. There's always food, too."

"What time does all of this start?" a voice asked from the doorway.

Bessie looked over at the girl who'd just arrived. She had to be one of Elizabeth's friends. Her hair was platinum blonde and she was wearing a tiny silver slip of a dress that barely covered anything. Incredibly high heels made her legs look impossibly long, and Bessie guessed that she had to be at least six feet tall in her shoes.

"Wow," the inspector said under his breath before letting out a long wolf whistle. "Maybe the island docs have some redeeming features," he said as he got to his feet.

The girl raised an eyebrow at him and then looked at Mary. "What time do we start?" she asked again.

"I believe Elizabeth is planning to start things around seven," Mary told her. "Why don't you have a glass of wine and something to eat while you wait?"

"I'm going to get the others," the girl replied. She spun on her heel and disappeared just moments before the inspector would have reached her.

He watched her go and then ambled back over to the food table and began to fill another plate.

"It's going to be a long night," Mary whispered to Bessie.

Bessie nodded and then finished the last of the food on her plate. "Maybe we should go and help Elizabeth greet guests," she suggested.

"I suspect Vivian will be back in a minute or two," Mary said. "Now that she knows drinks are available, she won't be gone long."

The words were barely out of Mary's mouth when the girl in the silver dress came back into the room. She was dragging several other people behind her, and they all quickly congregated around the food table. One of the young men nearly knocked the inspector over as the older man reached for a glass of wine.

"Oh, sorry," Elizabeth's friend said carelessly.

Inspector Rhodes gave him an angry look and then took his plate and walked over to an empty chair.

Bessie slid closer to Mary. "Tell me who everyone is," she requested.

"All of the young people are Elizabeth's friends from London. I believe they're all part of the same social circle as the group that came for New Year's Eve, but none of those people have come again."

"I can't blame them for that," Bessie said, thinking about the murder investigation that had followed that party.

"Yes, well, let's see now. The girl in the silver dress is Vivian Walker. She's a model when she can be bothered to work, but there's loads of family money, so that isn't often. The other girl is called Madison Fields. Again, lots of family money. I don't know that she does much of anything, besides attend parties and that sort of thing."

Bessie looked at the brunette, who was sipping a glass of wine and staring at the sea. She was considerably shorter than Vivian, but she was probably still taller than Bessie, who wasn't much over five feet tall. Madison was wearing a long blue dress that did nothing for her slender figure, and from where Bessie was sitting, didn't appear to be wearing any makeup. Compared to her friend, the girl almost seemed to disappear into the background.

"What about the two young men?" Bessie asked.

"One of them is Sean Rice and the other is Richard Long," Mary told her, "but I can't really tell them apart."

Bessie chuckled. While the two men didn't exactly look alike, she could see what Mary meant. They were both very much of a type. They both looked like the sort of young men who worked in banking or investments in London and received multi-million-pound bonuses each year. One of them had hair that was beginning to thin, but beyond that, their brown hair was cut in identical styles and their suits looked exactly the same, at least from a distance.

"And here are Ernest and Norma McCormick," Mary whispered, nodding towards the door.

Bessie looked at the pair. They both had short brown hair and brown eyes. Ernest was wearing a suit similar to the ones worn by the other men, but his had more style somehow. Or maybe it was the bright red and blue tie that he'd worn with it that made it seem more stylish. The tie seemed to match his companion's dress. It was also stylish, but reasonably modest, especially when compared with Vivian's. Bessie felt that the girl was wearing too much makeup, but it had clearly been expertly applied. "They're married?" she asked Mary.

"No, brother and sister," Mary told her. "Actually, twins. Another family with a great deal of money, although I understand they both work in the family business."

The pair joined the others at the food table as Elizabeth walked into the room. "Has everyone received his or her character cards?" she asked loudly in the doorway.

"Yes, and I don't like mine," Vivian complained. "I don't want to be the nanny."

Elizabeth laughed. "It's only pretend," she said. "Everyone has to be someone. You needn't worry that anyone will think you really are a nanny. Not in that dress."

Vivian glanced down at her dress and then laughed. "I don't own anything more nanny-like," she said.

"Or anything less nanny-like," Ernest suggested with a wink.

"The other guests have all arrived and are just getting character cards," Elizabeth announced. "We'll sit down to dinner in a few minutes."

"That means my friends are all here," Mary said, getting to her feet. "I should go and greet them and make sure they're all happy to play Elizabeth's little game."

"Take me with you," Bessie requested. "I don't want to stay here with the young people. I might have to talk to Inspector Rhodes again."

Mary laughed. "Come on, then, although I suspect they'll all be here before we get too far."

She was right. As Mary and Bessie crossed the room, four more people walked into it. Bessie was slightly surprised as she recognised one of the new arrivals.

"Elizabeth Cubbon, I should have expected to see you here," Mona Kelly said. "I'd heard that you and Mary had become friends, and you do live right down the beach, don't you?"

"I do," Bessie agreed as she took the other woman's hand. While Bessie was something of a Laxey institution, Mona Kelly was something of an island legend. Bessie reckoned that the woman was probably somewhere in her seventies, but she didn't look much older than sixty. She was always beautifully dressed and perfectly made up, and even when she drove her expensive convertible around the island or got caught in the rain, her hair was always exactly in place.

"This is my dear friend, Michael Higgins," Mona said. "He was with, well, a government agency, let's say, for many years. When he heard about tonight's little gathering, he thought it might be fun to attend."

Bessie shook hands with the very handsome and distinguished-looking gentleman. That was the other thing about Mona. She was nearly always on the arm of one handsome and wealthy man or another. There was a group on the island that didn't approve of Mona and her lifestyle. She had no visible means of support, though she lived lavishly, but Bessie didn't think such things were any of her concern. Bessie herself had no visible means of support, either, although most people on the island knew her story. Mona preferred to keep things to herself, and Bessie wasn't one to pry.

"It's lovely to meet you," Bessie told the man.

"Likewise, I'm sure. Mona has told me a little about you, and I had a long conversation with John Rockwell about you as well," the man replied.

Bessie opened her mouth to ask him why he'd been talking to John, but she was interrupted by Mona.

"And you know Leonard and Liza, don't you?" she asked Bessie.

Bessie nodded and then greeted the couple. Leonard Hammersmith was an island businessman who'd made a great deal of money buying and selling parcels of land over the years. His wife, Liza, liked to pretend that they'd always been well off, but Bessie had known the man when he'd first started out, borrowing money from his mother to pay the deposit on an empty field. He sold the field a few months later for a huge profit to a large UK retail chain that wanted to open an island branch, and his success had continued from there.

"Good evening," Liza murmured to Bessie. "I would have thought that you'd have had enough of murder in real life."

"I have," Bessie assured her. "I'm just here for dinner. I'm not taking part in the murder game."

"Oh, that is disappointing," Mona said. "I was hoping we might match wits against one another. You've more real-world experience, but I'm sure I read as many detective novels as you do."

"It really isn't for me," Bessie told her, "but I hope you all enjoy it."

"Does everyone have their character cards?" Elizabeth asked from the doorway.

A chorus of yeses came from around the room.

"Excellent. We can sit down to dinner, then," Elizabeth told them. "The gentlemen will be rotating around the table after each course so that people will have an opportunity to speak with everyone else. Please make sure to stay in character at all times."

"I would prefer to sit with my husband," Liza Hammersmith said.

"But he isn't your husband tonight," Elizabeth laughed. "I believe he's the doctor from the neighbouring village and you are a spinster woman who's never quite recovered from being slighted by your first love."

Liza sighed. "And you expect us to play these parts all through dinner?" she demanded.

"That's how it works," Susan said from behind Elizabeth. "It's only fun and successful if everyone takes part and tries to follow the rul, er, guidelines. Of course, some of the dinner guests aren't playing." She glanced at Bessie and Mary and then frowned. "I do hope they will still do their best to help the other guests remain in character anyway."

Bessie and Mary both nodded, while Bessie began to seriously regret agreeing to come.

"Before you all take your seats, I should introduce Inspector Jerome Rhodes," Susan continued.

The man in question stood up, and then rocked a bit unsteadily before putting a hand on the back of the chair he'd just vacated. He cleared his throat and then shrugged. "I'll be conducting the investigation after the murder takes place," he said. "Until then, I'm just another guest."

"If you'd like to find your places at the table," Susan said brightly. "There are place cards at each seat."

CHAPTER 3

$\mathcal{A}$s everyone made their way towards the table, George Quayle rushed into the room. "I'm not late, am I?" he asked in his booming voice. "I had to take a phone call about a merger and then my advocate rang and..." he trailed off and smiled at everyone. "But I'm here now. Let the murder and mayhem begin."

Bessie shuddered at his words before continuing on to the table. She found her seat next to George, who was at the table's head. When she noticed that Inspector Rhodes was on her other side, she frowned as she slid into her chair.

"After the soup course all the gentlemen will move two seats to the right," Susan said in an annoyingly perky voice. "Please remember to stay in character. You've all been given some background information about your character. Try to share some of that with the people on either side of you. Some of it may be relevant to the murder when it happens."

Bessie picked up her napkin and put it in her lap. Coming tonight had been a bad idea, she thought as she took a sip from the water glass in front of her. A moment later two waiters began pouring wine into glasses. Bessie hesitated and decided that one more glass of wine wouldn't hurt. It had already been a long evening and it was only just beginning.

The potato and leek soup smelled delicious as a second set of waiters began to distribute soup bowls. Bessie turned to George and smiled at him. "How are you tonight?" she asked.

"Oh, I'm very well. Thank you," he replied. "You aren't playing, are you?" he asked as he leaned close to Bessie. He probably thought he was lowering his voice, as well, but George's whisper was still loud by most standards.

"I'm not," Bessie agreed.

"I'm meant to be the owner of a country house," George told her. "Several of our guests are meant to be my children, but I've no idea which ones they are. I don't think Elizabeth explained it all very well. I'm endlessly confused."

Bessie hid a smile. No doubt Elizabeth had done her best. George was generally too busy with his businesses to pay much attention to his wife and children. Everything Elizabeth said had probably gone in one ear and out the other. "I'm afraid I can't help you," she told George, "but as I'm not playing, we can talk about anything. Tell me how you are."

George shrugged. "Busy, working too hard according to my lovely wife, but otherwise fine. I've just bought another little company in the south of the island. They wanted me to invest, but it seemed to make more sense to simply buy them outright. They manufacture some-thing tiny that goes inside something else that isn't very big, either. I own the company that makes the bigger thing, you see, so now I own both parts. It should be a good investment."

Bessie nodded. "And how are the children and grandchildren?"

"Oh, you'd have to ask Mary about that," he replied. "As far as I know, they're all fine, but she keeps track of them. I think one of the grandchildren had a birthday recently and one of my sons had a holiday in the US, but I can't remember any of the details."

Bessie took a few bites of her soup and sighed happily. While the company might be less than ideal, the food was excellent.

"I'm not much for soup," Inspector Rhodes said from Bessie's other side.

"No? I think it's delicious," Bessie told him.

"It's not bad, I just prefer food that I can chew," he explained.

"I see," Bessie replied.

"Did I hear that you aren't playing the game, then?" he asked.

"That's right. I'm not," she agreed.

"So there's no point in my interrogating you, is there. I'm meant to be forming opinions of the various suspects, but you won't be a suspect, will you?"

"I should hope not," Bessie replied.

"I can't talk to her, though," he said, tilting his head towards Vivian, who was sitting to his left. "She can't remember what her card said or who she's meant to be."

"Oh, dear, that isn't good," Bessie said.

"It happens," the man shrugged. "Some people get quite caught up in the game and others just sit around and watch, more or less. I don't know that I've ever been to one of these where people didn't actually have a part or anything, like you're doing, but I think that's better than taking a part and then refusing to actually play along."

"Perhaps she didn't realise what she was getting herself into," Bessie suggested.

"Yeah, I suppose," the man said. He finished the last of the wine in his glass and then turned his attention back to his soup. As he loudly slurped up the last of that, Susan clapped her hands together.

"Two more minutes, I think," she said. "Everyone has just about finished his or her soup. I hope you've all talked to the people around you. If you haven't spoken to one of your neighbours, now is the time."

Bessie sipped her wine and looked up and down the table. A few people were speaking quietly, but most of the guests were looking vaguely uncomfortable behind their empty bowls. The waiters cleared the table before Susan spoke again.

"Gentlemen, if you could please take your drinks with you and move two seats to your right, I would appreciate it," she said loudly. "The waiters will be serving the salad course momentarily."

"Good evening," Ernest said as he took George's place at the head of the table. "I'm meant to be some sort of disreputable rouge, I believe."

Bessie grinned as he made a face. "I'm not actually taking part, so you may tell me anything you like and it won't matter a bit."

The man laughed. "It will probably be easier if I just be myself. I'm already finding the whole murder mystery thing confusing."

"It does seem rather more complicated than I was expecting," Bessie replied as the waiter put her salad in front of her.

"I'm Ernest McCormick," the man said.

"I'm Elizabeth Cubbon, but you can call me Bessie; everyone does."

"It's a pleasure to meet you, Bessie. I assume you are one of Mary's friends?"

"Yes, and her neighbour, as well."

"You have a mansion on the cliff?"

Bessie laughed. "No, I have a tiny cottage on the beach, but it isn't far from here."

"I would love to live right on the water. London is shockingly expensive, though. I keep telling my sister that we should buy a cottage in Cornwall or a house in Blackpool or something like that just so we can be on the water."

"You could look at buying property on the island," Bessie suggested.

"That's a thought. I've never been to the island before, but so far I like what I've seen very much. I wouldn't want anything as extravagant as this, but probably something more than a cottage. Perhaps Elizabeth would let Norma and me stay for a few extra days so that we could do some house-hunting."

He took a sip of wine and then turned his attention to Elizabeth, who was on his right. As they began to talk, Bessie turned to the man on her left.

"Good evening," she said.

"Oh, yes, good evening," he replied.

"I'm Elizabeth Cubbon, and I'm not playing the murder mystery game, so you don't have to worry about being in character with me," she said.

The man laughed. "I wasn't all that worried," he said. "I'm not especially interested in the game. I just came over to get away for a few days."

"Away? I hope nothing is wrong at home."

"Just working too hard," the man replied. "I should introduce myself, though, shouldn't I? I'm Richard Long. I'm one of Elizabeth's thoroughly unsuitable friends."

Bessie chuckled. "She does seem to have rather a lot of friends. I'm surprised how many of them have been willing to come and visit her here on the island, as well. There doesn't seem to be that much for young people to do here."

"I was invited for the murder mystery. She promised it would be fun and exciting, but she also told me I could stay for the weekend. It's nice to get out of London once in a while."

"What do you think of the island so far?"

"I haven't seen much. We didn't arrive until last night, but it looks lovely so far. And Thie yn Traie is stunning."

Bessie nodded. "And it has incredible views of the sea."

"It does. I could sit and watch the water for hours," the man agreed.

"Right, I think we're about ready to move on," Susan announced. "I hope everyone is making sure to share a few facts about their characters with everyone else. You never know which facts might be important later."

Richard rolled his eyes at Bessie. "I'm meant to be a solicitor, here to help the owner of the country house rewrite his will. Surely that doesn't give me any motive for killing anyone."

Bessie shrugged. "I suppose you'll have to see who the victim is before you can judge," she said as waiters cleared empty plates.

"And now, if the gentlemen could move again, I'd appreciate it," Susan announced loudly.

This time there were a few grumbles as the men got to their feet. Elizabeth glanced up and down the table. "Come on, everyone. This is meant to be fun. You all need to get into character and enjoy yourselves."

Leonard Hammersmith dropped into the chair at the head of the table and glanced at Bessie. "At least the food is good," he said loudly.

"Andy Caine does a brilliant job," Bessie agreed.

"Is that who did the food? I should hire him for one of my restaurants."

"I didn't realise you have restaurants."

"I do now, but I probably won't for long," the man replied. "I was talked into investing in two in Douglas and a third in Castletown, but they're all losing money hand over fist, really. The biggest problem is getting good help, but I don't want to bore you with all of that. I'm meant to be telling you all about my character, right?"

"I'm not actually playing the game," Bessie said quickly. "You can talk to me about anything you like."

"Maybe I'll just eat," the man said as his plate was put in front of him.

Bessie looked down at her own meal and could understand the sentiment. Andy had made chicken in some sort of sauce, with roast potatoes and steamed vegetables. It looked and smelled delicious and Bessie's mouth began to water as she picked up her knife and fork.

"I'm Sean Rice," the man on Bessie's left said a few minutes later. "I'm one of Elizabeth's friends from London."

Bessie introduced herself and explained that she wasn't taking part in the game. "I hope you're enjoying your visit to the island," she added.

"It's okay. A bit quiet, but it's nice to get away from London once in a while. It's only for the weekend, anyway. I can put up with anything for a weekend. I go and stay with my father and his fourth wife for that long at least twice a year. If I can get through that, I can get through anything."

"Oh, dear," Bessie exclaimed.

The man shrugged. "Got to keep Dad happy, that's the key to staying in the will."

Not being sure how best to respond to that, Bessie took another bite of her dinner. The food was excellent, anyway.

"Liza was talking about having one of these parties at our house later in the year," Leonard said suddenly.

"Was she?" Bessie replied.

"Yeah, that's why we came. I can't say I'm overly impressed with what I've seen so far, though. It seems like too much fuss and bother. We could just have people around for drinks without everyone having to pretend to be someone else. That would make more sense."

"It's nice to try different things sometimes," Bessie said, trying to be diplomatic. She didn't want to agree outright and possibly lose business for Elizabeth.

"What was that inspector like, then?" Leonard asked. "He's meant to solve the murder, isn't he? Seems like he's been doing an awful lot of drinking, but maybe that's part of his character. I mean the character that he's playing, obviously."

Bessie thought that drinking too much was probably very much a part of the man's character, and not just the one he was playing. "I only just met him briefly," Bessie replied. "I'm not sure I heard where he used to work."

"It must have been London, mustn't it?"

"I don't know. I believe that's where Susan is from, anyway. She's the one who found the man."

"Maybe sleeping rough outside a bus terminal," Leonard muttered, looking over at the inspector, who was finishing off yet another glass of wine.

Bessie did wonder how well the man would do with the pretend murder investigation after all he'd drunk, but that was for Susan and Elizabeth to deal with. Once again she was glad that she wasn't taking part.

"Do you think I'd ever have a chance with her?" Sean said suddenly.

"I'm sorry?" Bessie said.

"Vivian, the girl in the silver dress. Do you think I have a chance with her?"

Bessie glanced at Vivian, who was across the table from her. "I haven't the slightest idea," she said honestly. "I haven't even met the girl."

"She's gorgeous, obviously," Sean sighed. "You'll think I'm shallow, but that's all I really want from a girl."

Bessie bit her tongue.

"I understand they're going to put out the lights so that the murder can take place," the man said. "Maybe I'll try talking to her when it's dark."

"You won't have a chance with her if you don't talk to her."

"I'm usually very confident with women, but she's something else. I'm sure she must be a model."

"I was told that she has done some modeling," Bessie replied.

"I came over because I was hoping to get closer to Elizabeth, really, but she seems to be involved with the guy that made the food. I didn't know Vivian was going to be here."

"You've met her before?"

"Once or twice. I've only ever admired her from afar in crowds, though. This is the first time we've been together in such a small group. Of course, Richard is probably thinking the same thing that I am. Did he mention her when you talked to him?"

"No, not at all."

"So maybe she isn't his type. I hope not."

Bessie wasn't particularly interested in the romantic entanglements of Elizabeth's friends. She ate the rest of her dinner while Sean talked about several of his former girlfriends. Every once in a while Leonard would say something random to her, but his comments never required anything more than a single-word reply. It was something of a relief when Susan clapped her hands together again.

"Right, now we're ready for the sweet course. If you'll just wait until the plates have been cleared, the gentlemen can move again," she announced.

Bessie grinned as she realised that she'd have Andy to sit next to during pudding. He'd told her that he'd based it on her shortbread recipe, but she had no idea what that meant.

A few minutes later, she found out as she was served her beautiful pudding.

"It's a shortbread bowl," Andy told her. "Filled with freshly made vanilla ice cream and caramel sauce."

Bessie used her spoon to crack her bowl into pieces. "It's delicious," she said after her first bite. The shortbread crumbled into the ice cream, allowing the caramel sauce to hold everything together. Bessie only just stopped herself from licking the plate when she was finished.

"Everything was truly delicious," she told Andy.

"Thank you. It was fun putting it all together, and even better that I did all of the work and then left it to the kitchen staff to serve everything. The staff have been great, and the kitchens at Tea and Try are fantastic."

"Thie yn Traie," Bessie said, gently correcting his pronunciation.

Andy laughed. "You'd think I would know that, having grown up on the island."

"Manx is a difficult language," Bessie told him. "I've taken the introductory class in the language four times now and I still can't say much."

"Maybe I'll take a class once I'm finished with school," Andy said. "I'd really like to do my restaurant menus in both Manx and English."

"I can point you in the right direction if you need them translated," Bessie told him.

"I may take you up on that. I just have to get through school first."

"How are you finding the evening?" Michael Higgins asked Bessie when she turned to speak to him.

"It's been unusual, with people changing seats every few minutes," Bessie said. "But the food has been very good, and I've enjoyed talking with everyone."

"Of course, we're all meant to be talking to one another in character, but you've not had to bother with that."

"No, and I'm quite relieved, really."

"I'm meant to be a retired army colonel or something like that," the man told her.

"You do rather look the part," Bessie said.

"As the parts were assigned before anyone met me, I think we'll have to assume that it wasn't planned that way," he shrugged. "I'm the only man here who is about the right age, I suppose."

"There's George, but he probably insisted on being the wealthy estate owner," Bessie said.

"And Inspector Rhodes is busy playing himself."

"Yes, well, yes," Bessie said, not wanting to complain about how much the man had been drinking, even though she didn't approve.

"I'm a bit concerned that he might not make it through the rest of the evening, though," Michael told her in a low voice. "I hope that Susan knows what she's doing."

"Have you been friends with Mona for long?" Bessie asked.

The man looked over at Mona and nodded. "We've been friends for many years. There was a time when I hoped we might be more than that, but it never worked out. She was kind enough to invite me to join her tonight, anyway."

"Do you live on the island?"

"I live in London mostly, but I have a cottage in Port St. Mary as well. I come across for a fortnight now and again. I was in London this afternoon when she rang about tonight, and I couldn't resist flying over."

"All right, everyone," Susan said loudly. "I think we're about ready for the next part of the evening. Has everyone finished with pudding?"

Waiters moved in to remove all of the plates. Bessie finished the last sip of her wine as Susan continued.

"We'll all move into the sitting area now," she said. "There you'll all have a chance to talk amongst yourselves for a while longer. The idea is for everyone to get acquainted with everyone else, so please try to speak to anyone you haven't already spoken with. As I said, you never know what might be a clue. And remember to stay in character."

Bessie slid her chair back and stood up. Now would probably be a good time for her and Mary to remove themselves from the room.

"I don't want to leave them," Mary whispered when Bessie made that suggestion to her. "If you don't mind terribly, can we just sit in the corner and keep an eye on everything? I feel that might be for the best."

Although Bessie didn't agree, she didn't argue. The room was huge, so there was plenty of space for her and Mary to settle in, out of the way of the rest of the crowd.

Susan and Elizabeth ushered everyone away from the table towards the windows. Several couches and chairs had been arranged in a rough circle, with tables between them. A long table had been set up as a bar nearby. Inspector Rhodes headed straight for the bar, getting himself yet another glass of wine before planting himself firmly in one of the chairs.

"We can sit over here," Mary told Bessie, leading her to a small couch that was some distance from the others. The couch was aligned with the windows, but because it was dark outside and the room was brightly lit, they acted as mirrors, rather than allowing Bessie to see the beach below them. She settled in and watched the large group reflected in the windows.

"Would you like some wine or something else to drink?" Mary asked her.

"No, I'm fine, thank you," Bessie replied.

Mary sat down next to her. "I hope this murder mystery thing works out," she told Bessie. "Elizabeth is really excited about the idea. She seems to think that there will be a lot of demand for this sort of party once the word gets out."

"Leonard Hammersmith said he and Liz were thinking about doing one, but he wasn't sure that it wasn't too much bother."

"Yes, I did hear a few complaints about how much effort it was to remember to stay in character during dinner," Mary agreed. "I understand that Susan wanted everyone in fancy dress, which would have been more work, and that she wanted to use names for the characters, rather than letting people use their own names."

"That all sounds as if it would be a great deal of work. I can't imagine trying to remember who everyone was and a second set of names as well."

Mary nodded. "Elizabeth was surprisingly sensible for once and told Susan that neither fancy dress nor made-up names were necessary, at least not for tonight's trial run."

The pair fell silent for a few minutes as they watched the group across the room. Bessie spotted Sean, standing behind Vivian and simply staring at her. Vivian was having what looked like an intense conversation with Norma. Madison Fields was sitting on a couch next to Richard, but they seemed to be ignoring one another. Ernest was at the bar, sipping what looked like whiskey and talking to Elizabeth and Andy.

"At least George is having fun," Mary murmured.

George was standing with Mona Kelly, and as Bessie watched, he seemed to be whispering something in her ear. Mona shook her head and said something back that made George flush. A moment later Michael joined them, handing them each a drink.

"I didn't realise you and Mona were friends," Bessie remarked.

"I'm not sure that we are," Mary told her. "Elizabeth asked me to invite her, though. Mona has a reputation for having fabulous parties, you see. Elizabeth is hoping Mona might be interested in hosting her own murder mystery if she enjoys tonight's gathering."

"Mona's parties are special because of the people she invites," Bessie said. "I haven't been to more than a couple, but at the last one I went to I met the US ambassador to the UK, a former Soviet cosmonaut, and a Hollywood actor who couldn't tear his eyes off of Mona all evening."

Mary nodded. "She seems to know an incredible number of people, and they all seem to love her."

Norma had joined her brother at the bar as Susan moved into the centre of the circle of chairs and couches.

"All right, everyone, it's nearly time for the game to begin. We're all at a large country house. You've all had a chance to get to know one another, but someone here has murder on his or her mind. In a few moments the lights are going to go out, thanks to the horrible storm outside." She glanced over at the window and then chuckled. "We'll have to imagine that part as well."

"We get a lot of rain, but very few thunderstorms," George said apologetically.

"It's fine," Susan smiled. "We're all using our imaginations anyway. So, the storm will knock out the power and we'll all have to sit in the dark while we wait for the power to come back on."

"What about torches?" Sean asked.

"We don't have any torches," Susan replied. "Instead, we'll simply have to wait out the storm. It should only take fifteen minutes or so for the power to come back on."

"Everyone make sure they have a full drink before the lights go out," Leonard suggested.

"Yes, of course," Susan said. "You'll all want to be sitting down comfortably. Once the lights go out, the only person who should be moving around is the murderer. He or she knows what to do."

"What's that?" Madison asked.

"He or she will make his or her way to the victim and tell him or her that they have been murdered," Susan explained.

"Does the victim know that someone is coming for them?" Sean asked.

"In this game, we've chosen not to tell the victim," Susan replied. "Sometimes we do, but this time only the murderer knows whom he or she intends to kill."

"I'm not sure that sitting around in the dark for fifteen minutes is going to be much fun for everyone," Bessie said softly.

"If it's too dark for anyone to see anything, it will be dangerous for the pretend killer go wandering around," Mary replied, frowning. "If he or she falls over something and breaks an arm, it won't be difficult to work out who the killer was meant to be."

"We can all point him or her out as we wait for the ambulance," Bessie suggested.

Mary laughed quietly. "I'm not sure that Susan has thought this through."

"I thought she did these evenings all the time."

"That's what she told Elizabeth, anyway," Mary shrugged.

"I would suggest that our murderer find a convenient place to position him or herself near the victim," Susan called out.

"Which makes sense, but will also make it easier for people to find the killer," Bessie murmured.

"This is never going to work," Leonard said. "If it's so dark that we can't see who the murderer is, then the poor murderer will probably break his neck trying to get to the victim."

"His or her," Vivian said with a giggle.

"Maybe we could put everyone in chairs in a row," Elizabeth suggested. "Then the killer could simply walk down the row, find the victim, and then return to his or her seat."

No one else had any better ideas, so Elizabeth had some of the staff set up a long row of chairs. Then she had everyone move over onto them.

"The chairs are arranged so that they are exactly two paces apart," she said. "My paces, anyway. If you are taller or shorter than me, you might have to adjust that. Why don't you all walk around the chairs a few times so you can get a feel for how many steps you need to take to get from one chair to the next and from your seat and back again?"

Mary looked at Bessie and they both rolled their eyes. The murder mystery evening was turning into another sort of game altogether.

Inspector Rhodes moved over to the bar and got himself another drink while the others dutifully walked around the chairs a few times.

"Okay, everyone can take their seats now," Susan announced. "Although he's been here all along, the inspector is now going to leave the room."

"He is?" Norma asked.

"Just in case our murderer does have some trouble in the dark, we don't want to give the game away to our police inspector," Susan said.

"I'll just lock the inspector in the library," Elizabeth said. "I'll be right back."

"Maybe, when the lights are out, we should all walk around the chairs a few times," Sean suggested. "I mean, otherwise we might be able to work out who moved and who didn't."

"That's not a bad idea," Susan said. "Let's do that. Once the lights go out, everyone can walk carefully around the chairs. At some point, the murderer will have to stop and then tell the victim that he or she is dead."

"How will he or she find the victim if everyone is walking around?" Liz asked.

"At the beginning of the line, each of you should call out your name," Susan said. "The murderer can step out of line and then stand nearby. When he hears the victim, he can step in and tell him or her to die."

"He or she," someone shouted.

"Yes, of course," Susan said, flushing.

"Won't we be able to guess that the crime has been committed once someone stops shouting out his or her own name?" Madison asked.

"There must be a better way to do this," Elizabeth said as she rejoined the party. "What do you usually do?" she asked Susan.

"Different things, depending on the venue," Susan replied. "Let's try this and see how it works. Everyone up and start walking slowly. In a minute I'll kill the lights and we'll see what happens next."

Bessie and Mary exchanged glances. It was obvious what was going to happen next. The whole thing was going to fall apart.

The group began their circuit of the chairs, each one calling out his or her name as they went past the first chair. After a moment, Elizabeth left the room. A minute later the room went dark. Bessie blinked several times, and then sat back and waited for her eyes to adjust. Eventually she felt as if she could make out movement around the row of chairs, but she couldn't be certain.

People were still shouting out their names, but it seemed entirely random. After a few minutes, Bessie heard one of the women shout out "Richard." Everyone laughed and then, from what Bessie could tell, began shouting out random names, including that of the prime minister and the island's governor.

"When do the lights come back on?" someone asked loudly.

"I've told Elizabeth to leave them off for fifteen minutes," Susan's voice called back.

"That's a bloody long time," someone snapped.

"Hey, watch your hands," another voice said.

"This is crazy," Mary whispered. "If I could see anything, I'd go and tell Elizabeth to turn the lights back on right now."

"Surely it won't be too much longer," Bessie replied.

"That's it, I give up," someone said. "I'll be sitting quietly in one of the chairs; watch you don't trip over me."

"That's a good idea," came another voice. "I'm finding a chair, too."

The last five minutes or so of darkness were oddly quiet. From what Bessie could tell, everyone had taken seats and they were all simply waiting out the clock.

When the lights came back on, Bessie was surprised to see Vivian lying on the floor just a few feet away from the row of chairs. She was giggling softly to herself.

Elizabeth walked back in and looked at Susan.

"It appears Vivian has been murdered," Susan said dramatically. "No one move. We must ring for the police."

Elizabeth nodded. "I'll go and ring for Inspector Rhodes. I'm sure he'll be here soon."

"Can we all get drinks while we wait for the police?" Richard asked.

"Especially me," Vivian said from her spot on the floor.

Susan opened her mouth to reply, but the loud scream stopped her. Bessie was on her feet, heading for the corridor before anyone else moved.

CHAPTER 4

*E*lizabeth was standing in the corridor outside the great room
with her hand covering her mouth.

"What's wrong?" Bessie demanded.

"The inspector," Elizabeth said. "He's, that is, I mean, I can't."

The girl burst into tears and then threw herself into Mary's arms
as Mary joined them.

"In the library?" Bessie asked.

Elizabeth shook her head. "I couldn't find my key earlier today, so
we decided to put him in the room next door. The key for that room
was in the lock."

"You locked him inside?" Mary wondered.

"It was just a precaution so that no one could say he cheated," Elizabeth told her.

Bessie crossed to the door to the room in question and looked
inside. It appeared to be a small study. There was a small desk in the
centre of the room with a large and comfortable-looking chair behind
it. A second chair had been placed in front of the desk. Inspector
Rhodes was sitting in that second chair with a large knife protruding
from his chest. From the amount of blood on the floor, Bessie had to
assume that the man was dead.

"I gather this wasn't part of the game," Bessie said to Elizabeth as she pulled out her mobile phone.

"No, not at all," Elizabeth said, shuddering.

"What's going on?" Susan demanded from the great room doorway.

"Inspector Rhodes isn't well," Mary said. "Just get everyone a drink. We're calling for an ambulance now."

"He's just drunk," Susan snapped. "I warned him that if he drank too much tonight I'd never use him again, but he never listens to me. Let me talk to him."

"Not right now," Bessie said. She'd rung John's home number, but no one was answering.

Susan took a step forward. "I want to see him," she said loudly.

Bessie caught Mary's eye. "You have guests to worry about," Mary reminded her. "Let's get back to the party."

"I invited the man. If he's ill, I need to know about it," Susan insisted.

Mary was struggling to deal with the still sobbing Elizabeth and an angry Susan when John answered his mobile.

"John, it's Bessie. We have a situation at Thie yn Traie," she said.

"At the murder mystery evening? What sort of situation?"

"You need to come," Bessie replied, not wanting to say too much in front of Susan.

"Do I need a full crime scene team?"

"Yes, I think you do."

"Someone is dead?"

"Sadly, yes."

John sighed. "I'll send the closest uniformed constable. He or she should be there in a few minutes. I'll follow with my team. How many guests are at the party?"

"Maybe a dozen or so," Bessie replied.

"And how many of them could have committed the murder?"

"Maybe a dozen or so," Bessie repeated herself.

John sighed again and then ended the call. Susan was still loudly demanding to see the inspector.

"The police are on their way," Bessie said loudly.

"The police? Oh, no, what's he done now?" Susan asked.

"What do you mean?" Mary asked her.

"What has Inspector Rhodes done that has made you ring the police? Whatever it is, I'm sure we can work things out without involving the police," Susan replied.

"Let's go and sit down in the other room," Mary suggested.

Susan hesitated and then nodded. Elizabeth took a few deep breaths and then wiped her eyes.

"I should go and do something about my face," she murmured.

"I think it would be best if you didn't go anywhere right now," Bessie told her.

The foursome walked slowly back towards the great room. As Bessie crossed the threshold, Susan suddenly turned away and ran back into the corridor. She pushed her way through the partially open door to the study where the body was located and then began to scream.

Bessie quickly grabbed her arm and tried to pull her out of the room. Michael Higgins was at her side a moment later. He succeeded where Bessie hadn't, nearly dragging the still screaming woman back into the corridor.

"Daddy," Susan sobbed. "Someone killed my father."

A dozen questions flashed through Bessie's head, but she didn't let herself ask the girl anything.

"Maybe you should take her into another room," Michael said. "Is there a key for the door to the room where the body is?" he asked Elizabeth.

Elizabeth nodded and fished a key out of her pocket. Michael shut and locked the door to the study and then turned around to face Bessie.

"Take Susan somewhere and try to calm her down," he told her. "I'll go back in and deal with the party guests. I assume someone has rung 999."

"I called John Rockwell," Bessie told him.

He stared at her for a minute and then nodded. "That will do," he said before he turned and his heel and strode back into the great room.

"You should be in there with the guests," Mary told Elizabeth. "Don't tell them what's happened, though. That's for the police to deal with."

Elizabeth nodded and made her way through the door to the great room.

"Madam?" Jonathan Hooper said.

"The police will be here soon," Mary told him. "Please bring them to me here."

"Of course, madam," he replied. He bowed and then disappeared in the direction of the front door.

"I need to take Susan somewhere," Bessie said.

"There's another study down the hall," Mary told her. "The key should be in the door." She led Bessie down the corridor. Bessie kept a tight grip on Susan's arm as they went.

Mary opened a door and switched on the lights. The room was small and held only a few chairs and a large table.

"What did the Pierce family do with this room?" Bessie wondered.

"I believe Mrs. Pierce used it as a sewing room," Mary told her. "There were some other lamps and things in here when we bought the house, but we've reused them elsewhere."

Bessie nodded and then guided Susan into a chair. "Sit," she said firmly.

Susan complied, her face still buried in her hands.

"I'll wait in the corridor for the police," Mary said. She shut the door behind her, leaving Bessie alone with Susan, who was still crying quietly.

"I'm sure I have tissues in my bag," Bessie told the woman. She found a small packet and held it out towards Susan. The other woman peeked out over her hands and then reached out to take the tissues.

She blew her nose loudly and then wiped her eyes. "Thank you," she said softly.

A knock on the door startled them both. Bessie opened it to one of the uniformed waiters, who was carrying a tray. "Mrs. Quayle sent me," he told them as he put the tray on the table. The tray held a large box of tissues, a pitcher of ice water with two glasses, and two pots of tea with teacups. A plate of biscuits sat in the centre of the tray.

"I don't want anything," Susan said flatly.

"Have a drink of water," Bessie suggested.

Susan looked as if she wanted to refuse, but after a moment she took the glass that Bessie offered. After a few sips, she sat back in her seat and sighed. "I don't imagine you'll keep your mouth shut about what I said when I saw the body," she said to Bessie.

"About the inspector being your father? Surely that's something you'll want the police to know."

"I'd rather no one knew," Susan replied. "Although it's mostly Elizabeth and her mother that I'd like to keep it from, and they were both standing there when I fell apart. It probably doesn't matter who else knows now."

"I don't want to pry," Bessie said, desperately wanting to pry, "but why wouldn't you want Elizabeth and Mary to know?"

Susan sighed. "I may have exaggerated slightly when I said he was a retired senior police official. And I may have exaggerated slightly when I said I'd done lots of these parties before."

"May have?" Bessie echoed.

"Yeah, okay, I lied," Susan snapped. She took a sip of water and then shook her head. "I'm sorry. I don't mean to shout at you, but, well, I am a party-planner, at least part time, but it's hard to find jobs. One of my friends heard about how Elizabeth was starting up a party planning business over here and suggested I get in touch and offer to give her a hand. I couldn't see any harm in it, really."

"I assume you're charging Elizabeth for your assistance," Bessie said coolly.

The other woman flushed. "Not as much as I charge for proper party planning," she said defensively. "I have been helping her quite a lot, too. I did nearly all of the planning for tonight, you know. It was my idea from the start."

"Was it, now?"

"Yes. I kept hearing about these sorts of parties and I thought they sounded like fun. I suggested to Elizabeth that we try one here on the island and see how it went."

"Except you told her that you'd already done several," Bessie pointed out.

"I don't think I said that exactly," the girl muttered.

"Where does your father fit into all of this?"

"We needed a proper police inspector to take on that role. Elizabeth thought she had someone lined up, but he couldn't make it at the last minute, so I asked my father to step in."

"He was with the police?"

"He, well, he's done a lot of security work," the girl said quietly, "and he watches a lot of detective shows on the telly. It was only a pretend murder, so it didn't much matter anyway."

Bessien nodded. It wasn't her place to question the woman. It would probably be smart for her to stop doing so before John arrived. "I'm sorry for your loss," she said.

"Thank you," Susan replied. "I'm devastated, obviously, surprisingly so. My father and I didn't exactly get along well. I'm surprised at how I feel, really."

"I think we're often surprised by the emotions that we feel when we're faced with tragedy," Bessie told her. Someone tapped on the door. After a moment, Mary pushed it open and looked inside.

"John's here with the crime scene team. He'll be ready to start taking statements in a few minutes. He'd like to start with you, Bessie, and then talk to Susan next," she said.

Bessie nodded. "I'll wait here for him. Maybe you could find someone else to sit with Ms. Haymarket while I'm with John. I'm not sure she should be alone."

"Who's John?" Susan asked.

"Inspector John Rockwell is the head of the Laxey CID," Bessie told her.

"CID?"

"Criminal Investigation Department," Bessie explained. "He's a police inspector, a proper one."

"Police? I don't want to talk to the police," she replied.

"Your father was murdered," Bessie said as gently as she could. "We will all have to talk to the police, probably several times."

"It must have been an accident," Susan said insistently. "No one would have murdered him on purpose. I'm the only person who hated him that much."

"Why not save all of that for Inspector Rockwell," Bessie suggested. "He'll have a great many questions for you."

"Can I refuse to speak to him?" the woman asked.

Bessie looked at Mary, who shrugged. "Surely you want to do everything you can to help the police find the man or woman responsible for your father's death," Bessie replied eventually.

"I don't know what I want," Susan said, "or rather, I do. I want to wake up and have this all be a horrible nightmare. I think I need to get some fresh air."

The woman got to her feet and took a step towards the door.

"It's raining quite hard," Mary told her. "You're better off staying inside."

"I don't care about rain. I'm feeling quite claustrophobic in this little room," Susan said sharply. She kept walking, forcing Mary to step back out of her way. Bessie followed the woman into the corridor.

"I'll just go get some air," Susan told them both, heading towards the front door.

Mary looked as if she wanted to say something, but Bessie shook her head at her. Bessie knew John well enough to know that there would be a constable at the door, stopping people from leaving. Susan strode down the corridor, stopping short as she walked into the foyer. Bessie followed and was relieved to see that she was correct. Not only was there a uniformed constable at the door, it was someone she knew well.

"Good evening," Hugh Watterson said politely to Susan. He caught Bessie's eye and gave her a smile.

To Bessie, the young man still looked not much more than fifteen, even though he'd been with the police for several years and had recently married. He and his wife, Grace, had a baby on the way, and

Bessie was delighted for them. They were in the process of buying one of the new houses that had been built along the beach some distance from Bessie's own cottage, and Bessie was looking forward to having them nearby.

"Hi there," Susan said. She walked over to Hugh and said something in a low voice.

He shook his head. "I'm awfully sorry, but for now the inspector wants everyone to remain in the house."

"But it was my father who was killed," Susan said, tears beginning to stream down her face again. "I just need a minute or two to clear my head before I talk to the police about it, that's all."

"I'm very sorry for your loss," Hugh told her.

"So I can go for a short walk?" the woman asked.

"Perhaps in a little while," Hugh said. "Maybe after you've spoken to the inspector."

"Please, please, just give me two minutes," the woman begged. "I'm so devastated that I'm barely able to think straight. I just need a few minutes to myself."

Hugh nodded. "I understand that," he said. "I'm sure Mrs. Quayle can find you somewhere quiet where you can gather your thoughts."

Susan opened her mouth again, but she was interrupted by a new arrival. "Is there something wrong out here?" John Rockwell asked in a serious voice.

Bessie was grateful to see the man. He looked incredibly handsome in a dark suit that made her wonder where he'd been when she'd rung him. His brown hair looked as if it had been recently cut, as well. His bright green eyes focussed on Susan.

"You're Susan Haymarket?" he asked.

"Yes," she replied. "Are you in charge here?"

"I'm Inspector John Rockwell. I will be conducting the investigation into your father's death, if that's what you mean."

"Good. Then you can tell this man to step aside and let me get some fresh air," the woman replied. "He's refusing my very simple request."

"I'm afraid it isn't quite that simple, not during a murder investigation," John told her. "Until we've had a chance to question everyone, no one is going to be going anywhere."

"You can't make me stay here," the girl said angrily.

"I can, actually," John replied evenly, "but as you're so eager to get away, why don't I talk to you first, before anyone else? Then once we're finished, you can take your walk in the rain."

Susan frowned. "I don't want to talk to you," she told him.

"Surely you want the police to work out what happened to your father," John replied. "Someone killed him. You don't want them to get away with murder."

For a moment Bessie thought that Susan was going to argue, but instead she sighed deeply. "Okay, then, let's get this over with," she said.

John nodded. "Mrs. Quayle has kindly provided me with a temporary office. If you'll come with me, please."

Bessie, Mary, and Hugh all watched as John led the woman away.

"How are you?" Bessie asked Hugh as the pair disappeared.

"I'm fine, thanks. How are you?" he replied.

"I've been better," Bessie sighed. "I really didn't want to get caught up in another murder investigation."

"I'm sorry, Bessie," Mary said.

"It isn't your fault in any way," Bessie told her, "and it isn't Elizabeth's fault, either. The only person who should be sorry is the murderer, and he or she probably isn't at all sorry."

"I shouldn't have talked you into coming, though," Mary protested.

"I made my own decision to come. If you want to blame someone, you should blame Andy for being such a wonderful chef. I only came because of his food, you know," Bessie replied.

"Poor Andy. He looked very shaken when I saw him last," Mary told her.

"Is everyone else in the great room?" Bessie asked.

"Yes, with a handful of constables watching over them," Mary replied.

"Maybe we should go and join them," Bessie suggested. She gave Hugh a quick hug and then she and Mary walked back to the great room. As they entered, everyone looked up, and Bessie thought they all looked disappointed as she and Mary entered the room.

"Bessie, what is going on?" Mona called from her seat on one of the couches. Michael was sitting next to her, holding her hand tightly.

Having no idea what anyone knew, Bessie simply shook her head and then took a seat on the nearest couch. Elizabeth had been standing at the bar. Now she walked over to join Bessie and her mother, who'd sat down next to Bessie.

"Where's Susan?" she asked in a low voice.

One of the police constables crossed the room. "The inspector would prefer it if you didn't talk," he said in an apologetic tone.

"I was just checking on the whereabouts of my friend," Elizabeth told the man.

"She's with John," Bessie said quickly, earning herself a stern look from the constable.

The silence in the room was oppressive and Bessie found herself feeling desperate to speak, even though she had nothing to say. She looked around the room, taking time to study the partygoers, who were sitting together in an awkward cluster.

Vivian was sitting between Richard and Sean. The girl looked bored, but unconcerned. Richard was tapping his foot and staring at his watch, seemingly unaware of Vivian, while Sean appeared to be watching her closely through half-closed eyes. Bessie wondered if she were imagining it because of the things Sean had said to her earlier about his feelings for the girl, and then decided it didn't really matter.

Madison was sitting on a chair next to the trio, staring straight ahead. Her face was pale and she looked as if she might cry if anyone spoke to her. On the next couch, Liza and Leonard Hammersmith were sitting with their hands tightly clasped. Liza was staring at the window while Leonard looked at the floor.

Norma and her brother, Ernest, were standing at the bar with drinks in front of them. Bessie hoped they were soft drinks. No one needed any more alcohol at this point. George and Andy were sitting in chairs next to one another a short distance from the others. Bessie caught Andy's eye and gave him a smile that she hoped was reassuring. He shrugged.

George suddenly looked around the room and seemed to notice Mary for the first time. He silently got up and crossed to his wife, sitting down next to her. She leaned against him as he slid his arm around her. Elizabeth moved over to sit on the other side of her father and he quickly put an arm around her as well.

What felt like several hours but was only about twenty minutes later, John spoke from the doorway. "Ladies and gentlemen, on behalf of the Isle of Man Constabulary, thank you for your patience. I'm Inspector John Rockwell with the Laxey Criminal Investigation Department. I understand you were all here for a murder mystery evening, but unfortunately a real murder investigation takes precedence. For those of you who don't know, the gentlemen who was introduced to you as Inspector Jerome Rhodes was murdered."

John stopped there and waited as gasps and murmurs went through the crowd. "I will need to speak to each of you individually, and I appreciate your patience as I conduct my investigation."

"Surely you don't need to speak to me or my wife," Leonard Hammersmith said loudly. "We didn't know the man and had no reason to want to kill him. Anyway, we were both here, playing at the ridiculous murder game, when he was killed."

"As I said, I need to speak to each of you, individually," John replied. "I've requested assistance from Douglas CID so that we can get through the interviews more quickly, but for now I'm asking you to be patient with us."

"I have better things to do than sit here and wait while you talk to a dozen people, one at a time," Leonard objected.

"A man is dead," John said sharply, "and it's highly likely that someone in this room killed him."

Vivian began to laugh and then stopped abruptly as everyone looked at her. "But none of us would have killed him," she protested. "We didn't even know who he was."

"Nevertheless, I have to speak to each of you," John replied. "Mary, if I could start with you, I'd appreciate it."

Mary nodded and then rose to her feet. As she began to walk towards the door, George called after her.

"Do I need to ring for our advocate?"

Mary shook her head as she kept walking. George settled back in his seat with a sigh. As soon as John and Mary were out of sight, it seemed as if everyone began to fidget in their places. Whenever anyone moved around, however, a police constable followed them. Bessie was grateful when Peter Corkill strode into the room.

"Good evening, everyone," he said. "I'm Inspector Peter Corkill from the Douglas CID. Because there are so many of you to interview, John requested my assistance. Miss Cubbon, if I could start with you, please?"

Bessie nodded and got to her feet. She'd been to the man's wedding only a month earlier. It felt strange hearing her friend call her Miss Cubbon. They walked into the corridor. Once they were out of sight of the others, Pete gave her a hug.

"Are you okay?" he asked.

"I'm fine," Bessie replied. "How are you? I saw your lovely wife in Douglas the other day and she told me all about your fabulous honeymoon."

"It was amazing," he told her. "Everything that we'd hoped it would be and more. We even enjoyed Las Vegas, and Helen won over five hundred dollars playing the slot machines. We were smart, and quit after that, as well."

"How wonderful for you," Bessie smiled.

"John really wants to talk to you himself, but I know you'll be our best source of information tonight," Pete said.

"I can wait and talk to you both at the same time, after you've spoken to everyone else," Bessie offered. "I know many of the others are eager to get away."

"It's up to you," Pete said. "I can take your statement now and you can go home, or you can wait until the end."

"If I go home, I won't sleep," Bessie told him. "I may as well wait."

Pete nodded. "Thank you," he said. "There are some people in there who think they are quite important. The sooner we can deal with them and let them go, the better."

Bessie knew he was talking about Leonard and Liz, although she wondered about Michael Higgins as well. Mona had been vague about the man's occupation, but she'd said something about him working for the government. He's certainly been quick to take charge earlier.

Pete led Bessie back into the great room. She returned to her seat near Elizabeth and George and then waited to see which person Pete would take next.

"Mr. Higgins, if I could speak with you, please," Pete said.

The man stood up and then pulled Mona to her feet. "My friend is tired. Perhaps you could talk to her at the same time?"

Pete hesitated and then nodded. "Come along. I'm sure we can make it work."

Mona gave Michael a satisfied smile, and then the pair walked out of the room behind Pete. When John returned a short while later, he took Elizabeth and George away to be interviewed. Bessie sat on her own, trying to guess who would be the next to be summoned. She'd just settled on Leonard when Hugh appeared in the doorway.

"Mr. Hammersmith, if you could come with me, please?" he said.

"Why do I only get a lowly constable?" the man demanded. "What are the inspectors doing?"

"The inspectors are interviewing witnesses," Hugh replied. "Inspector Rockwell asked me to come and collect you for him while he finishes writing his notes from his last interview. He was hoping that this might save a bit of time, but you'd prefer to wait for him to come to collect you, I can go and tell him that."

The man pressed his lips together and then stomped across the room. "You should talk to my wife at the same time," he said.

"If you'd like to wait here, I can go and ask the inspector if that's possible," Hugh said cheerfully.

Leonard shook his head. "Let's just go and get this over with," he snapped.

When Hugh returned a few minutes later, he took Liza away. Andy was next, and Norma and Ernest followed him in quick succession.

"This is boring," Vivian complained loudly as Ernest followed Hugh out of the room. "We should be allowed to drink at the very least."

"You don't want to be drunk when you talk to the police," Sean suggested.

"Why ever not?" Vivian replied. "I've nothing to hide and it's going to be a boring conversation. Maybe if I'm a little bit drunk, it will be more fun."

"You really aren't meant to be talking together," a young constable that Bessie barely knew said to Vivian.

"You're cute," Vivian replied. "Do you like being in the police?"

The man blushed and looked at the ground. "Very much," he replied.

"Wouldn't you rather do something more exciting that pays better?" she asked.

The man shook his head. "I'm quite happy where I am," he said.

When Hugh walked back into the room a moment later, the young constable crossed over to him and said something. Hugh frowned and then nodded. "Ms. Walker, you're next," Hugh announced.

"Ha, you're just trying to stop me from chatting up the other constable," she said as she rose to her feet. "He's awfully cute, but so are you. Are you single?"

Hugh shook his head. "I'm married and we have a baby on the way," he said proudly.

Vivian sighed. "And I so love a man in uniform," she simpered as she followed Hugh out of the room.

Bessie looked over at Sean, who was watching the girl leave with a sad expression on his face. When Bessie caught his eye, he shrugged and then flopped backwards on the couch. Bessie found that she could no longer be bothered with guessing who might be next. The evening was dragging on, seemingly endlessly, and she was beginning to regret telling Pete that she'd wait.

"Has anyone seen Susan?" Hugh asked from the doorway a minute later.

Bessie looked around the room. Everyone was staring blankly at Hugh. "She hasn't come back in here," Bessie told him.

"I was afraid of that," he sighed, pulling out his mobile phone.

After a few minutes, Hugh returned to collect Madison. Richard and Sean weren't far behind, which left Bessie on her own in the great room with three uniformed constables. Unusually for her, Bessie didn't feel up to making conversation with the men, even though she was acquainted with two of them. When Hugh finally came in to collect her, Bessie was more than half-asleep in her seat.

"Bessie? John and Pete are ready for you," Hugh said.

CHAPTER 5

*B*essie struggled to her feet, shaking her head to clear the cobwebs. What she really needed was some strong coffee. A chocolate biscuit or two wouldn't have gone amiss either. Thinking dreamily of chocolate biscuits and sleep, Bessie followed Hugh down the corridor and into yet another small room that she'd never noticed before. It appeared to be an office, with a large desk that stretched nearly the entire length of the room. John was sitting behind the desk in a huge well-cushioned chair. Pete was in one of the two chairs opposite John. Both men got to their feet as Bessie entered.

"I'm sorry that you had to wait so long," John said as he came around the desk to give Bessie a hug.

"I offered," Bessie reminded him. "I was hoping you might get a confession from someone before you got around to me, anyway."

John smiled tightly. "That would have been nice," he said as he returned to his chair.

"Knock, knock," Jonathan Hooper said from the doorway. "Mrs. Quayle sent me," he told them as he carried a large silver tray into the room. He set it on the desk and then bowed before exiting the room.

"Coffee," Bessie said excitedly.

"And biscuits," Pete added, his eyes lighting up like a small child's.

"I needed this," John admitted as he poured himself a cup of the hot, dark liquid.

"Don't we all?" Bessie asked as she took her turn with the pot. She added a tiny drop of milk to her cup and took a sip. Even though she knew the caffeine couldn't possibly work that quickly, she felt better immediately. The first bite of chocolate biscuit also improved her mood dramatically.

"So let's start at the very beginning," John said after he'd washed several biscuits down with two cups of coffee. "Tell me about your day, starting with the time you got up."

"I think it might be better if I start with Thursday and work forward," Bessie told him. "That was when I first heard about tonight's little gathering. I don't know that any of that is relevant, but it might be."

John nodded. "Start with Thursday, then," he said, sounding a little tired.

"I'll condense it," Bessie promised.

She told both men about her conversation with Elizabeth and her subsequent talks with both Elizabeth and Mary about the party. Then she told them everything that she'd done that day, starting with when she'd woken up and moving through the party. When she was done, she sat back and took a long drink of coffee.

"So who killed Inspector Rhodes?" Pete asked her.

Bessie blinked in surprise. "I've no idea," she exclaimed.

"I was hoping you might have a guess," he told her.

"Was he even an inspector?" Bessie asked. "From what Susan said, I got the impression that he wasn't."

"No, he wasn't," John told her. "Of course, no one was who they were pretending to be at the party, isn't that right?"

"Yes and no," Bessie replied. "Mary and I weren't playing, and Susan wasn't either, from what I could see. As I already told you, when I talked to people at dinner, I told them all that I wasn't taking part. No one bothered to try to stay in character with me once they knew that."

John yawned. "I'm too tired to think straight," he said. "I've taken statements from everyone. I think it's time for all of us to go home and get some sleep. Who knows, maybe the technicians will find fingerprints on the murder weapon or something useful like that."

"What was the murder weapon?" Bessie asked.

John glanced at Pete and shrugged. "I'm sure it will be all over the papers tomorrow, anyway. It was one of the knives from the kitchen here. From what I can tell, everyone in the house had access."

Bessie sighed. "Why aren't these things ever easy?"

John nodded. "It would be nice, for once, to turn up and find someone still standing over the body holding the knife or something like that, but I've never known it to happen." He yawned again. "I'm going to come and see you some time tomorrow, and I'll warn you now that I'm going to want to go back through the party in greater detail. I'm afraid if we try to do it tonight I'll miss something."

"It's better to let the technicians finish before we go too far, anyway," Pete said. "They may not be able to solve the crime, but they may well be able to narrow the field for us."

"I certainly hope so," John replied. "Right now there are far too many suspects."

John had Pete give Bessie a ride home. "I have a few more things to do here and then I'll be going home as well," he promised Bessie before she left. "I know I'm better off getting some sleep tonight and tackling the case in the morning when I'm fresher."

When Pete pulled up to Treoghe Bwaane, he insisted on parking and going inside with Bessie. "After what happened last month, I'm not just dropping you off and driving away," he said firmly when Bessie tried to protest.

"The man who broke into my cottage is safely tucked away in prison," Bessie reminded him as she opened her cottage door.

He nodded, and then, as she switched on the lights, he walked across the kitchen and into the sitting room. Bessie stood by the door and listened as he climbed the stairs and stomped around the first floor. When he came down, she smiled.

"Did you find anyone hiding in my wardrobes?" she asked.

"Only a few stray cuddly toys who must have wandered off from your bedroom," he replied. "I rounded them up and sent them back where they belong."

Bessie grinned. Her bedroom was bright pink, a colour she'd thought she would love when she'd selected it in the shop. She'd been far less thrilled with it once she'd painted the walls, but she'd decided to give herself time to get used to it. Many years later, she was still waiting for that to happen. One day she'd get around to repainting, but that day hadn't come yet. To go along with the pink walls, Bessie's bedroom was filled with piles of cuddly toys. Many of Laxey's children seemed to believe that cuddly toys were the perfect present for their honourary auntie, and the more toys Bessie had accumulated the more children seemed to appear with further new additions.

She let the man out of the cottage and then carefully locked the door behind him. As she climbed the stairs, she admitted to herself that she was grateful that he'd checked over the cottage for her. Last month's break-in had made her home feel slightly less safe and it was taking her a while to feel at ease there again. In spite of that and the amount of coffee she'd recently drunk, Bessie was asleep as soon as her head hit her pillow. Her dreams were a confused mix of friends and strangers, and when she woke at six the next morning she was happy to leave them all behind her and get out of bed.

After tea and toast, Bessie headed out for her morning walk. It was overcast but not actually raining as she made her way past the holiday cottages. An unhappy-looking police constable was standing at the foot of the stairs to Thie yn Traie.

"Good morning," Bessie greeted the man. She remembered seeing him at Hugh's wedding, but she didn't think they'd ever been introduced.

"Good morning," he replied.

"How are you this morning?" she asked.

"I'm fine, thanks. Just hoping the rain holds off until I finish my shift."

Bessie chuckled. "When do you finish?"

"I just got here," he sighed. "I'll probably be here all day."

"You can't complain about the view," Bessie pointed out.

"You're right about that. It's somewhat less attractive in the rain, though."

"Do you have an umbrella?"

The man shook his head. "Someone is meant to be bringing one out to me, but they haven't yet. I was assigned to patrol today, but got pulled to do this. I hadn't expected to be outside."

"I'm going to go and get you an umbrella," Bessie told him. "You can't stand out here in the rain without one. Perhaps once you have it the rain will hold off."

The man laughed. "That's usually how these things work, isn't it."

Bessie walked back to her cottage and picked out one of the sturdiest umbrellas in her collection. There was already a stiff breeze blowing, and that was sure to pick up if it did start to rain. While she was at it, she slipped a few biscuits into a bag for the man as well.

"Here we are," she said as she rejoined him on the beach below Thie yn Traie. "An umbrella and a little snack for later."

"Thank you so much," the man said. "I hope I don't need the umbrella, but I will definitely need the biscuits."

"You can drop the umbrella back off at my cottage or simply give it to John or Hugh," Bessie told the man. "I have several, so I don't need it back in a hurry."

"If you don't mind, I might let my replacement use it as well. I believe the inspector wants someone here for a day or two."

"By all means, pass it along to whoever follows you," Bessie said. "Are you here to keep people in or out?"

The man shrugged. "A bit of both, I think. A reporter tried to get up the steps last night to get some pictures of the house and its occupants, but then someone from inside the house snuck out and climbed down to the beach to get away, as well. I'm meant to stop both things from happening again."

Bessie knew better than to ask any more questions. The young man probably shouldn't have told her that much, really. She wished him a good day and then turned and headed back towards home. As she walked, a light rain began to fall. She increased her pace and then walked even more quickly when she spotted John Rockwell's car outside her cottage.

"Good morning," he called as he climbed out of the car.

"Good morning," Bessie replied. She didn't stop at the car, but headed straight for her door. The rain was getting heavier and she didn't want to get any wetter than she already was. A few minutes later she and John were sitting together at Bessie's kitchen table with steaming cups of tea in front of them.

"I was just chatting with the young constable on the beach," Bessie told John as he helped himself to a biscuit.

"I hope someone got an umbrella down to him," John said. "I should check on that, really."

"I took him one, and a few biscuits."

John chuckled. "That was very kind of you," he said. "I suspect everyone else has forgotten him with everything else that's happening."

"I was surprised to see him there. Are you stopping people from going in or going out?"

"Both," John echoed what the constable had already told Bessie. "Dan Ross from the *Isle of Man Times* tried to get up the stairs late last night to get some pictures to go along with his story. Luckily, one of my men spotted Mr. Ross before he'd managed to get his camera out."

"I don't like that man," Bessie complained.

"I think he does a valuable job, but he doesn't always do it in the best way," John said diplomatically.

"And you need to keep everyone in the house?" Bessie asked.

"Susan snuck out last night after I'd spoken with her. She went down the stairs and then walked into Laxey. From there, she took a taxi to the airport, where she was arrested," John told her.

"My goodness, I suspected she wanted to get away, but sneaking off in the middle of a murder investigation seems odd. Especially when it was her own father who was murdered."

"I think we're going to find out a great deal more about both Susan and her father that will explain why she felt the need to disappear. Anyway, in light of both incidents, it seemed wise to have someone posted at the bottom of the stairs. I'm hoping they won't have to be there for long. I'd really like to get this case wrapped up quickly."

"You're meant to be taking the children on holiday again, aren't you?" Bessie asked.

"I'm hoping to take them away for a few days, just across to a holiday park, but everything is on hold at the moment. Murder takes precedent over holidays, unfortunately."

"Well, then, let's work out who killed Inspector Rhodes, shall we?"

John nodded. "If you can do that for me, I'd be grateful."

"Surely there can't be many people who had motives for killing the man? Most of us didn't even know him."

"Let's start at the beginning," John suggested. "Take me back through the party, minute by minute. I'm hoping I missed something last night."

Bessie nodded and then took a sip of tea. "I arrived early, because I'd been told the party started at six," she began. An hour later, she finished.

"It sounds as if it was an interesting evening," John said.

"I'm not sure I'd use that word. I'm a little bit sorry that I didn't get to see the rest of the murder mystery play out, though. Susan made such a mess of it, I can't help but wonder what would have happened next."

"From what I've heard, I think it would have all simply disintegrated into chaos," John told her. "Mr. Rhodes was far too intoxicated to conduct any sort of investigation, even a pretend one. From what I've been told, I don't believe that anyone at the party was particularly interested in staying in character or working out what happened to the victim."

"Did you find out who was meant to have killed Vivian?" Bessie asked.

John flipped through his notes. "According to Susan, Vivian was killed by Elizabeth. Vivian was meant to be the illegitimate daughter of the owner of the house, but apparently she didn't know that. Only Elizabeth was aware of who she really was."

"But that doesn't work at all," Bessie complained. "Elizabeth wasn't even in the room when the pretend murder took place. How did she manage to get Vivian to play dead? I thought she was in the corridor the whole time."

"Apparently Elizabeth told Vivian to play dead before she went into the corridor with Mr. Rhodes."

"So all the walking around the chairs and whatever was a waste of time," Bessie sighed, "and there was no way that anyone could have solved the crime, because Elizabeth couldn't have actually done it."

John shrugged. "You'll have to take that up with Susan."

"I will do, if I ever see her again," Bessie replied.

John nodded. "The lights were out for fifteen minutes. What we need to work out is who left the great room in that time."

"Were the lights out all over the house?" Bessie asked, "or did they just switch off the lights in the great room?"

"They turned off all of the ground floor lights."

"So someone had to walk out of the great room into the corridor, open the door to the study, stab the inspector, and the return to the great room, all in the dark and without making any noise."

"Except Elizabeth was in the corridor with a torch," John sighed. "She swears no one left the great room."

"So the killer wasn't someone at the party?" Bessie asked, feeling confused.

"Or Elizabeth is covering for someone, or she wasn't really paying attention the entire time," John replied. "We're taking a good look at the staff, but Jonathan Hooper insists that none of them were involved."

"I know Jonathan. He's a good man and an excellent butler."

"I got that impression. He didn't want any of his staff to get hurt when the lights were out, so he had them all gathered together in the kitchen. He insists that every member of staff was there when the lights went out and that no one left until the lights came back on and Elizabeth started screaming."

"If he's right, then that leaves Elizabeth as the only person who could possibly have killed the man," Bessie said.

"Unless she's covering for someone," John added.

"She wouldn't," Bessie said firmly. "Not for murder."

"Then someone sneaked past her and got into a locked room under her nose."

"Where was the key?"

"In Elizabeth's pocket. They felt it was important that Mr. Rhodes not have any chance to see the crime scene until the victim was dead, so they locked him in the study and Elizabeth pocketed the key."

"How many keys are there to that room?"

"According to Mr. Hooper, only that one. It was normally kept in the lock, the same as all of the others on that corridor. Apparently the doors were always simply left unlocked and the keys left in place."

"Maybe one of the other locks is the same, but only the killer knew about it," Bessie suggested.

"That raises the question of how the killer knew something about the house that the butler doesn't," John pointed out, "but even if we put that aside, we have the problem of motive."

"Someone must have known the man from across," Bessie said.

"Yes, but which someone? No one is admitting to it now, of course."

"You keep calling him Mr. Rhodes. Susan told me he wasn't really a police inspector."

"No, he wasn't. He had no connection with the police in any capacity, unless you count being arrested several times."

"Oh, dear," Bessie exclaimed. "The man was a criminal?"

"He drank too much, and when he was drunk he tended to lose his temper," John explained. "He never got into fights with other people, but he seems to have had several arguments with inanimate objects."

"Such as?"

"Windows were a particular favourite, it seems. He would have a few drinks too many, get upset about something and then throw a glass through the pub window."

"My goodness, what a dreadful man."

"I spoke to the landlord at the pub near his flat and he seemed surprisingly fond of the man, actually. He told me that Mr. Rhodes always paid for the damages and was always quite apologetic once he was sober again. After the first few incidents, the landlord had reinforced glass installed at Mr. Rhodes's expense. Apparently glasses just bounce off of it now."

"You said Mr. Rhodes had been arrested, though?"

"Not all pub landlords are as understanding as the one at Mr. Rhodes's local," John replied. "And Mr. Rhodes didn't always drink in his local."

"He had some nerve pretending to be a police inspector. Surely he could have found himself in a lot of trouble for that."

"As it was a private party, he was probably okay," John said. "If challenged, he could simply have insisted that he was simply staying in character. That's his daughter's argument, anyway."

"She told everyone he was a police inspector."

"To make Elizabeth happy because Elizabeth couldn't find one here on the island who was willing to take part. At least that's how Susan tells it. As I said earlier, I suspect there's more to it than that, but for now I'm taking her at her word."

"She'd also told Elizabeth that she'd done this sort of party before, but she told me she hadn't," Bessie said.

John nodded. "And that's for her and Elizabeth to discuss. I believe it was fairly obvious to everyone at the party last night that Susan didn't know what she was doing."

"It certainly was, and her solution to the case isn't a proper solution, either. I'm sure I could do a better job with such things, if I wanted to try."

"I'm sure you could, but don't let Elizabeth hear you say that. She'd probably try to talk you into helping her with the next party."

"I can't believe there will be a next party, not like that one, anyway."

"You're probably right about that," John agreed.

"So what happens next?" Bessie asked.

"We're doing background checks on everyone who was at the party. We're hoping to find a link between Mr. Rhodes and one or more of the guests."

"What about working out how they did it? I mean, if Elizabeth was outside the door the whole time, how did someone get to Mr. Rhodes and then back out again?"

"I have two constables searching the study for any sign of a hidden door. Beyond that, I simply don't know. At the moment, I'm working on the assumption that everyone had access because that gives me more to work with than believing that no one did."

"Clearly someone did," Bessie said. "If there is a hidden entrance to the room, how would anyone know about it, though?"

"As I said, we're doing background checks on everyone. Maybe we'll find that someone at the party had previously visited Thie yn Traie."

Bessie sighed. "It's all incredibly complicated. Are you sure fifteen minutes was enough time for someone to leave the party, kill Mr. Rhodes, and return?"

"We tried timing it a few different ways, and it can be done," John told her. "The killer had to have moved quickly and also had some measure of luck on his or her side, but it is possible, especially if he or she already had a key ready."

"And assuming Elizabeth didn't notice anything."

"Yes, assuming that. She was pacing up and down the corridor, apparently. It's just possible that she missed someone slipping past her, even though she did have a torch with her."

"Whoever it was had incredibly good luck," Bessie sighed.

"Tell me what you thought of the different guests. You've told me about your conversations with each of them, now tell me your impressions of them. You spoke to them only a short time before Mr. Rhodes was killed. Who do you think was contemplating murder?"

Bessie shook her head. "I've been asking myself that very question all morning. I can't help but feel as if I should have spotted the killer, but I really don't have any idea. I didn't know most of the guests, of course, but none of them seemed strangely nervous or anything, and I didn't notice anyone paying special attention to Mr. Rhodes, either."

"Let's go through them one at a time," John suggested. "I'll give you a name and you tell me your thoughts." Bessie nodded. "Let's start with Leonard Hammersmith," John said.

"I've known Leonard for years. He's a successful businessman, but not my favourite person."

"Why?"

"I just don't much like him," Bessie said, waving a hand. "He's arrogant and demanding and I wouldn't go out of my way to spend time with him, although I wouldn't avoid him at a party, either."

"And his wife?"

"Liza is worse. She seems to think that every pound her husband makes moves her another notch up in social standing. Her I would avoid at parties."

John smiled. "Any reason to think that either of them might have known Mr. Rhodes or had any previous connection to Thie yn Traie?"

Bessie shook her head. "They may have gone to summer parties there when the Pierce family had the estate, but I doubt it. When Mr. Pierce first had the house built, he and his wife used to have lots of parties each summer, but over the years they had fewer and fewer. Leonard and Liza probably weren't wealthy enough in those early days for Mr. Pierce to have noticed them. I could be wrong, of course, but if they had been invited to parties when the Pierce family had the house, I can't imagine that they'd lie about it now, no matter what the circumstances. It seems as if that's something that could easily be checked and they wouldn't want to be seen to be lying to the police."

"What about Mona Kelly?"

Bessie smiled. "I'm sure you've heard of her," she replied.

"I have, yes," John agreed. "She's on the short list of men and women about whom I was briefed when I arrived."

"There's a short list?"

"It's very short."

"So I'm not on it."

"No, you aren't, although you should be on the Laxey-specific version. It's really a list of very wealthy individuals, many of whom have the ear of the lieutenant governor or other politically connected individuals."

"And Mona is on the list?"

"Yes, I understand she's a personal friend of the chief constable, among others."

Bessie nodded. "She's a personal friend of a great many men," she said dryly.

John grinned. "I take it you don't like her?"

"On the contrary, I like her a great deal. It isn't my place to approve or disapprove of the choices she's made in life. She's lived an interesting life, that's for sure, and she's done so with considerable style."

"Would she have been at Thie yn Traie before?"

"Oh, undoubtedly. I'm sure Mrs. Pierce wouldn't have approved of her, but I'm sure she would have been taken along to parties on several occasions."

"How much time does she spend in London? Would she have had an opportunity to meet Mr. Rhodes somewhere?"

"I imagine she used to travel to London regularly, no doubt in the company of one wealthy man or another. I've no idea where she might have met Mr. Rhodes, though. He doesn't seem the type to have spent time in the same sorts of places that Mona haunts."

"What did you think about Ernest and Norma McCormick?"

"I barely met them. They both seemed nice enough. Neither mentioned having been on the island before or knowing Mr. Rhodes, but that doesn't mean anything."

John nodded. "What about Sean Rice and Richard Long?"

"Again, we barely spoke. Sean was quite attracted to Vivian Walker. She was just about the only thing he talked about over dinner."

"Yes, you mentioned that. And Richard?"

"He said something about finding the island nice, which suggests he hadn't been here before. Beyond that, I simply don't know. I under-stand both men work in London, though, so it's possible they may have met have met Mr. Rhodes before last night."

"Tell me about Madison Fields."

"Who?" Bessie asked, frowning. "I mean, I know who you mean, but really, she was barely there last night. I don't think I spoke to her at all and I don't remember anything about our conversation."

"Perhaps that was deliberate on Madison's part," John suggested.

"It could have been, I suppose. If it was, she was very good at being vague. I can't tell you anything about her."

"And Vivian?"

"She wanted to make sure she made an impression. I'm not sure why, as she didn't seem particularly interested in any of the men at the party."

"Did she seem to know her way around Thie yn Traie?"

"I've no idea. I was already in the great room when she arrived there. She went off to find her friends and was back fairly quickly, but that may be because they were already in the corridor behind her, for all I know."

"I won't ask you about Elizabeth, Mary, or George. I'm pretty sure I know what you think of all of them."

Bessie grinned. "And you should know that you can eliminate them from consideration. None of them will have had anything to do with Mr. Rhodes's untimely death."

"I assume you'll say the same about Andy Caine?"

"Of course I will. Andy wouldn't hurt a fly."

"That just leave Susan Haymarket," John said. "What did you think of her?"

"I thought she was terrible at event planning, and that she behaved oddly after her father's death."

"Do you think she could have killed him?"

"I don't know. I'd hate to think that a child could kill his or her own parent, but they didn't seem particularly close, even if she did break down when she found out he was dead. She was angry at him for drinking so much, I know."

"She is the only susp, er, witness that we know knew the man before last night," John said. "For that reason alone, we're taking a very hard look at her."

"And then she tried to run away," Bessie added.

"Yes, that was a mistake on her part."

"She seems the most likely to have had a motive, but she didn't seem like a killer to me," Bessie said. Before John could speak, she held up a hand. "I know, I know, very few of the murderers I've met in the past year or so have seemed like murderers, at least when I've first met them, but that's how I feel, anyway."

"If you had to choose one or two likely suspects, whom would you choose?" John asked.

Bessie frowned. "One of Elizabeth's friends, probably. They're all from London, so they have the greatest chance of having met Mr. Rhodes before. I can't believe that Elizabeth is covering for anyone, but I suppose if she were that she'd be more likely to cover for one of her friends than anyone else."

"Except maybe her parents or Andy?"

"Maybe, but they didn't do it, so we don't have to worry about them," Bessie said dismissively.

John nodded. "My thoughts are running along the same lines, although I'm keeping a more open mind than you are."

As he started to get to his feet, Bessie put a hand on his arm. "You didn't ask me about Michael Higgins," she said.

"Ah, yes, well, Mr. Higgins is a rather special case. He may well be working with us on this, and he certainly isn't a suspect."

Bessie tried to find out more, but John wouldn't say anything further on the subject. She was frustrated when she let him out a few minutes later. A glance at the kitchen clock showed that she had about an hour to fill before lunch. Maybe another walk on the beach would do her some good.

CHAPTER 6

*I*t was still raining lightly, so Bessie went to find herself an umbrella before she headed out. She'd found an old favourite in the back of her wardrobe, and was almost at the door when the phone rang. While she considered letting the answering machine pick up, she knew she wouldn't be able to leave until she'd heard whatever message might be left. It was probably faster and easier to simply answer the phone.

"Bessie? It's Mary. I know you probably don't want to talk to me after last night, but I wanted to see how you are."

"I'm fine, and I'm always happy to talk to you," Bessie replied. "How are you holding up?"

"I hate being caught up in the middle of another murder investigation, but otherwise I'm fine. Feel free to refuse, but I was wondering if you'd like to join me for lunch? We have a house full of guests, none of whom are inclined to go out anywhere, and I would love to have someone my own age to talk to while we eat."

Bessie hesitated. She liked Mary a lot, and she knew the woman was painfully shy. Having to sit through lunch with all of Elizabeth's friends would be difficult for her. While Bessie wasn't particularly eager to see the young people again, it was also remotely possible that she might pick up a clue or two for John over lunch. "Of course I'll come," she said after a moment.

"Should I send a car?"

"No, don't. I was just going out for a walk. I'll come up from the back, assuming the police constable will let me."

"I'll let him know that you're expected," Mary promised. "He's not meant to stop legitimate visitors, just uninvited ones."

"I should be there in about twenty minutes, unless that's too soon," Bessie said.

"No, that's perfect. We can have a few minutes of peace and quiet together before lunch."

Bessie put the phone down and glanced at her clothes. She was far too casually dressed for lunch at Thie yn Traie. No doubt Mary would be wearing something gorgeous and expensive. Bessie slipped off her raincoat and headed back upstairs. She changed into a nice skirt and a matching jumper.

The constable was expecting her when she arrived at the bottom of the stairs to Thie yn Traie a short while later.

"Miss Cubbon, if you could just wait here, please," he said. "Someone is coming down to escort you up the stairs."

Bessie frowned. "I'm quite capable of walking up stairs all by myself," she said tartly.

"But you'll let me fuss over you because you know I care," Hugh said from above her.

Bessie hadn't noticed his approach, as her umbrella blocked her view. She took the arm he offered and let him lead her up the long and winding flights from the beach to the back of Thie yn Traie.

"I could have managed on my own," she repeated herself as they went.

"The stairs are very slippery when they're wet," Hugh said. "I thought coming down to get you was better than standing at the top and worrying about you."

Bessie might have argued further, but just then Hugh's foot slipped slightly and he nearly lost his balance. Bessie held on to him tightly until he was steady again. "See," he muttered.

"Good thing I was here," Bessie laughed.

At the top, Hugh led Bessie into the house through the back door. Jonathan Hooper was there to take her coat and umbrella.

"Mrs. Quayle is waiting for you in the great room," he told Bessie in his formal tone. "If you'd like to come with me?" He held out an arm and Bessie took it.

"How are you coping with all of this?" Bessie asked as they walked through the corridor.

"It's quite trying, really, but I'm surviving. At least the staff should all be out of it, as we were all together in the kitchen during the relevant time."

"I hope you're right," Bessie said.

"I'm spending every spare moment trying to find that hidden door," he whispered. "It's the only thing that makes any sense, so it has to be here somewhere."

"Just be careful," Bessie told him. "If there is a hidden door and the killer did use it to get to Mr. Rhodes, he or she isn't going to want anyone else to find it."

"I'll be careful," Jonathan promised.

Mary was sitting on a couch in front of the windows. The rest of the room looked very much as it had the previous evening, with the long dining table still in place. Bessie frowned at the row of chairs that had been set up before the lights had been turned off. Why hadn't anyone tidied them away?

"Bessie, thank you so much for coming," Mary said, getting to her feet and crossing the room to give Bessie a hug. "I wouldn't have blamed you one bit if you'd told me you never wanted to come to Thie yn Traie again."

"Are we having lunch in here?" Bessie asked.

"No, we're leaving this room exactly as it was last night, at least for the time being," Mary sighed. "I managed to persuade Inspector Rockwell that he didn't need to put police tape all over everything, but effectively the room is considered a crime scene, or rather, that half of the room is."

"I'm surprised he's letting you use the rest of the room."

"He probably would rather we didn't, but George rang the chief constable and got permission for us to use it if we promise to stay away from the table where we ate and the chairs that were used during the pretend murder," Mary told her. "I probably should just have had the butler lock the doors and keep everyone out, but it's my favourite place to sit and think. I'm being very careful and I'm not letting anyone else in."

Bessie nodded. Not doubt John would have preferred that the room was locked and inaccessible, too, but George and the chief constable were friends. The chief constable would probably prefer if John let Mary and George move the furniture back where it belonged entirely. "I think I'd rather sit somewhere else, if you don't mind," she told Mary.

"We can go through to the dining room," Mary said. "Our chef is just putting out a buffet lunch for people so that they can help themselves whenever they're hungry."

Bessie followed Mary down a long corridor, past the kitchen where a handful of staff were hard at work. The dining room was enormous, with a long rectangular table at its centre. Bessie quickly counted the seats. There were twenty chairs around the table, but Bessie imagined that many more could be fit into the gaps between the chairs. Sean Rice was sitting on his own with a plate of food in front of him. As Bessie and Mary walked into the room he jumped to his feet.

"The butler said I could just help myself," he said apologetically. "I didn't realise anyone else was coming."

"I'm hoping everyone is coming down," Mary told him. "I'd hate for the kitchen to have to make individual meals for everyone throughout the day. Mr. Hooper has gone to invite everyone to lunch."

"I should have waited, then," Sean said.

"Not at all. It's meant to be an informal buffet luncheon," Mary assured him. "Bessie and I will be eating now. We aren't waiting for the others either."

Mary walked over to the table along the far wall. The vast quantity and variety of food on offer surprised Bessie.

"Everything looks wonderful," she told Mary.

"I won't promise it all will be wonderful," Mary said in a low voice. "Our chef is often more ambitious than successful, but she's trying. I would love to hire Andy in her place, but he's not interested in the job."

"He still has to finish culinary school."

"He's already one of the best chefs I've ever known. I'm not sure that culinary school is going to be able to teach him much more."

"I believe he's learning about a great deal more than just cooking. He said something about learning business management and how to deal with staff and all manner of things."

"As he's independently wealthy, I can't imagine why he'd want to go to all of the trouble to open his own restaurant. I've seen how hard Dan and Carol have to work. It's a very difficult business."

"But it's all that Andy has ever wanted to do," Bessie told her. "Maybe he'll modify his plans and simply do catering or open a bakery or something, but he gets enormous satisfaction out of what he does."

"And he's incredibly talented. I should be encouraging him to open that restaurant. George and I would eat there every night."

"You want Elizabeth to find something useful to do with her life," Bessie reminded her friend, "and she's quite wealthy, isn't she?"

Mary laughed. "You're right, of course. And we make both of our sons work hard as well. It just seems as if Andy has chosen such a difficult career for himself when he doesn't have to work that hard, that's all."

"Food, how nice," Ernest McCormick said from the doorway. "I don't suppose it will be as good as what we were served at the party, but I shouldn't complain, as I haven't had to make it myself."

His sister laughed. "As if you ever cook anything yourself," she said. "I cook whenever we eat at home in our flat, which isn't very often, I must say. We both prefer restaurants to my cooking," she said to Bessie and Mary.

"I didn't realise you shared a flat," Bessie said. She'd filled her plate, so she stepped away from the table to let the brother and sister have their turn.

"Oh, yes, our parents set it all up," Norma replied. "They gifted us with a gorgeous flat in a wonderful location in London on the condition that we live together. I believe they want me there to keep on eye on my little brother."

"If they only knew," Ernest said with a wink. "Norma is the one who's out every night until the wee small hours, running around with unsuitable men. I'm usually tucked up in bed by nine."

"With some cheap blonde or other to keep you company," Norma shot back.

Ernest laughed. "Well, there may be some truth to that, but at least I'm home if Mummy rings to check in on me."

"If Mummy would learn to ring my mobile instead of the flat, she would be able to check in on me as well," Norma sighed.

"She's rung my mobile three times already today," her brother told her.

"Yes, I've talked to her twice and let the third call go to voice mail. Why she should suddenly start using that number today, after all these years, I'll never understand."

"I hope nothing is wrong," Bessie said as she found a place at the table. She deliberately sat near the centre of the table, hoping she'd be able to talk to everyone as they came in.

"Mummy is incredibly worried about there being a murderer running around at tiny tray," Ernest explained.

"Thie yn Traie," Bessie corrected his Manx.

"Yeah, there," he shrugged. "Anyway, she's been ringing everyone she can think of to ring, from the island's lieutenant governor to her own member of parliament. None of them have managed to get us permission to leave, however."

"We all need to be patient with the police as they try to work out who killed Inspector Rhodes," Mary said. "You know you're all more than welcome here as long as you need to stay."

"That's very kind of you," Vivian said as she strode into the room. Today the girl was wearing a tight T-shirt and a miniskirt that just barely covered her bottom. Bessie held her breath as the girl leaned over the food table to inspect what was on offer. Across from her, Sean sat up and took in the view.

"I don't know that I can eat any of this," the girl said with a sigh. "I have to watch everything I eat so carefully. I can't afford to gain an ounce, you know. I've several modeling gigs booked for when I get back to London."

"I can have our chef make you whatever you'd like," Mary said. She got to her feet. "What can I get for you?"

Vivian shrugged. "I'm not especially hungry, really. I was just lonely in my room, so I thought I'd come down and hang out in here for a while. Maybe I'll just have some salad."

The girl piled a few lettuce leaves onto a plate and then sat down next to Sean. Ernest and Norma had taken seats on Bessie's side of the table, but had left a few empty chairs between themselves and Bessie.

"Everything smells wonderful," Richard said from the doorway. He crossed the room and began to fill a plate with what looked like a little bit of everything. Vivian jumped back up and joined him at the table.

"I have to be very careful of what I eat at the moment," she told Richard, "but it all looks so good. You'll have to tell me what's nicest and maybe I'll try a bit of it."

Richard glanced at her and shrugged. "I'm sure it will all be good," he said.

"I was wondering where everyone was," a quiet voice said from the doorway.

Bessie smiled encouragingly at Madison Fields. "Come and get some lunch," she told the girl.

Madison nodded and then crossed to the food table. Richard was still loading up his plate, with Vivian watching his every move. As Madison arrived, Richard smiled at her.

"Good morning," he said softly.

"I believe it's afternoon now," Madison replied, "so good afternoon."

Richard chuckled. "I'm afraid after last night I've lost track of time."

"Me, too," Vivian said loudly. "It definitely feels as if we should be drinking wine with whatever meal this is."

Mary stood up again. "I can have someone open a bottle of wine, if you'd like," she offered.

"I would definitely like," Vivian said.

"Yes, wine would be good right now," Sean agreed.

"It's a bit early in the day," Richard said. "I think I'll stick to coffee for now."

"There's coffee?" Vivian asked. "I'll have coffee, then. We can drink wine with dinner."

"Did you want some wine?" Mary asked Sean as Vivian pulled Richard into the other seat next to hers.

"No, I'm fine," he said shortly.

"Madison, sit here," Richard suggested as the girl turned around with her plate. She'd taken tiny portions of only a few things, Bessie noted.

"Thank you," she said as she dropped into the chair next to Richard.

"How are you?" Bessie asked the girl.

She looked startled as she looked at Bessie. "Fine, thank you."

"I'm sure everything that's happened has been unsettling," Bessie suggested.

"Oh, yes, I'm unsettled, but, I just thought..." she trailed off and looked down at her plate.

"I'm here," Elizabeth announced from the doorway. When everyone was looking at her, she swept into the room and then rushed around the table, giving everyone air kisses as she went. "It's so good to see you all," she said when she'd finished. "I was worried that you'd all be hiding in your rooms complaining about the party."

"The party was fine," Sean said. "The murder mystery part went a bit off track, but the food and drink were excellent."

Elizabeth nodded. "Well, you can't blame me for the murder mystery part. That was all Susan's doing."

"Gee, thanks," Susan said as she walked into the room.

Elizabeth flushed. "Even you have to admit that there were a few flaws in the execution of the murder mystery," she said to the other woman.

Susan raised an eyebrow. "Besides the fact that my father was murdered while we were all playing silly games in the dark?"

Elizabeth opened her mouth to reply but then snapped it shut again. She turned and made her way over to the food table and began to fill a plate.

"Susan, I'm glad you came down to get something to eat," Mary said in a gentle voice.

"I'm not hungry," Susan said. "I only came down because I couldn't stand staring at the walls in my room any longer."

"You should eat something," Mary said coaxingly. "At least try something light."

Susan shrugged as Mary got to her feet. Elizabeth quickly moved away from the food table and slid into an empty seat near Ernest and Norma. Mary took Susan's arm and led her to the table. As Susan looked on, Mary filled a plate for her with a little bit of just about everything available.

"Come and sit with me," Mary suggested as she turned away from the table. "Bessie and I were just chatting about the weather. It's been so rainy the last few days, hasn't it?"

Susan sat down next to Mary and took a tentative bite of something from her plate. Mary looked over at Bessie.

"I'm not sure I ever remember an August quite this wet," Mary said.

"The island is always rainy," Bessie replied. "I don't pay much attention to which month we're in, really. I just always expect rain."

"That's very pessimistic of you," Elizabeth said.

"I don't think so. I quite like the rain, when it isn't too heavy or too cold," Bessie replied.

"And you truly enjoy sunny days if you're always expecting rain," Mary added.

"Exactly. I have a number of umbrellas and several raincoats, and there's nothing better than being able to take a long walk and not need either," Bessie said.

"The south of France has lovely weather," Norma interjected. "I shall be planning a long holiday there once we get out of here."

"Portugal is better," Sean said.

"I hate Portugal," Vivian said, making a face.

"Why?" Sean asked.

"Oh, it's just not for me," she replied vaguely. "I've been thinking about moving to America, actually. I think somewhere like Los Angeles would suit me perfectly. I could do some modeling and spend my spare time at the beach."

"That's where my mother is now," Sean said. "She married an American, and they've settled in LA. It's very hot, but no one ever goes out of their air-conditioned homes, so it doesn't matter."

"Do you ever visit her?" Vivian asked.

Sean looked surprised that she'd spoken to him. "I haven't yet, but, well, I mean, I'd quite like to, but my father would prefer that I didn't. Their divorce was not friendly."

Vivian shrugged and then looked over at Richard. "Do you have family in America anywhere?" she asked.

He stared at her for a minute. "I might have a few distant cousins over there somewhere. My grandfather's brother moved to the US when he was young, and he married and had children, but I've never met any of them."

"Are they in California?" was Vivian's next question.

"I believe they are somewhere in Montana, if that's a place in the US," he replied.

"I have family in Michigan," Susan said. "Maybe I should go and visit them once this is all over. I've never been to the US."

"I grew up there," Bessie said.

"Really?" Vivian gasped, "and you moved to the Isle of Man? Why would you want to do that?"

"I was born on the island, but we moved to the US when I was two," Bessie explained. "My parents decided to move back here when I was seventeen. As I wasn't an adult yet, I didn't have any choice in the matter."

"I would have stayed in the US anyway," Vivian said airily. "I'd love to live there. It looks so exciting on telly and in the movies."

"It isn't really that different from here," Bessie told her.

"Of course it is. They have Hollywood and year-round sunshine," Vivian said.

"We lived in Cleveland," Bessie replied. "We didn't have Hollywood, but we did have snow for six months of the year."

"You should have moved to California," Vivian said.

"California was a long way from all of our family and friends. I can't imagine my parents ever gave it a single thought. In those days people tended to settle where they had family connections," Bessie told her.

"My father always wanted to move somewhere warm," Susan said in a low voice. "He was saving up for it. He had all sorts of plans."

"That's good news for you, then, as you'll inherit, right?" Vivian asked.

Susan looked stunned. "I would much rather have my father back than inherit money," she said after an awkward pause.

"Really? No offense, but your father wasn't the most likeable man I've ever met. He drank a lot and he kept leering at me every time I walked past him," Vivian replied.

"Maybe if you didn't dress like a whore he wouldn't have leered at you," Susan snapped.

"I wear what I like," Vivian said. "It isn't my fault that men seem to like it as well."

"What is everyone enjoying from the buffet?" Mary asked in a loud voice.

"It's all fine," Ernest said after a moment. "None of it is outstanding, but it's all fine."

"Our chef isn't as good as Andy," Elizabeth said with a frown, "but Andy doesn't want to come and work here."

"He still has to finish culinary school," Bessie reminded the girl.

"Yes, I know, but even after that, he doesn't want to be a private chef. He keeps insisting that he wants to open a restaurant, even though he has enough money now to just sit around and do nothing," Elizabeth sighed.

"Not everyone is lazy like you," Vivian said. "I have plenty of money, but I still work."

"You do an hour of modeling once a month or so and then complain about it for weeks afterwards," Elizabeth replied. "Standing in front of a camera looking bored while someone snaps your picture isn't working, anyway. You know I'm putting a lot of time and effort into my party planning business."

Vivian laughed. "And it's going so well, isn't it? Wasn't someone murdered at the wedding you planned last month? And now again at your murder mystery evening, someone has ended up dead. Having you plan a party is like writing a death warrant for some unsuspecting individual."

The colour drained from Elizabeth's face as she jumped to her feet. "I don't have to listen to this. You're meant to be a guest here. Maybe you should leave."

"I so wish I could, darling," Vivian drawled, "but the police aren't letting anyone go anywhere at the moment. We're all stuck here together like miserable peas in a horrid little pod."

"Perhaps you'd all like to move to a hotel," Mary suggested in a cool voice. "We can arrange that for you if you'd prefer, at our expense, of course."

Vivian looked around at the others. "What do you think?" she asked them. "Should we stay or should we move to a hotel?"

"I like it here," Madison said so quietly that Bessie could only just hear her.

"I do as well," Richard said. He smiled at Madison. "And I like the company."

Vivian narrowed her eyes at the man and then looked over at Sean. "What about you? Are you happy here, too?"

"I'm not unhappy," he said with a shrug. "I don't want to put Mrs. Quayle to any expense or bother, either."

"I'd like to leave," Susan said loudly. "Right now, if that's possible."

Mary nodded. "I'll just ring Inspector Rockwell and check with him," she said. "If you'll excuse me."

"Are you happy here?" Ernest asked his sister as Mary left the room.

"Not especially, but we're stuck, really. I certainly wouldn't expect Mrs. Quayle to make other arrangements for us. I'm sure the police will have everything worked out in a day or two, anyway," Norma replied.

"I wish I shared your confidence in the local police," Vivian said. "I rang Daddy last night and asked him to send someone from Scotland Yard, but he said it wasn't that easy." She sighed. "They do it on telly all the time."

"This isn't telly," Susan snapped. "This is real life and a real person has been murdered. That person was my father, and I think you should all stop worrying about yourselves and think about other people for once."

"I'm sorry for your loss," Madison said in her quiet voice.

"Thank you," Susan said.

"We're all sorry for your loss, although you and your father didn't seem terribly close earlier in the evening," Sean said. "You barely said two words to each other."

"We were working," Susan replied through gritted teeth. "He was playing a part, and I was trying to keep the evening running smoothly. We didn't have time to sit and chat together."

"I can't understand why anyone killed him," Vivian said. "I mean, are the police sure it was murder? Maybe he simply drank himself to death."

"He was stabbed," Susan said flatly.

"Maybe he was just holding the knife and it slipped out of his hand or something," Vivian suggested. "Maybe he was cutting something and his hand slipped."

"Or maybe he was stabbed by someone who took advantage of the murder game to sneak away and kill him," Susan shot back.

"But none of us even knew the man," Sean said. "We didn't have any reason to kill him."

"Maybe one of us is a serial killer," Vivian said. "They just kill people at random, right? I see them on telly all the time."

"I don't think anyone here is a serial killer," Sean said.

"Then why do you think someone killed Inspector Rhodes?" Vivian demanded.

"Maybe the killer knew him from London," Sean replied. "We all live in London, after all."

"Did he tell you that he'd seen someone he knew?" Vivian asked Susan.

The girl shook her head. "We didn't really talk during the party. He was in character."

"Surely he would have said something if he thought his life was in danger," Vivian said. "Maybe he didn't recognise the person, but the person recognised him."

"Or maybe it was a case of mistaken identity, or maybe one of the other guests knew my father from somewhere, or maybe a dozen other things," Susan snapped. "This is why I want to go and stay somewhere else. I can't stand listening to all of this."

"I'm terribly sorry," Mary said as she walked back into the room, "but Inspector Rockwell doesn't want anyone going anywhere just now. He's actually on his way here to talk to each of you again."

"I won't talk to him," Vivian said. "I've already told him everything I know. Then again, he was really cute, even if he is really old. Maybe I will talk to him. Maybe I'll talk him into running away with me to some exotic island in the South Pacific or something."

Bessie smiled at the thought of the girl trying to talk John into anything like that. While Vivian was pretty, John was far too sensible to let his head be turned by her questionable charms.

"I don't want to talk to him, either," Madison said softly.

"You'll be fine," Richard said, patting her hand. "All we can do is keep repeating what we've already said. Eventually, the man will get tired of hearing the same thing over and over again and give up."

"I hope not," Elizabeth said. "I hope he doesn't stop asking questions until he's found the killer."

Richard shrugged. "Maybe someone was trying to break into the house and the inspector spotted them, or some such thing. I'm sure it was nothing to do with any of us."

The suggestion was impossible, but Bessie didn't bother to point out all of the flaws in it. None of the ideas that anyone had offered had seemed likely to her, but it was interesting to hear what Elizabeth's friends were thinking.

She finished the last of her lunch and then sat back in her chair. "I should be going," she said to Mary, who'd rejoined her at the table.

"Stay until John gets here," she requested. "I told him you were here and he mentioned that he'd like to speak to you."

"I already talked to him this morning," Bessie said in surprise.

Mary shrugged. "He asked me to keep you here. He didn't give me any reason why."

Bessie nodded. "I don't mind waiting for him, I was just surprised by the request."

"Inspector Rockwell has arrived," Jonathan Hooper announced a short while later. "He'd like to speak to Miss Cubbon first."

Bessie got to her feet and followed the butler out of the room. She could feel the curious stares of the others on her back as she went.

CHAPTER 7

"*A*h, Bessie, I should have expected to find you right at the centre of everything," John said with a smile as Besise joined him in the small office that Mary had provided for him.

"Mary invited me to lunch," Bessie explained.

"Yes, she told me that she had. And how has lunch been?"

"The food was okay, but not great. The company was, well, interesting."

John grinned. "Go on then, tell me everything that was said over lunch."

Bessie took a deep breath and then did her best to recount the various conversations that had taken place over the past hour or so. John made several notes as she spoke.

"They seem to have several interesting theories about the murder," he commented when she finished.

"None of them are plausible, but, yes, they do."

"It could have been a serial killer. At the moment, the killing certainly seems random, anyway."

"And are there other, similar cases to it elsewhere?"

John sighed. "No, that's one of the flaws in that theory," he admitted. "There are other reasons why a serial killer is unlikely as well, but we're trying to keep an open mind at the moment."

"Do you think one of Elizabeth's guests killed the man?"

"We're investigating everyone who was at the party, and the household staff," John replied.

"So one of Elizabeth's friends, or Leonard and Liza Hammersmith, or Mona Kelly," Bessie concluded.

"We've eliminated Ms. Kelly from our enquires."

"Because she was with Michael Higgins and he's above suspicion?"

"I wouldn't have put it that way, but I can't stop you from drawing your own conclusions."

"I wouldn't necessarily count Susan Haymarket as one of Elizabeth's friends, of course. And she must be a suspect."

"Everyone who was in the house is a suspect."

"Except Mona Kelly, Michael Higgins, and me," Bessie said.

John nodded. "I'm not sure the chief constable has crossed you off of his list yet, but you definitely aren't on mine."

"Surely Susan must be near the top of the list, if only because she actually knew the man," Bessie mused.

"I don't think this is a good time for us to start discussing the case," John said. "I need to talk to each of the guests individually, and then I have a plane to meet."

"A plane to meet?" Bessie repeated. "Sue hasn't decided to come back from Africa early, has she?"

"No, not at all; in fact, she's been talking again about staying longer. The poor kids don't know what to do about school, but I'm just about ready to register them here for September. If Sue wants to argue about it, she can do so when she gets back, whenever that is."

Bessie patted the man's arm. "I'm sorry. This isn't easy for any of you."

"It isn't easy, but I really love having the kids here. Amy has started making dinner for us all every night. Some attempts have been more successful than others, but she's trying. After a long day at work, I don't much care if things are a little bit overdone or whatever, anyway, I'm just glad to have a meal on the table."

"She seems like a good girl."

"She's great, and Thomas has actually decided that he should be able to cook as well. He's making dinner tonight, with his sister's help. I'm really proud of both of them for dealing so well with everything that has happened."

"You should be proud. Should I not ask whom you are meeting at the airport, then?"

"I can't tell you," John replied. "I will tell you that it's business, not pleasure, though."

Bessie nodded. "I won't ask any more questions, then."

"I have one more for you and then I'll let you go," John said. "Can you remember Susan saying anything about her mother or about any women in her father's life?"

"Not at all," Bessie said after a minute's thought, "but then, she didn't tell anyone that Inspector Rhodes was her father until after he was dead."

John nodded. "Okay, that's all I need for now. Thank you for your time. Are you going home now or staying here?"

"I suppose I'll go home. Maybe I'll see if Mary wants to come back to Treoghe Bwaane with me. She might like a chance to get away from here."

"I'll talk to her next," John said.

"Maybe I'll wait for her, then," Bessie said thoughtfully. "It might be interesting to see how everyone is holding up under the pressure of waiting to speak to you again, anyway."

"Maybe you should go home now," John suggested. "I don't want you in any danger."

"I won't do anything silly," Bessie promised. "I'll just do what I've done all day, sit quietly and observe."

Bessie walked back into the dining room. It seemed as if everyone jumped as she entered. Two members of staff were clearing the food away as Bessie sat back down next to Mary.

"They'll be bringing in pudding in a minute," Mary told her. "You'll want to stay for that."

"Oh, yes, please," Bessie said.

"Mrs. Quayle? The inspector is ready for you now," Jonathan said a moment later.

Mary gave Bessie a nervous smile and then followed the man out of the room. No one said anything as the staff carried in trays full of fairy cakes, biscuits, and other sweets. As soon as they were finished setting up the table, Sean was on his feet.

"Pudding," he said happily.

"What did the police want now?" Susan asked Bessie.

"Inspector Rockwell just asked more questions about last night," Bessie said as she stood up. "He did tell me I could leave, but I wanted to wait until I had a chance to speak to Mary first."

"If the police had told me I could leave, I'd be out of here so fast your head would spin," Susan muttered.

"Well, I do only live a short distance down the beach," Bessie told her. "Inspector Rockwell knows exactly where to find me if he has more questions."

She put two fairy cakes and a few biscuits on a plate and then made herself a cup of tea. When she sat back down, Madison stood up.

"Everything looks delicious," she said in her whispery voice. "Maybe just one fairy cake would be okay."

"If you aren't watching your figure, neither is anyone else," Vivian said. "I never eat sugary treats."

"One fairy cake won't hurt a bit," Bessie told Madison firmly. "I'm having two and biscuits besides."

Vivian looked as if she was about to say something, but she was interrupted by a new arrival. The woman who walked into the room appeared to be around fifty. She was wearing a black dress that was two sizes too small and her frizzy brown hair had several inches of grey roots showing. Her makeup had been applied with a heavy hand, seemingly with little care or attention. She stood at the head of the table, looking around the room.

"Who are you?" Vivian snapped after a minute of uncomfortable silence.

"You aren't Susan, are you?" the woman shot back. "Goodness, I hope not."

"I'm Susan," Susan said, getting to her feet. "Who are you and what do you want?"

"I should have recognised you from your father's photos," the woman said brightly. "You don't look like your father, but that can only be a good thing, right?" She laughed and then stopped abruptly. "I was so looking forward to meeting you, but under different circumstances."

"Who are you?" Susan repeated.

"Oh, darling, I'm Clara Rhodes, your stepmother."

Susan looked as stunned as Bessie felt. For a long moment the room was completely silent as everyone stared at the new arrival.

"Your father didn't mention me?" the woman asked, eventually breaking the silence. She sounded hurt.

"No, no, he did not," Susan said slowly, clearly struggling to keep her emotions under control.

"Oh, baby, I'm so sorry. I shouldn't have just blurted it out like that. I thought you knew. I thought Jerry would have told you."

"Don't call him that," Susan said tightly.

"Oh, that's right, that was your mother's pet name for him, wasn't it? I am sorry. He did tell me not to call him that in front of you, but, well, I mean, it was my pet name for him, too."

Susan shook her head. "I don't know who you are, but I don't believe you're who you claim to be. I think you should leave."

"Oh, you poor little thing," the woman said. "Jerry, er, Jerome really didn't tell you anything about me? Not even a hint?"

"Not even a hint," Susan repeated in an icy tone.

"I have our wedding photos, if you'd like to see them," the woman offered. "I brought a copy of the marriage license, too, for the police. They were meant to meet me at the airport, but I changed flights at the last minute. I simply couldn't wait to get over here and meet you."

Susan shook her head. "I don't want to see photos or anything else. I want you to leave."

"Oh, but I can't leave. The police want to speak to me about Jerry.

They need to know if he had any enemies and that sort of thing," the woman replied.

"Quit calling him that!" Susan shouted. "Elizabeth, make her leave before I drag her out of here myself."

Elizabeth stood up and took a step towards the woman. "Maybe it would be better if you left," she said softly, "or at least waited in another room, if you want to talk to the police."

"But I want to talk to Susan," the woman wailed. "She's the daughter I've always wanted, and I'm sure she'll come to care about me, given time."

Susan burst into tears as Elizabeth tried to take the woman's arm. "Let's find you a nice quiet corner where you can wait for now," she said. "You can talk to Susan later, when she's recovered from the shock."

"Jerry promised me he was going to tell you as soon as he saw you," the woman said. "I'd been nagging him about telling you for such a long time."

Susan's eyes were wild with rage. "Get out!" she shouted.

"Good afternoon," John Rockwell said to the new arrival in a low voice. "I'm sorry, but we haven't met. I'm Inspector John Rockwell."

"Oh, yes, you were going to meet my plane, but I decided I simply couldn't wait to get here. I found an earlier flight and here I am."

"I see," John said.

"I'm Clara Rhodes, of course, Jerry's wife. I'm ever so devastated by his sudden death. I came as soon as I heard so that I could help my poor stepdaughter with her grief, even though I am grieving terribly myself."

"I'll leave you to work that out with your stepdaughter," John said.

"She's not my stepmother," Susan snapped. "I don't know who she is, but she's not who she claims to be. My father wouldn't have married again, and if he did, it wouldn't have been to a woman like her."

"I'm not sure what you mean by that, but it sounded like an insult. I'm going to overlook it, though, since you're still upset about your father's death and all. But I can assure you that your father and I were married, and we had been for the past three years," Clara said sounding triumphant.

"Three years?" Susan echoed. She sat back down in her seat and put her head in her hands. Mary, who had come back into the room with John, found a box of tissues and put it next to the girl.

Clara looked around the room and then smiled at John. "It appears she didn't know about me. That's rather sad, but knowing Jerry, not all that surprising. He did like to keep secrets, that man."

"Perhaps you'd like to tell me more," John said, offering his arm.

"I'm a bit peckish," the woman replied. "They don't do food on planes anymore, you know, and I was so busy rushing over here that I missed lunch."

"I'll have someone bring you some sandwiches," Mary said, "and a cuppa."

"Oh, that would be nice," Clara beamed. "Thank you, my dear."

John turned around and led the woman out of the room. Bessie felt as if everyone else simply watched in shock as they disappeared.

"Well, there's a turn-up for the books," Sean said after a moment. "One has to wonder if the secret wife had a motive for murder."

"She just arrived, though," Vivian said. "She couldn't have killed her husband."

"Flights go back and forth all the time," Sean replied. "She could have come over and killed him and then flown back home, ready for the police to ring her and tell her the bad news."

"Surely the police would be able to find evidence of that," Vivian said.

"Maybe, but maybe she used a different name or something," Sean suggested.

"We would have seen her around the house during the party, wouldn't we?" Vivian asked.

"Maybe Jerome let her in and hid her somewhere. Maybe he was going to tell Susan about her after the party was over. Or maybe she pretended to be one of the maids. I never notice maids," Sean replied.

"I hope you weren't counting on inheriting a fortune from your father," Vivian said to Susan. "It will be his wife who inherits, no doubt."

"She wasn't his wife," Susan said dully as she lifted her head. "I don't know who she is or what her game is, but she wasn't married to my father, and I'll never believe otherwise."

"She doesn't have to convince you, though, just the courts. The police inspector seemed to believe her, anyway," Sean said.

"I'm going to my room," Susan announced. "If the police want to speak to me, they can speak to me there. I won't be coming back out and I definitely don't want to see that woman."

Mary nodded. "As soon as she's finished with the inspector, I'll have her taken elsewhere. I'll get her contact information in case you want to get in touch with her another time, but I won't share yours with her."

"I will never want to talk to her," Susan said firmly. She walked out of the room with her head held high and with tears still streaming down her face. Bessie was tempted to follow her, to offer a sympathetic ear, but she didn't want to miss the conversation in the dining room, either.

"I'm going to make sure that Susan gets to her room safely." Elizabeth solved the problem by following the other woman out of the room.

"How sad for Susan," Madison whispered.

"We all have stepparents," Sean said. "She didn't seem any worse than that father of Susan's, to be honest."

"He was a drunk," Ernest said. "She seemed exactly like the type of woman he'd be attracted to."

"What does that mean?" Norma asked.

"Oh, nothing, really," Ernest replied. "I'm just bored and desperate to get out of here. Oh, not out of your lovely home," he added, nodding at Mary, "just off this island."

"I can't imagine my father getting remarried and not telling me about it," Sean said. "He's on his fourth wife and I've been at every one of his weddings, well, except for the first, when he married my mother."

"I didn't get the impression that Susan and her father were close," Ernest said. "Let's face it, if she rang him to play the police inspector, she must have been desperate. She could have chosen a homeless person at random to do the job, and he or she probably would have done it better."

"That's harsh," Norma said. "He might have been good at the interrogation part of the evening; we just never got around to it."

"He was too drunk to interrogate anyone," Ernest replied. "Stabbing him was probably unnecessary. His liver probably would have given up soon anyway."

When the butler walked back in a short while later, Vivian and Norma were talking desultorily about some daytime soap that no one else watched. Bessie was contemplating leaving when he spoke from the doorway.

"The inspector is ready for Mr. McCormick," he said.

As Ernest left the room, Bessie looked over at Mary. "I think I'll go home now," she said. "Do you want to come over for a cuppa?"

"I wish I could, but I think I need to stay here," Mary replied. "I need to find out what happened to Clara Rhodes, though."

She and Bessie both stood up. No one else seemed to notice as they walked out of the room together. Mary picked up the nearest telephone and pressed a number.

"Jonathan? Is the inspector finished with Mrs. Rhodes?"

Bessie couldn't hear the response, but a moment later Mary said "thank you," and put the phone down.

"She finished her conversation with Inspector Rockwell and was given permission to leave," Mary told her. "She left all of her contact information in case Susan wants to get in touch."

"That's not going to happen," Bessie sighed.

"No, I don't believe that it will," Mary agreed.

"Thank you for lunch. It was, well, interesting."

Mary shrugged. "I hope John gets this case solved quickly. I'm not sure how much longer I can stand having all of these people here."

"I'm sure John wants it solved as badly as you do," Bessie replied. And I'm doing what I can to help, she added to herself.

Mary walked Bessie to the back door and then opened it for her. "It's still raining," she sighed.

"I have an umbrella here somewhere," Bessie said.

Mary found Bessie's umbrella and rain jacket. "Let me find someone to walk you down the stairs," she said. "You know how slippery they are when they're wet."

"I'm fine," Bessie said firmly. "I'll hold onto the railing and take my time. It's not a problem."

She walked out into the rain as quickly as she could so that Mary couldn't argue any further. While she was apprehensive about the steep and slippery steps, she was eager to get some fresh air and to get away from Thie yn Traie and its unhappy occupants. The stairs weren't as bad as Bessie had feared. She held the railing with one hand and the umbrella with the other as she wound her way down to the beach below.

"You should have had someone ring me," the constable at the bottom said. "I would have come up and walked you down. Those stairs aren't safe."

"They were fine," Bessie told him. "You have a job to do down here."

"I don't know about that. Mostly I've just been standing around all day. You're the only person I've spoken to since I've been here."

"If the weather was better the beach would be full of tourists," Bessie told him. "They probably wouldn't speak to you, but at least you'd have something to watch."

"That would be nice. I was watching the waves going in and out, but that only made me drowsy."

Bessie laughed. "Oh dear, we don't want you falling asleep on the job."

"No, that wouldn't be good. Dan Ross would probably sneak right past me as soon as my eyes were closed, too, knowing my luck."

"He's probably back in Douglas writing a lurid headline about someone's speeding ticket or something," Bessie said. "Do you need any more biscuits?"

"Oh, no, I'm good," the man assured her. "I'm only eating one each hour, so I have more than enough to get me through the day."

Bessie smiled and then walked away, wishing she'd put more biscuits in the man's bag. If he was stationed there again tomorrow she'd give him an entire packet, she decided.

She was nearly back at her cottage when she heard her name being called.

"Bessie, oh, Bessie," the voice shouted across the sand.

Forcing a smile onto her face, Bessie turned around and greeted Maggie Shimmin. "Maggie, how are you today?" she asked.

"I'd be a good deal better if we hadn't had another murder on the beach," Maggie snapped as she joined Bessie under her umbrella. "Having a uniformed police constable standing there all day has been raising all sorts of questions from our guests."

The woman was in her mid-fifties and plump. Bessie found herself holding the umbrella over Maggie more than herself. She swallowed a sigh. "No one was murdered on the beach," she said.

"No, I know that, but that isn't the way it looks when the police are on the beach, is it?" Maggie demanded.

"If someone had actually died on the beach, there would be more than a single constable out here. You know that."

"I do, but our guests don't. I don't believe any of them have ever had the misfortune to be caught up in a murder investigation."

"Yes, well, it's a good thing you're here to set their minds at rest, then."

"Hurumph," Maggie said, "but at least I was right about Thie yn Traie."

"Right about what?"

"It's cursed, clearly."

"Thie yn Traie has been there for a great many years," Bessie said. "I'll admit a few bad things have happened lately, but that does not mean that the house is cursed."

"George and Mary Quayle will never be able to sell the place, not now, not with all the murders associated with it. It's a good thing they got a low price from Mr. Pierce, but even so, the value of the property has plummeted, I'm sure."

"I don't believe that George and Mary are interested in selling the house, so it doesn't much matter," Bessie said. "What are you doing about that last cottage?" she changed the subject.

Maggie flushed. "Yes, well, that's another problem, isn't it? The curse on Thie yn Traie must have extended to that cottage. It is the one closest to Thie yn Traie, after all."

"Except there is no curse," Bessie said softly.

"Whatever the reason, someone died in that cottage and now no one wants to stay there. The letting agent that we are using in Douglas keeps on telling potential guests about the unfortunate incident that happened there, and no one will take it, even at a discount. We can't get her to stop, though."

"People really should be informed, don't you think?" Bessie asked.

Maggie shrugged. "I mean, I suppose I'd like to know, if I were hiring a holiday cottage, but people do die every day. I can't see why anyone has be told outright. I'm not suggesting that she lie to anyone, but if they don't ask, she shouldn't tell them."

"Have you worked out what you're going to do with that cottage, then?" Bessie asked.

"I think we're going to have to tear it down," Maggie sighed. "Thomas is trying to get planning permission for a larger cottage in its place. We could do with two or three more as well, but I'm not sure we'll get permission. I wish I'd known how successful the cottages were going to be. We'd have had better luck getting permission for the whole thing at once, I think."

"Well, good luck to you," Bessie said.

"Thanks, but what actually happened at Thie yn Traie? I heard that Elizabeth Quayle was having some sort of murder mystery party and that one of the guests got stabbed."

"I haven't seen the local paper today," Bessie replied.

"But you were at the party," Maggie challenged. "What really happened?"

"You know I can't talk about active police investigations," Bessie told her. "I'm sure Inspector Rockwell will make a statement as soon as it is appropriate for him to do so."

"I'm sure, but you can tell me," Maggie said. "Just tell me who died, at least. The police aren't releasing any details yet. It wasn't Elizabeth, was it?"

"No, it wasn't," Bessie told her, "or Mary or George, but beyond that I can't comment."

"Bessie, I thought we were friends," Maggie sighed. "You know I always share everything I hear with you."

Maggie always shared everything she heard with everyone she knew. That was just one of the reasons why Bessie wasn't willing to tell her anything. "I'm truly sorry," she said, "but I simply can't tell you anything."

Maggie protested again, but Bessie turned on her heel and took a step forward. She nearly tripped over the man who had been standing right behind her without her realising it.

"Dan Ross!" she exclaimed. "What are you doing here?"

"Hoping for an exclusive interview with the woman who keeps finding all of the bodies," the obnoxious reporter from the *Isle of Man Times* said with a nasty grin.

"You were eavesdropping," Bessie said angrily. "You should be ashamed of yourself."

"I'm sorry, Bessie," Maggie said. "I didn't see him behind your umbrella."

Bessie glanced at the woman. "It's not your fault," she said. She turned back to the reporter and glared at him. "I have no comment for you," she said firmly.

"Oh, come on," the man replied. "Do you have any idea how many bodies you've found in the past eighteen months? I counted them all up and it's quite an impressive total."

"I'm sure it's a good deal higher in your count than in reality," Bessie said coldly. "You tend to credit me with finding any body that turns up in the north of the island."

"Okay, I suppose some of them you didn't actually find, you simply happened to be there when they were found, but still, it's starting to look a bit odd. And then I got to thinking, what if you started to get a bit bored and thought you would liven things up a bit by murdering someone yourself?"

Bessie nearly dropped her umbrella as the man's words registered in her brain. "Are you accusing me of murder?" she asked.

"Oh, no, of course not," the man replied quickly. "I was just putting the idea out there."

It was only after counting to ten and taking several deep breaths that Bessie was able to reply. "As I said, no comment." She began to walk away, forcing herself to walk slowly and steadily, reminding herself that she had an umbrella and Dan Ross did not.

"You'd be good at it, I reckon," the man said as he kept pace with Bessie. "You could probably get into a locked room, kill a total stranger, and get back out again before anyone even realised you'd moved. After all the murder investigations you've been mixed up in, you could probably commit the perfect crime."

He's just trying to get a reaction, Bessie told herself as she bit her tongue.

"And it would be sensible to kill someone you didn't know. That way you wouldn't have a motive, so you'd look completely innocent," Dan continued.

Bessie had reached her cottage door. She turned and looked at the reporter. "Where were you last night?" she asked.

"Me? Home alone, like always," he replied.

"Maybe the police should check on that," Bessie suggested. "Maybe you got tired of not having headlines screaming about murder so you took it upon yourself to generate an interesting headline."

"That's a crazy idea," the man said hotly.

Bessie just smiled and then slipped into her cottage, shaking her umbrella several times in the doorway before shutting the door in the man's face. It took her several minutes of slow and steady breathing to calm down. She put her umbrella in the downstairs bathtub and then hung her rain jacket above it. What she needed was a cup of tea and a good book, she decided.

An hour later she was feeling much better. The tea had warmed her from the inside out, and chocolate biscuits always improved her mood. Even better, she'd lost herself in one of her favourite mystery novels, choosing one where the first victim of the fictional killer was a nasty reporter from a small-town newspaper. She knew it was childish, but she still felt better when she read about the fictional man's demise.

After her buffet lunch, Bessie wasn't particularly hungry for dinner, so she made herself some soup and toast and then finished her meal with a few more chocolate biscuits. As she did the washing-up she could hear children's voices outside the cottage. Having been lost in her book, she hadn't noticed that the sun had finally come out. An evening walk was just what she needed to finish her day.

She packed a bag with a dozen custard creams for whatever police constable might be stationed behind Thie yn Traie now and headed out across the sand. The sun felt warm and Bessie breathed in deeply the sea air that she credited with keeping her alive and healthy for so many years.

There were only a handful of people on the beach, mostly small children who were busily building sandcastles and digging holes in the sand. A few parents were scattered among them, watching their offspring, reading books, or simply staring off into the distance. Bessie kept to the water's edge until she was behind Thie yn Traie.

"Just a few biscuits to keep you going," she told the uniformed constable on duty.

"Ah, thanks, Aunt Bessie," the young man replied. Bessie vaguely remembered him as having grown up in Laxey. No doubt he'd spent some time playing on the beach where he was now standing guard.

Still feeling full of energy, Bessie kept going past the mansion steps along the beach. She walked as far as the new houses, waving to one or two of the residents there, before turning back towards home.

The sun was starting to set and Bessie found herself walking more quickly as it grew darker. The police constable had switched on a powerful torch as Bessie walked past him.

"I was just starting to worry about you," he called.

"I feel as if I could walk forever," Bessie replied.

The beach in front of the holiday cottages was deserted now and Bessie found herself picking up her pace as she walked. Nearly all of the cottages had their curtains drawn, as their occupants presumably were settled in for the night.

Bessie was only a few paces from her door when she noticed the large rock behind her house. It was one of her favourite places to sit and enjoy the sea. Tonight, someone else was sitting on the rock, and as Bessie got closer to home, that person suddenly stood up and headed straight for her.

CHAPTER 8

*A*s the person approached, Bessie recognised Clara Rhodes. "Hello," she said softly.

The other woman jumped. "Oh, I didn't see you there," she said. "I was lost in thought, I suppose."

"Are you okay?" Bessie asked.

"No, not at all," the woman sighed. "I just lost my husband, you see."

Bessie wondered if the woman remembered her from Thie yn Traie earlier in the day. It didn't seem likely, really. "I'm very sorry," she said, not sure if she should remind the woman of their earlier encounter or not.

"Are you? That's very kind of you to say. No one else seems to be the least bit sorry."

"Goodness, but that's dreadful."

"It is rather, but I suppose the circumstances are rather odd. I was just sitting out here watching the sea and trying to think, but it wasn't working."

"No doubt your emotions are all over the place right now," Bessie said soothingly.

"That's for sure. I can't even think straight, you know? And I'm feeling ever so alone right now. I was hoping that my stepdaughter and I could mourn together, but she's not, well, she's rather upset."

"Would you like to come in for a cuppa?" Bessie asked, knowing that John would disapprove, but feeling unable to resist the opportunity to speak to the victim's wife.

"Oh, that would be lovely. Is this your cottage? It's adorable. I was wondering who lived here and whether they'd get cross that I was sitting on their rock."

"It isn't my rock. The beach is public and anyone can come and sit on the rock."

"Really? I'm not sure I'd like having people behind my house all the time," Clara said, frowning. "I quite like my privacy, and Jerry was the same way. He was worse than me, if I'm honest. He was almost obsessive about privacy."

"The beach is only busy in the summer months, and most people stay down near the holiday cottages rather than the beach behind my cottage, but I'm quite used to it anyway. I've lived here since I was eighteen."

While she'd been speaking, Bessie had continued walking towards her home. The other woman followed.

"Oh, that's a good long time, then, isn't it?" she replied.

Bessie frowned at the comment as she unlocked her door. "Have a seat," she suggested, waving towards the kitchen table. She washed her hands and then filled the kettle before stacking some biscuits onto a plate. A few minutes later the women were sitting opposite one another with tea and biscuits.

"I'd love a little cottage like this," Clara sighed. "Are houses expensive on the island?"

"Prices have gone up rather dramatically of late," Bessie told her. "A great many banks and financial services companies have opened branches here, and they've been bringing a lot of staff with them. Greater demand for housing has driven up prices very quickly."

"So how much would a cottage like this cost?"

Bessie shrugged. "I've no idea, really, but I suspect most of the value is in the land. When the cottage next door to me was sold, the new owners tore it down and built a row of holiday cottages in its place."

"I am expecting to come into some money soon," Clara said. "Are you thinking of selling, by any chance?"

"Absolutely not. This is my home and I intend to stay here for a good many years to come."

"But there must be other cottages like this one on the island, right?"

"I can give you the name of a good estate agent if you really want to consider buying property on the island," Bessie said. "They'll be able to answer all of your questions."

"Yes, I suppose that would be for the best. I will have to wait and see exactly how much I inherit, as well."

"I'm Elizabeth Cubbon, by the way," Bessie said as she realised she hadn't introduced herself.

"I'm Clara, Clara Jennings, well, I was Clara Rhodes, really, but I kept my maiden name for the most part."

"It's very nice to meet you. Your husband was Jerome Rhodes, then?"

"Yes, how did you know that?"

"I was at the party at Thie yn Traie last night," Bessie admitted.

"Oh, goodness, it is a small island, isn't it?"

"Mary Quayle, the owner of the house, is a friend of mine," Bessie added.

"It's a beautiful house. I wish I were going to get enough money to be able to buy something like that, but I can't see that happening. Still, any inheritance is better than nothing."

"Indeed. I didn't realise that Mr. Rhodes was wealthy."

"Oh, he wasn't exactly wealthy, but he did have some money put away for a rainy day. He was always talking about moving away to somewhere warm and sunny and he was doing what he could to save up for that."

"Had you been married long?"

"About three years, but we split up and got back together about a dozen times over those years," the woman said with a laugh. "We fought like cats and dogs, we did. But we always made up eventually."

"That must have been difficult," Bessie suggested.

"Oh, no, I was used to it, really. We'd get together and have some fun and then we'd fight over something stupid and I'd move back home with me mum for a month or two. When she started to drive me batty, I'd move back in with Jerry until our next fight. It wasn't like a conventional marriage, but it worked for us."

Bessie took a sip of tea while she tried to think of how to reply.

"Sadly, we were fighting again just before he died," Clara continued. "We would have made up soon, but it was our worst fight ever."

"That must be difficult," Bessie murmured.

"He changed the locks on his flat," Clara said angrily. "As soon as I heard what had happened, I headed over there to, well, check on things, and I found out he'd changed the locks. I hope he didn't give his daughter a key. She'll take everything for herself, she will."

"You don't get along with his daughter?"

"Jerry didn't get along with his daughter. They fought like he and I did, really. One minute they wouldn't be speaking to one another, and then they'd make up and she'd be over visiting for days on end. They were only together when he and I weren't, though. That was one of the things that Jerry and I fought about."

"Oh, dear," Bessie said softly.

Clara nodded. "He never even told her about me," she said, blinking rapidly and then wiping her eyes with the back of her hand. "When I met her this afternoon, she didn't even know I existed."

"How awful for you both."

"Ha, she'll be sorry because now she won't get the money, but it's awful for me because I'd really like to get to know her. She's the only connection I still have with Jerry, you know?"

Bessie nodded. "Maybe she'll come around, given time."

"Or maybe she'll go to prison," Clara snapped.

"Prison?"

"Oh, she must have been the one who killed Jerry, I reckon. She's the only person on the island who knew him. No one else had any cause to kill the man. He was just a harmless drunk."

"Have you shared your theory with the police?"

"Oh, yes, but they wouldn't admit that she was their main suspect. I can't imagine why anyone else would have killed him, though. I'm just lucky I wasn't on the island when he died, otherwise I might be a suspect."

"Did you know he was going to be here?"

"Oh, yes, I rang him a few days ago to talk about getting back together. Me mum is making me crazy again, but that's nothing new. Anyway, he told me that he was thinking about filing for a divorce and that he'd let me know what he'd decided when he got back from a little trip he was taking with his daughter. He wouldn't give me any details, he just said he was going to the Isle of Man and that the trip was going to be very lucrative for him."

"What did he mean by that?"

Clara flushed. "I don't know, I suppose he meant that he was going to be getting paid for his time."

"Was he? I didn't realise."

"I assume so. His daughter would have made sure of that, I reckon. She's like her father, always looking for ways to make a bit of extra money."

"I understand she runs a party planning business."

"Does she, now? That's interesting. I thought she just sponged off of her father and whatever desperate man she could ensnare."

"My goodness, I wonder how Elizabeth Quayle managed to get mixed up with the woman."

"No doubt Susan, that's her name, by the way, in case you didn't know. Anyway, no doubt Susan managed to convince Ms. Quayle that she was a professional party planner. She's very good at pretending to be things she isn't, or at least that's what Jerry always told me. She took after her father in that regard."

"Did she?"

"Jerry was very good at pretending to be something he wasn't," Clara confirmed. "I'm sure that's why Susan had him come with her and pretend to be with the police. He'd spent his life trying to avoid the police. I'm sure he found the whole thing funny."

"I met Susan at the party. She seemed very nice," Bessie protested.

"Well she wasn't very nice to me when we finally met. She refused to believe that her father and I were married, for one thing. I can't believe Jerry never mentioned me, though we were married for three years and we were together for two years before that."

"What did Jerry do in London?"

"Oh, a little of everything," the woman shrugged. "He was never one for holding down a job for long, but he was very clever. He could turn his hand to just about anything, really."

"How did you meet?"

"Down at the pub, of course. How else would we have met? When he wasn't working at some odd job or other, Jerry was pretty much always at the pub. He'd get out of bed around midday and head there for lunch. Most nights he'd still be there at closing time. I'm not much of a pub goer myself, but once in a while, when I'm between jobs or whatever, I'll stop in my local for a drink or two."

"And your local was also his?"

"No, not at all," Clara said, sounding cross.

Feeling as if she wasn't following the conversation, Bessie took another sip of tea and waited to see if the other woman would continue. After a pause, Clara spoke again.

"I was shopping with a friend one day, and just for fun we thought we'd drop in at a pub and have a drink. That's where I met Jerry. He told me he was a solicitor with lots of important celebrity clients, and I was dumb enough to believe him, at least for a few days. By the time I found out the truth, I was crazy about him, regardless."

While Bessie couldn't imagine falling for someone who had lied to her, she didn't want say as much to Clara.

"But that was Jerry, through and through. Why tell the truth when a lie will work and be more interesting? It made life more fun and exciting."

"And complicated, surely?"

"Oh, yes, it was complicated," Clara laughed. "The more he drank, the more elaborate his lies became, but then he'd forget what he'd said and have to tell more lies to try to get himself out of trouble. It was all very funny, really, and mostly harmless."

"Mostly?"

Clara frowned. "It was harmless. He didn't mean anything by it, really. He just felt like a boring person leading an ordinary life, so whenever he had the chance, he'd invent a new life for himself. Most people didn't mind at all when they found out the truth."

"He should have tried writing fiction," Bessie suggested.

"He didn't have any qualifications," Clara told her. "He could talk eloquently, but he couldn't write stuff down very well."

"I wonder if someone at the party last night had met him before, then," Bessie said thoughtfully. "If someone had, goodness only knows what he might have told that person."

"That's true. I hadn't thought of that, but I can't imagine any of the people at that fancy house ever spent time in the pub in Jerry's neighbourhood."

"Maybe they crossed paths elsewhere."

"Jerry didn't go anywhere else. Maybe to the corner shop to buy some food, but he usually just ate at the pub. Anyway, he certainly didn't often go outside of the area, and it wasn't the sort of neighbourhood that posh people visit."

"Where does his daughter live?"

"I suspect she was living with Jerry lately, but before that she had a flat with some guy she was seeing. It wasn't anywhere fancy, though."

Bessie thought about Elizabeth's friends. What might any of them have been doing in the part of London that Jerry inhabited?

"Anyway, Susan must have killed him; that's the only thing that makes sense," Clara said. "Since she didn't know about me, she probably thought she was going to inherit her father's fortune. Too bad she killed him for no reason, isn't it?"

Bessie got up and refilled the teacups and the plate. Clara was munching her way through another biscuit when Bessie sat back down.

"Surely there can't be much money," she suggested.

"Oh, there's more than you'd expect," Clara said smugly. "Jerry had a way of making money. He was very observant, you might say, even when he was drinking heavily."

"Observant?"

"Like he noticed everything that went on around him," Clara explained, "and then he remembered it the next day, even if no one else did."

Bessie nodded slowly. "So if someone were doing something they shouldn't have been doing at the pub..." she trailed off.

"Jerry would remind him or her of what he saw," Clara said. "He was just trying to help, really, by letting people know that their behaviour had been noticed. People were usually really grateful."

"I'm sure they were," Bessie said dryly.

"A lot of times they'd be so grateful that they'd buy Jerry a round of drinks or two the next time he was in the pub," Clara continued. "Or they'd just give him the money so he could buy his own drinks. That was sometimes easier."

"He was blackmailing people," Bessie said flatly.

"Oh, no, I wouldn't call it that," Clara said quickly. "Like I said, he was just trying to help, and people could be incredibly generous when they were grateful, that's all."

"Have you told the police all of this?"

"The police? I mean, I told them all about me and Jerry and our relationship, but they didn't ask for specifics on where his money came from or anything. I wouldn't want them to get the wrong idea like you did. They might start to think that Jerry was a criminal."

"While Jerry might not have meant to do anything wrong, it's possible that his vict, er, the people he talked to didn't see it that way," Bessie suggested. "Someone might even have been upset enough about it to kill him."

"You're making it out to be far more serious than it was," Clara protested. "It wasn't like that. Anyway, I'm sure it was Susan who killed him."

"Except I believe she was in the corridor with Elizabeth Quayle the entire time," Bessie said. "I don't think she could have done it."

"Ms. Quayle probably wasn't paying attention. She was probably quite drunk, too. I know how these high society parties go. Everyone drinks too much and sometimes there are even drugs around. Ms. Quayle probably didn't even lock the door properly when she put Jerry in that room."

"I was there," Bessie reminded the woman. "Elizabeth had no more than a single glass of wine all evening. She was working, helping to run the party and trying to learn about running such an event. Elizabeth may be wealthy, but she takes her job very seriously."

Clara shrugged. "Then she's lying to protect Susan," she suggested. "Or maybe they were in on it together. Or maybe Elizabeth is now blackmailing Susan. She'll be disappointed to learn that Susan isn't actually inheriting anything, won't she?"

"If Susan didn't kill your husband, do you have any idea who might have?" Bessie asked.

"I didn't really get to meet anyone at the fancy house up the beach," Susan replied, "but everyone I saw there seemed far too well-off to stoop to murder. Surely, if any of them did want to kill someone, they would have had their staff take care of it."

"None of the guests have any of their own staff with them, and as I understand it, the household staff at Thie yn Traie were all together in the kitchen when the murder took place."

"Then it was Susan," the woman said. "As I said, I'm sure she was after Jerry's money. I suppose I must be careful now or she may come after me next."

"You should be careful, certainly," Bessie told her. "If your husband was blackmailing someone and he or she killed him, that person might think you'll continue the blackmail now that Jerry is dead."

"I told you, he wasn't blackmailing anyone," Clara said insistently. "People gave him money sometimes, but it wasn't blackmail."

Bessie wasn't about to start arguing semantics with the woman. "Where are you staying?" she asked.

"I don't really know," the woman replied. "I suppose I should find a place, shouldn't I? When I talked to the police, they offered to help me find a hotel for the night, but I got restless waiting for them to finish talking to everyone, and I just left. Do you know if there are any che, er, reasonably priced hotels in the area?"

"It can be difficult to find places to stay in the summer months," Bessie told her. "Let me ring a friend and see if he has any ideas."

"Hello?" The voice on the phone sounded very young.

"Is that Thomas?" Bessie asked. "It's Elizabeth Cubbon."

"Hello, Bessie. Yes, it's me. Did you want to talk to Dad?"

"If he's not busy."

"I was just beating him badly at cards. I'm sure he'll be happy to take a break," Thomas laughed.

"What can I do for you, Bessie?" John's voice came down the line.

"I met a woman on the beach this evening who needs a place to stay tonight. I don't know if you can suggest somewhere that would have vacancies?"

"A woman on the beach? What have I told you about talking to strangers?"

"We have mutual friends," Bessie told him. "Or, at least, mutual acquaintances at Thie yn Traie."

"If you have Clara Rhodes sitting at your kitchen table right now I'll, well, I don't know what I'll do," John said tightly.

"I do have just that."

Bessie wasn't sure what John said next because he said it in a very low voice. She was pretty sure that he'd also put his hand over the receiver and that his mutterings were inappropriate for polite conversation.

"I have three constables combing the island for her," he said a moment later. "One of them will be at your cottage in less than five minutes to collect her."

"I think we should have a chat in about ten minutes, then," Bessie replied.

"We'll definitely be having a chat," John said. "Don't tell Ms. Rhodes that the police are coming for her, please. I don't want to lose her again."

"That's fine. I really appreciate your help."

Bessie put the phone down and smiled at her guest. "My friend is going to come over and collect you," she said brightly. "Do you have a car on the island?"

"No, I took a taxi to the mansion up the beach and then I walked down here along the road. I left my suitcase in a locker at the airport in case I decided to go right back home again. I hope your friend won't mind going back down there to collect it before he takes me to a hotel."

"I'm sure you'll be able to work something out," Bessie said.

She cleared away the teacups and slipped the few biscuits that remained on the plate into a bag. Whoever came for Clara would surely appreciate them. It was Hugh Watterson who knocked on Bessie's door a short time later.

"Hugh!" Bessie exclaimed as she pulled the man into a hug.

"John rang and asked me to pop over to help your friend," he said.

Bessie wondered if John had really rung Hugh at home. The man was wearing jeans and a T-shirt, so maybe he was telling the truth. "I'm sorry you were bothered at home," she replied.

"You know I'm always happy to help a friend," Hugh grinned.

Bessie introduced him to Clara. "She's left her suitcase at Ronaldsway, unfortunately."

"We'll work it all out," Hugh said easily. He offered the woman his arm. "Shall we?"

"My goodness, I wasn't expecting such a handsome escort," Clara giggled. "Maybe we should go and get a drink before you take me to that hotel."

"I don't really have the time tonight," Hugh said, sounding apologetic.

"Oh, that is a shame," Clara sighed. "I so rarely get to spend time with handsome young men."

Bessie stood in the doorway and watched as Hugh escorted the woman to his car. When she was safely tucked inside, he moved around to the driver's door and climbed in. They drove away, but before Bessie could shut the door another car appeared on the road behind her house. It pulled into the space that Hugh had just vacated. Bessie wasn't surprised when John Rockwell got out of the car.

"I should have rung you as soon as I realised the woman was missing," he sighed once he was inside Bessie's kitchen with a cup of tea in front of him. "I don't know why I assumed she'd get a taxi somewhere. I never thought that she'd simply walk away from Thie yn Traie."

"Is she in a great deal of trouble?"

"Yes and no. I did ask her to stay Thie yn Traie while I spoke to some of the others. I had more questions for her, but I wanted to see what Susan in particular had to say before I finished with Clara. I didn't tell her that she had to stay there, though, at least not in so many words."

"So what will happen to her now?"

"Hugh is going to take her back to the station and sit with her until I get there. Then I will ask her the rest of my questions. Once that's done, we'll find her a place to stay for a few nights. I'd rather she didn't leave the island until the investigation is complete, but I can't actually make her stay here."

"Oh, dear."

"I'm hoping that the promise of posh accommodations and free food will be enough to keep her here for a while, anyway."

"She seemed like the type that would appreciate such things."

"What did she tell you, then?"

Bessie took John back through the conversation, trying her best to repeat the woman's exact words whenever she could. When she was done, John was frowning.

"What she described sounds a lot like blackmail to me," he said.

"And to me. She insisted it wasn't, however."

"Now I need to talk to Susan again," John sighed. "I didn't get a hint of any of that when I spoke to her earlier. Clara didn't say anything like that when we talked, either."

"What if Susan was part of it?" Bessie asked. "Clara suggested as much. If Susan really was planning parties for the rich and famous, she'd be perfectly placed to see things that might provide useful blackmail material."

"If she really was planning parties," John repeated. "From what she's told me, this party for Elizabeth was really the first party she'd ever planned. I gather she was an assistant to a party planner for a short while before she decided to go out on her own. I also got the impression that she may have exaggerated her involvement in the parties that were planned while she was working for the other planner."

"It seemed pretty obvious during the party that she didn't know what she was doing," Bessie said.

"Yes, just about everyone has made that same observation," John said with a grin.

"Clara was insistent that her husband couldn't have possibly crossed paths with any of the party guests, but if he didn't, there doesn't seem to have been any motive for anyone to kill him."

"Having heard what Clara said, it appears we have more possible motives than I realised," John said. "This will open up a totally new line of enquiry."

"I just hope Clara tells you the same thing she told me," Bessie said.

"Whether she does or not, I believe you," John replied. "It will be interesting to talk to her and to Susan again."

"Good luck," Bessie told him.

"And you saved me from losing yet another round of crazy eights with my kids," he added as he got to his feet. "When they were little, I could just about convince myself that I'd let them win, but now I have to admit that they're better at card games than I am."

Bessie laughed. "I'm glad you're getting to spend time with them this summer, but you'll really miss them when they go back to Manchester, won't you?"

"I'll cross that bridge when I come to it. For now, I'm just enjoying having them here. Doona came over to supervise after you rang. I told her put them straight to bed and not to get tricked into playing cards with them. I suspect they'll all still be playing when I get home, whatever time that is."

Bessie let the man out and locked the cottage door behind him. The washing-up didn't take long. After everything that had happened that day, Bessie was still feeling restless in spite of the lateness of the hour. She thought about a short stroll on the beach, but the rain had started again. After last month's break-in, she was reluctant to leave the cottage empty at night, anyway. After several minutes of looking, she finally found a book on one of her shelves about the women who were called into factory jobs in America during the Second World War. It had been years since she'd read it and she quickly got lost in the various stories.

When she looked at the clock again, it was well past her bedtime. Sighing, Bessie put the book to one side and switched off the downstairs lights. After washing her face and brushing her teeth, she crawled into bed and quickly fell asleep. Her dreams were all about airplane manufacturing plants and she was happy to wake up at six, even though she hadn't had nearly enough sleep.

"I must find something more relaxing to read at bedtime," she told her reflection in the mirror. Her tired eyes didn't argue with her. Setting her coffee maker brewing, Bessie headed out for a short morning walk. It was overcast again, as if it might start to rain at any minute, so Bessie didn't dawdle.

The constable standing by the stairs to Thie yn Traie looked even more tired than Bessie felt as she approached him.

"I thought you could use a few biscuits," she said as she handed him the packet.

"Oh, bless you, Aunt Bessie," he replied. "You've just saved my life."

Bessie chuckled and then turned back towards home. She was ready for some coffee and a few biscuits herself. After her odd dreams the night before, she left the history book on the table and pulled out a new thriller that the bookshop in Ramsey had recently sent. She didn't often read thrillers, but this one was by a favourite author who had switched genres for this title. The story was gripping from the first page and Bessie quickly found that her heart was racing as she turned the pages.

There were only two suspects that seemed likely to be behind the rash of murders in the story and as Bessie raced towards the climax she found herself hoping that the killer would turn out to be the unpleasant nephew rather than the penniless suitor. A glance at the clock showed her that it was nearly time for lunch as she reached the beginning of the end.

"Never mind, lunch can wait," she said to herself before plunging back into the story. The penniless suitor was standing on the balcony with the female protagonist. The unpleasant nephew was nearby, but the couple were unaware of his presence. As the suitor began to declare his feelings for the heroine, he was interrupted when a shot rang out. Bessie turned the page, unable to breathe from the suspense. Someone knocked on her door.

CHAPTER 9

*S*ighing deeply, Bessie put the book down and headed for the door. "This better be important," she muttered to herself as she crossed the kitchen floor.

"Good afternoon," Jonathan Hooper said, smiling at Bessie from the doorstep.

"Jack, what a lovely surprise," Bessie replied. "Do come in."

"I hope I'm not interrupting anything important," the man said. "I wanted to come after lunch and before dinner. I probably should have rung first."

"You're fine," Bessie told him. "I haven't actually had lunch yet, because I was reading a very exciting book, but I'm delighted you're here."

"Did you finish the book?"

"No, not quite yet, but I've only a chapter or two to go."

Jack smiled at her. "You sit down and finish your book and I'll make you some lunch," he said.

"Oh, no, I couldn't possibly."

"Of course you can. Remember how many afternoons I turned up on your doorstep with a badly skinned knee, desperately in need of a plaster and a biscuit? I'm sure I interrupted you in the middle of a good book nearly every day for years. Go and finish while I make you a sandwich or something."

Bessie wanted to argue further, but she was rather desperate to find out who had just been shot. "Maybe just a page or two more," she said.

"Or finish the book," Jack laughed.

It only took Bessie ten minutes to read the final pages of the novel. She put it down and stomped into the kitchen a moment later.

"Oh, dear, from the look on your face, I take it you didn't like the ending," Jack said, looking up from the hob.

"No, I most certainly did not," Bessie said stoutly. "If you're going to hint at someone being the killer for the entire book and only reveal that he's really a secret government agent on the last page, the least you can do is have the unlikeable character be the killer."

"And he or she wasn't?"

"No, she had the protagonist's best friend be the killer, and it was all wrong and deeply unsatisfying. I won't be buying any more books in that series, that's for sure. I may not buy anything else by her in any series, now that I think about it."

"I made you a ham and cheese toasty with soup," Jack said. "Sit down."

Bessie sat down at the kitchen table and shook her head. "I'm sorry. It isn't your fault that I didn't like the ending. And you've gone to all this trouble for me, as well."

"It wasn't any trouble at all," he told her. "My butler training included a course in making quick and easy meals for emergency situations, but beyond that, my mother made sure I could heat soup and make toasties. She considers basic cooking an essential life skill."

"She's right about that, and this is delicious," Bessie said after a few bites.

"The soup came out of a can in your cupboards. I can't take any credit for doing anything more than heating things up."

"But what brings you here?" Bessie asked after several more bites. Now that she'd finished the book, she was absolutely starving.

"I wanted to talk to you about what happened on Saturday night.

I've never been a witness to a murder before, but I know you have. I just wanted to talk through it all, if you don't mind."

"Of course not. Feel free to make yourself a cup of tea or whatever you'd like and then sit down and join me."

Jack nodded and then refilled the kettle. He made tea for himself and Bessie and got out some biscuits as well. By the time everything was ready, Bessie was finished with lunch, so he cleared her plates before he joined her.

"Where shall we start?" he asked.

"Maybe you should tell me about the evening as if I weren't there," Bessie suggested. "It will be interesting for me to hear about it from a different perspective."

"I'll start with Saturday afternoon," Jack said. "Susan Haymarket arrived around one o'clock. Elizabeth thought that the police inspector was going to be coming with her, but he was on a later flight for some reason."

Bessie nodded. "What about Elizabeth's friends? Were they already at Thie yn Traie at that time or did they arrive later in the day?"

"That's a good point. Most of Elizabeth's friends arrived on Friday evening. I'll tell you about them first, then, shall I?"

"I think that would be best."

"Okay, let me think. Elizabeth sent a car to the airport around seven. It brought back Vivian Walker and Ernest and Norma McCormick. I met them in the foyer and had their bags taken to their rooms while they went in to dinner with the family. After dinner, I escorted them all to their rooms in the east wing."

"And what did you think of them?"

"Oh, I couldn't possibly say anything about the guests in the house," Jack began. He laughed. "Okay, yes, I can, but only to you. I have told the police a few things as well, but I was more careful with them. I know the chief constable is friendly with Mr. Quayle. I can't have him finding out that I was talking about the guests, now can I?"

"I suppose not, but if you tell me anything that might be relevant, I will have to tell John Rockwell about it," Bessie warned him.

"He seems very reasonable. Maybe he could put whatever it is into his notes as coming from an unnamed source or something like that."

"I'll certainly ask him to do so."

"Okay, so what did I think of the first three arrivals well, let me see. Vivian Walker is a spoiled monster who thinks men should fall at her feet so that she can trample all over them and then laugh. When I didn't immediately become enslaved by her beauty, she got quite snippy with me, which I found amusing."

Bessie grinned. "So you didn't like her, but can you see her killing anyone?"

"Absolutely. I can see her losing her temper and stabbing someone with one of her ridiculously high heels, for instance. Do I think she killed Jerome Rhodes? No, I don't. It was far too cleverly done for her."

"What do you mean by that?"

"The man was alone in a locked room in the dark. The killer had to make his or her way out of the great room, find a way into the study, find and stab a man in the dark, and then get back to the great room without anyone noticing. I can't quite believe that anyone accomplished that, really."

"John said something about another way into the room?"

"I'm looking for it, but I haven't found it yet," Jack replied. "The police are still denying everyone access to the study itself, but I've been trying to find a sliding panel or something on the wall behind it every chance I get. I haven't found anything yet, though."

"Elizabeth was in the corridor with a torch. She would have seen anyone who walked out of the great room. There must be another way into that room."

"I agree, although I'm not sure that I'd rely too heavily on what Miss Elizabeth says, either."

"Why not?"

"I believe she and Mr. Caine spent some part of the time while the lights were out, um, let's just say, together."

"Together and not paying attention to anything else that was going on around them?" Bessie suggested.

"Exactly."

"I thought Andy was in the great room the whole time," Bessie mused. "I certainly didn't notice him leaving."

"The staff was all in the kitchen, but I can tell you we heard a lot of noise and shouting, even from that distance. You couldn't possibly have heard anyone leaving or entering the room."

"It was very dark, though."

Jack nodded. "I still think whoever it was found another way into the study, but he or she might have switched a torch on at some point outside of the great room. I don't know that anyone in the great room would have noticed."

"Probably not. But we were talking about the guests. You didn't like Vivian. What about Ernest and Norma?

"They seem slightly odd to me, but nice enough."

"Odd in what way?"

"Maybe it's a twin thing, but they seem to be together all the time. I don't have any siblings, but they seem much closer than most of my friends are with their brothers and sisters."

"Perhaps it is a twin thing," Bessie said. "I understand they work together in the company business, as well, so that may play a part in their relationship."

"I don't think either of them killed Mr. Rhodes, mostly because they are so close. If one of them wanted to commit murder, I think they both would have had a hand in it, and that would make things even more complicated."

"Maybe one of them stayed behind to provide an alibi for the other," Bessie suggested.

"Except as far as I know, neither of them has done so. Mr. McCormick said something at breakfast about not knowing where anyone was while the lights were out. I waited to see if he'd add something about his sister, but he didn't."

"Okay, so those three arrived and were given dinner. What happened next?"

"While they were eating, Sean Rice, Richard Long, and Madison Fields arrived by taxi. I believe there was some sort of confusion about their arrival, which is why Elizabeth hadn't sent the car again."

"And what did you think of them?"

"Mr. Rice and Mr. Long are nearly interchangeable. They're both London bankers with too much money and not enough personality."

"It's difficult to imagine either of them as a murderer, then."

"Yes and no. I suspect they're both quite capable of murder if suitably provoked, but I couldn't begin to guess what might provoke either of them."

"Sean is quite interested in Vivian," Bessie suggested.

"Only because she's gorgeous and the only woman around, well, aside from Madison, but we'll talk about her later. He wants her, but he wouldn't kill for her, and even if he would, why would he kill Mr. Rhodes? His only competition for Vivian's affections at the moment is Mr. Long."

"But you think either of them could be the murderer, if we could come up with a motive."

"It will have to be something to do with money," Jack told her. "That's the only thing men like that really care about."

"So we need to learn more about both men. Maybe one of them crossed paths with Mr. Rhodes in London."

"Maybe. Now let's talk about the quiet, shy, and mousy Madison, shall we?"

"You don't like her?"

"I wouldn't say that, exactly, but no, I really don't. She does her best to blend into the background everywhere, but in a showy way. It's almost 'look at me, here I am, standing in the corner, being all demure and silent.'" He shook his head. "I'm explaining myself badly, but there's something unpleasant about her. Her shy, quiet routine seems to be working on Richard Long, though."

"I thought he was paying her some attention at lunch."

"He is, which is driving Vivian mad. She wasn't interested in either man until Mr. Long started chasing after Madison, now she's chasing him while Mr. Rice is chasing her and it's all getting quite ugly."

"Can you see Madison as the killer?"

"She's certainly sneaky enough to have worked out a way to do it, but she's also curiously devoid of emotions. I can't see her caring enough to kill anyone. Still, with the right motive, yes."

"What happened after they arrived, then?"

"Elizabeth took them to the dining room and fed them. Eventually, they went to their respective rooms and everyone was tucked up for the night."

"Could anyone have been up exploring Thie yn Traie during the night?"

"We had a member of the security staff stationed in that corridor all evening," Jack told Bessie. "He was there in case anyone needed anything, not because we were worried about security, but he reported the next morning that no one had left their rooms before breakfast time."

"Did anything interesting happen at breakfast?"

"Not that I recall. I can tell you all about it if you'd like, but I really don't think it's relevant."

"When you started earlier, you started with Susan's arrival at one. Can we safely jump to that, or is there anything you need to tell me about the morning or lunch?"

"Not a thing. As I said earlier, we were expecting the police inspector to arrive with Ms. Haymarket, but she told us that the man had had to switch to a later flight for some reason. Miss Elizabeth might know more about that. All I know is that I had to ring all of the guests to change the time of the party from six to seven."

"All of the guests?"

"I didn't ring the guests who were staying at Thie yn Traie, just everyone else."

"You didn't ring me, either. I still arrived at six."

"Miss Elizabeth told me that she would ring you herself. I'm sorry that she didn't do so."

"It wasn't a problem. Elizabeth sent a car for me before six, anyway. I'm not sure why she didn't let me know about the change."

"I suspect she wanted her mother to have some company while she was waiting," Jack said with a grin.

Bessie nodded. Elizabeth knew how nervous her mother got before social occasions. She also knew that having Bessie there would make Mary feel better. "Susan arrived at one, and then what happened?" she asked.

"She and Miss Elizabeth directed the staff as to how they wanted the great room set up. They worked out where Mr. Rhodes was going to stay while the lights were out, and basically just rushed about shouting at everyone."

"And where were Elizabeth's friends during all of this?"

"They mostly stayed out of the way, although I'm pretty sure they all drifted through at least once or twice during the afternoon. The kitchen staff was kept busy taking them all food and drinks, mostly to the television room in the east wing. That seems to have been where the group spent most of their time on Saturday."

"Why didn't they go out and see some of the island?" Bessie demanded.

"Miss Elizabeth did suggest that, but no one was interested in doing so. Apparently it was more fun to sit around and complain about being bored."

"You said Elizabeth and Susan worked out where Mr. Rhodes was going to be while the lights were out. How many of Elizabeth's friends were around when she and Susan were discussing that?"

"I know Mr. Rice and Mr. Long wandered through during that part of the discussion, because they were together and they were looking for a photocopier for some paperwork that Mr. Long needed copying to give to Mr. Rice."

"Did they seem particularly interested in the study?"

"I wish I could say yes, but they were just looking for Miss Elizabeth so that they could ask about a photocopier. I don't recall either of them paying any attention to the various rooms outside the great room, or even being there when Miss Elizabeth and Ms. Haymarket were discussing using the office."

Bessie made more tea and added more biscuits to the plate. "What was the next thing that happened, then?" she asked as she sat back down.

"You arrived," Jack grinned, "and you know what happened from there."

"So talk to me about the people we haven't already discussed. Tell me about Leonard and Liza Hammersmith for a start."

"They're guests at Thie yn Traie at least once a month. Mr. Quayle has some business interests that Mr. Hammersmith shares."

"But what do you think of them?"

"She's a social-climbing snob who thinks she's better than everyone else, and he's a ruthless businessman who would steal from his own grandmother if he thought it would help him make a pound or two."

"My goodness, you really don't like them, do you?"

Jack shrugged. "I don't really like them, but at least I know where I stand with them. I can't see either of them killing anyone in such an elaborate way. If Mr. or Mrs. Hammersmith wanted someone dead, they'd simply hire someone to do it for them. Neither of them would get their hands dirty."

"What about Mona Kelly?"

"She's a dear," Jack said with a smile. "I know she's a little bit older than I am, but, well, there's something very attractive about her."

"She's considerably older than you," Bessie pointed out.

Jack shrugged. "I'd still ask her to dinner if I thought she'd say yes."

Bessie chuckled. She didn't understand it herself, but she knew that Mona generally had that effect on men. "So you don't think she killed Jerome Rhodes?"

"No, although if she wanted him dead there's no doubt in my mind that her escort could have had it taken care of in no time."

"Michael Higgins?"

"Yes, although I doubt that's his real name. He's MI5 or MI6 or maybe even with some government department about which we know nothing."

"And you think he could have killed Jerome?"

"I think he could have had the man killed, but if he did want him dead, he would have done a better job of it. Mr. Rhodes would have fallen off a cliff or taken an accidental overdose of something. He wouldn't have been stabbed. Mr. Higgins is far too clever to have done something so crude."

"I think that's everyone," Bessie sighed. "We don't need to discuss George, Mary, or Elizabeth, and I won't consider Andy as a suspect either."

"I could never say a bad word about my employers," Jack said. "Anyway, Mrs. Quayle was with you and Mr. Quayle is far too loud and bumbling to have walked anywhere when the lights were out. From the kitchen doorway, I could see Miss Elizabeth for most of period in question, as she had that torch, and Mr. Caine was with her nearly the entire time."

"And the staff were all in the kitchen?"

"That seemed the safest place for everyone," Jack explained. "I warned Miss Elizabeth that I was going to have them all join me in the kitchen, which meant leaving the bar unattended for a short while, but she didn't mind."

"What about the security staff?"

"They were monitoring the house from the outside, but didn't have any staff inside Thie yn Traie during the party," Jack replied.

"That's a shame. And they were warned about the power cut?"

"Yes, Miss Elizabeth set it all up with them so that they didn't worry. Security arranged for the power to be cut to the ground floor, but the external cameras and alarms continued to function throughout the outage. I'm afraid there's no way anyone broke into the house to kill the man."

"I can't imagine how anyone from outside would have found their way to Jerome in the dark, anyway," Bessie said. "The killer has to have been someone who was at the party. What did you think of Susan?"

"When she first arrived, she seemed very competent and a bit bossy. Miss Elizabeth didn't seem quite certain of how to deal with her. As the afternoon went on, however, it became increasingly obvious that she was slightly out of her depth, shall we say? The plans kept getting more and more convoluted as they went along and I believe Miss Elizabeth was getting quite fed up."

"And what did you think of Jerome Rhodes?"

"I didn't believe he was a police inspector, that's for sure, not after he started drinking, anyway, and he started drinking almost as soon as he arrived."

"Did he mention why he'd taken a later flight?"

"Not to me, but he didn't say much to me at all. He mostly looked right through me as if I weren't worthy of his notice. That was the first thing that gave him away, really. Real police inspectors know that the staff always know everything that happens in a home and pay them particular attention. That's one of the reasons why I'm so frustrated about this murder. It happened right under my nose and I almost feel responsible."

"Don't be silly. You are in no way responsible."

"I feel as if I should know who did it, though. I was there, right down the corridor from the study. I should have seen something or heard something."

"As you said earlier, the party was very loud and there was all manner of shouting going on. Jerome could have shouted out his killer's name and we all would have missed hearing it. As for seeing something, well, if Elizabeth missed it all while practically standing in the doorway, it's hardly surprising that you missed it."

"Which is why I'm quite determined to find the alternate way into the room that has to be there," Jack said. "I was hoping you might know about it, actually, as you were around when the house was being built."

"I didn't really know the Pierce family," Bessie said. "I certainly wasn't invited over to Thie yn Traie while they lived there. I do know someone that I could ask, though. If anyone would know about secret doors at Thie yn Traie, it's Bahey Corlett."

"Is it?"

Bessie grinned. "She was nanny to the Pierce boys when they were growing up. She's retired now and lives in Douglas."

"Can you ring her right now?" Jack demanded.

"I can try. I don't know that she'll be home."

She wasn't. Bessie let the phone ring a dozen times, but no one picked up, and Bahey didn't seem to have an answering machine. "I'll just try her friend, Howard, as well," Bessie told Jack. "She's often with him."

Howard didn't answer either, but at least he had a machine. Bessie left a message, asking him to have Bahey ring her back before she put the phone down. "I'm sorry, but that's all I can do."

"Now I'm even more eager to get back to the house," Jack said. "I really want to find that secret door myself, if I can. Mrs. Quayle gave me the afternoon off. If I go back now, I can spend a few hours searching before I have to return to work."

"I hope you find something," Bessie said. "I'm sure John will feel better when he knows how the killer got access to his or her victim."

"It was lovely to see you, Aunt Bessie," the man said as he got to his feet. "I shall have to make a point of visiting you more often. I'm sure we could find more pleasant things to talk about."

"Definitely. I must ring your mother, as well. I've been meaning to do that. How is she?"

"She's fine and very happy to be back on the island. Let me give you her mobile number as she's never at home. I know she'd love to hear from you and would enjoy visiting with you." Jack scribbled a number on a piece of paper and handed it to Bessie.

"I'll ring her later in the week, maybe once the case is solved," Bessie said.

"That might be best. Mum hates that I'm wrapped up in a murder investigation. She'd probably complain to you about it for hours."

Bessie let the young man out, watching as he let himself into a small black car. It looked very like the car she'd sometimes seen Elizabeth driving, so perhaps it was part of the fleet of cars that George Quayle owned. Jack waved as he drove away. Bessie did the washing-up while she thought back through everything that Jack had told her. While it was all very interesting information, none of it seemed at all helpful when it came to the investigation. Still, that wasn't really for her to decide. She needed to share everything she'd learned with John Rockwell.

"John? It's Bessie," she said a short time later when the man answered his office phone.

"How are you?"

"Oh, I'm fine. I just had a lovely chat with Jack, er, Jonathan Hooper. He shared his thoughts on everyone at Thie yn Traie, perhaps telling me things that he shouldn't have. I wondered if you'd like to hear them, strictly off the record so that Jack isn't in any trouble for talking about his employers and their friends."

"I'd very much like to hear what he said. And I'd really like to talk through the case with you, as well. Are you free for dinner? Maybe we could meet at your cottage? I could see if Hugh and Doona are available to join us."

"That sounds good, but someone will have to bring food. I don't have anything I could make for four people."

"I'll bring pizza and garlic bread," John told her, "and I'll have Hugh or Doona bring pudding."

"Perfect. Six o'clock?"

"Or maybe a little bit later, depending on what time I finish here. I'll ring you if I'm going to be more than twenty minutes late or if either Hugh or Doona can't make it."

Bessie put the phone down and looked at the clock. She had a few hours to fill before her friends would arrive for one of their traditional gatherings. It had been a few days since she'd done any housework, so she cleaned the bathrooms, dusted, and ran the vacuum through the entire cottage. She felt better when that job was done.

The rain had stopped, but it was still overcast. Bessie decided that a walk to the shop at the top of the hill was just what she needed. The local paper was bound to have an article or two about the murder, although she doubted that it would tell her anything she didn't already know.

The girl behind the till was a stranger. Bessie grabbed a basket and put a loaf of bread and a carton of milk into it. A few glossy magazines of the sort she didn't normally read made their way into the basket as well. A chocolate bar and the local paper rounded out her purchases.

The total was just under ten pounds and Bessie handed the girl a twenty pound note. She was shocked when the girl gave her a few coins in change.

"I gave you a twenty pound note," she said sharply.

"Nah, you gave me a tenner," the girl replied.

"I'm quite certain I gave you a twenty," Bessie said firmly.

The girl shrugged. "Are you calling me a liar?"

"I'm suggesting that you're mistaken," Bessie replied.

"Well, I'm not," the girl said, shutting the till.

"I'm sorry, do you think I'm just going to leave and let you pocket my ten pounds?" Bessie asked.

"Yep," the girl smirked.

Bessie raised an eyebrow and then pulled out her mobile phone.

"Laxey neighbourhood policing, this is Doona. How can I help you?"

"Ah, yes, this is Elizabeth Cubbon. I'm at the shop at the top of the hill in Laxey. I gave the shop assistant a twenty pound note and she's only given me change for a ten pound note. I wasn't sure whom I should ring about the matter."

"I'll send a constable," Doona said, "and I'll let the shop's owner know that there's an issue. I'm sure he'll want to come out and help get things sorted."

Bessie put her phone away and stood and watched the girl closely. There was no way she was going to sneak any money out of the till while Bessie was watching her.

"Rang your answering machine to make me think you'd rung the police, did you?" the girl asked. "You didn't ring 999, that's for sure."

"No, I rang the police non-emergency number," Bessie explained. "Someone is on the way."

"Yeah, sure," the girl said, looking slightly less confident.

A minute later the shop door swung open. Bessie grinned as Hugh Watterson strolled in.

"I understand we have a problem," he said.

"She's just a confused old lady," the girl behind the till snapped. "She thinks she gave me a twenty, but she only gave me a tenner."

"So let's count the drawer and see what it says," a voice behind Hugh suggested.

Bessie didn't really know the man who owned the shop, but she had reason to dislike him. When he'd purchased the shop, he'd replaced her friend Anne Caine with his grumpy teenaged daughter. At that time Anne had really needed the job and Bessie had stopped shopping there as a show of support.

Anne had never held a grudge, though, and now that her son had inherited a small fortune and she didn't need to work she occasionally helped out at the shop when the man needed assistance. His daughter had gone across and done some work at a bakery. When she'd returned home, she decided that she wanted to bake cakes for a living rather than work at the shop, so she was rarely if ever there. It seemed to Bessie as if every time she came in the shop lately there was a different person behind the till.

"It'll balance, or nearly," the girl said firmly. "She's wrong, that's all. She's just confused."

The man punched a few buttons on the machine and it spit out a long receipt. While Bessie and Hugh watched, he carefully counted all of the money in the drawer.

"It's a few pennies off, but not ten pounds off," he told Bessie.

Bessie felt her face flush. "But I gave her a twenty pound note," she said quietly.

The owner of the shop looked from Bessie to the shop assistant and back again. The girl was smirking as she leaned against the wall.

"Let's check the camera footage," the owner suggested.

"Camera footage?" the girl repeated.

"Yes, there's a camera trained on the till for just such a problem," the man explained. "Constable Watterson, if you'd like to come with me, we can watch it in the back room."

Hugh followed the owner through the door marked "staff only," leaving Bessie alone with the girl. Another customer came in and bought a paper and a few other things before Hugh and the owner emerged. When the girl saw the looks on the two men's faces, she shook her head.

"It isn't how it looked," she said quickly. "I mean, I didn't do anything wrong."

"You're going to have to come with me," Hugh told her. "We'll talk about what the videotape shows down at the station."

"But I can explain," the girl replied.

"Good. You can do that down at the station," Hugh told her.

He left a moment later with a videocassette and the girl. The owner of the shop looked at Bessie and sighed. "Do you have any idea how hard it is to get good help?" he asked.

"I'm sure it isn't easy," Bessie said politely.

"Here, let me give you your money back," the man said. He opened the cash drawer and handed Bessie a twenty pound note.

"I should only be getting ten pounds," she said.

"Take twenty and consider it a token apology and a thank you. I'm sorry she tried to cheat you, and I'm grateful that you caught her at it so that she can't cheat anyone else."

Bessie put the note into her handbag and then picked up her shopping and headed for the door. The man followed her out, turning the sign to "closed" and locking the door behind them.

"This won't be good for business, but I need to go down to the station and give a statement of my own. Maybe it's time to sell the stupid shop," he said, mostly to himself, as he walked away from the building.

CHAPTER 10

*B*essie walked home slowly, wondering how anyone could ever think that cheating someone out of money was okay. She was still shaking her head over it as she let herself in Treoghe Bwaane. It was closer to six than she'd realised, so she quickly put her shopping away and refilled the kettle. People would probably rather have cold drinks this time of year, but it was always good to have the kettle ready, just in case.

Doona was the first to arrive. Although she was Bessie's closest friend, at first glance the pair seemed to have little in common. Doona was in her mid-forties and had been married twice, but was currently single. Her hair was red, thanks to a recent dye job, although she was thinking about going blonde next. Her bright green eyes were mostly due to coloured contact lenses. She'd gained some weight as her second marriage had fallen apart, but that weight had disappeared when her second husband had been murdered and she'd been a suspect in the killing.

"Hugh is probably going to be late. He has a lot of paperwork to get through," she told Bessie as they hugged.

"And that's my fault," Bessie sighed.

"You did exactly the right thing, ringing me," Doona assured her. "That girl tried to steal ten pounds from you."

"Yes, I know, but I might have been willing to let her have it if I'd known it was going to make Hugh late."

"He'll only be a little bit late, you'll see," Doona said, laughing. "John won't make him finish everything tonight, just the preliminary report."

John was at the door a few minutes later, laden down with pizza boxes. "The top two have garlic bread in them," he told Bessie as she and Doona moved the boxes onto Bessie's counter. "I promised Hugh that I would get extra of everything because he's going to be a little bit late."

"I feel guilty for making him late," Bessie said.

"It's the girl from the shop who is at fault, not you," John told her. "Be angry with her, not yourself."

"Oh, I'm plenty angry with her," Bessie replied.

"She was very clever, really, or nearly. It was just lucky for the shop's owner that he had that camera there," John said.

"So you could see that I gave her a twenty pound note?" Bessie asked.

"Yes, among other things," John replied.

"Like what?" Doona demanded.

John shook his head. "It will all come out in court, but I can't say any more for now."

"I wouldn't be surprised if she wasn't taking money right out of the till," Bessie said, watching John's face closely. "That would explain why the money was right even though she'd shortchanged me."

John winked at her as someone knocked on the door.

"Hugh, I was worried you'd never get here," Bessie said as she hugged the young man.

"So was I," he grinned. "I could smell the pizza from the station."

"Maybe it was the garlic bread," Doona suggested. "It's very strong."

They all filled plates while Bessie got drinks for everyone. "What shall we talk about?" she asked as she joined the others at the kitchen table.

"We need to talk about the case, but that can wait until after we've eaten, if you'd prefer," John said.

"Why don't I give you a quick run-through of what Jack had to say when he was here?" Bessie suggested. "Then we can talk properly about the case over pudding."

"Oh, no!" Hugh exclaimed. "I forgot to bring pudding."

"That's hardly surprising under the circumstances," Bessie said. "But never mind. I can throw some shortbread together in two minutes."

She finished a slice of pizza and then got up and pulled out flour, butter, and sugar. After all of her years of experience it didn't take her much longer than the two minutes she'd suggested to get the shortbread mixed up and into the oven. While she worked, Bessie told the others about her conversation with Jack.

The shortbread was ready to come out of the oven by the time everyone had finished second helpings of pizza. Bessie cut it into crumbly squares and spooned vanilla ice cream on top of it before serving.

"This is delicious," Doona sighed. "I shall have to eat nothing but lettuce for the rest of the week, though."

"Don't say that in front of Amy," John said. "She's already worrying about her weight, and I don't want her to think that she has to diet."

"I'm very careful what I say in front of her, actually," Doona said, "and I keep reminding her that she needs to keep her body healthy and that that is more important than what the numbers on the scale say."

"You've been terrific with both kids, and I don't thank you enough," John told her. "Thank you."

Doona blushed. "I like them both a lot. They're more fun to spend time with than most adults I know, present company excepted, of course."

Everyone chuckled. "And now we should talk about the case," Hugh suggested. "I'd like to get home before it gets too late."

"How is Grace?" Bessie asked.

"She's doing well and looking forward to getting into the new house and getting settled before the baby arrives. The whole thing seems a bit unreal to me, but I suppose it feels more real to her since the baby seems to be kicking her constantly."

"I can't imagine," Bessie murmured.

"Me, either," Doona said. "I think I quite prefer looking after teenagers, really."

"Every stage of parenting has its own unique challenges and rewards," John said. "For fathers, pregnancy is the easy part, of course. It's something of a shock to the system when the baby actually arrives, of course. Then the sleepless nights begin. Poor Grace is probably already having trouble sleeping, though."

"She is, and her mother told her it will only get worse."

Bessie and Doona exchanged glances. "Does anyone want more shortbread?" Bessie changed the subject.

Of course, Hugh did, and when John decided to have a bit more, Doona and Bessie found that they couldn't resist, either.

"I found what Jack, er, Jonathan, had to say quite interesting," John said as Bessie put the second round of puddings on the table. "I think we should talk about each of the, um, witnesses in turn."

"What about means, motive, and opportunity?" Hugh asked.

"Let's leave those for last, as they're possibly the most difficult part," John suggested. "For now let's assume that everyone had all three and talk about each of the party guests individually. Let's start with Leonard and Liza Hammersmith." John pulled out one of the notebooks he always carried and flipped to a blank page. With his pen ready, he looked at Bessie expectantly.

"I know them both, but only slightly," she said. "He made his money from buying and selling property around the island. She married him when he was just starting out, although she tries to act as if they're old money."

"Do either of them spend much time in London?" John asked.

"Not that I know of, but, as I said, I don't know them well," Bessie replied.

"How well do they know George and Mary?" was John's next question.

"Jack said that they visit Thie yn Traie regularly. I don't know if that's mostly social or mostly business. I believe that Liza is friendly with Elizabeth as well."

John nodded. "Were they friendly with the Pierce family?"

"We talked about this before," Bessie reminded the man. "I don't believe so, but it's possible."

"We talked about everyone before, but that was just the two of us. I want Doona and Hugh to have all of the background. Anyway, it helps hearing it all again," John explained.

"I don't mind repeating myself," Bessie said with a grin. "I was just worried that you were testing my memory."

John laughed. "I'm pretty sure your memory is better than mine. Anyway, does anyone have anything else to say about Leonard or Liza?"

"I knew Liza years ago," Doona said. "We had some mutual friends, but I didn't get to know her well. Once she married Leonard and he made a few pounds, she dropped all of her former friends."

"That's Liza," Bessie sighed.

"Let's talk about Elizabeth's friends, then," John said. "Tell me about Sean Rice."

"I don't really know anything about him, except that he's hoping to get involved with Vivian Walker but she doesn't seem interested. She's too busy chasing after Richard Long." Bessie replied.

"Who's Vivian Walker?" Doona asked.

"I forgot that you haven't met any of the people involved," Bessie said. "Vivian is a very beautiful part-time model with family money. She seems incredibly spoiled and I wouldn't be surprised if she was only chasing Richard to annoy Sean."

John sighed. "I'm not sure we're going to get anywhere talking about Elizabeth's friends. The things that Jack said were interesting, and might help, at least."

"I simply don't know them very well," Bessie said apologetically. "I could ring Elizabeth and see if she'd come down and talk about her friends with us."

"I've already interviewed her," John said. "I don't think she'd tell me anything more than what she's already said in her statement. Maybe you could try talking to her, though. She might be willing to tell you more about her friends than she told me."

Bessie nodded. "I'll ring her in the morning and see if she'd like to come over for a cuppa."

"So if we aren't going to talk about them, who's left to discuss?" Doona asked.

"Mona Kelly?" Bessie suggested.

"As I said earlier, she's been eliminated from our enquires. She and her friend, Mr. Higgins, have given one another an alibi," John said.

"And that's sufficient for you to cross them both off the list of suspects?" Bessie asked.

"In this case, yes," John said firmly.

"I hope you've at least been able to question them both about the evening. Maybe they saw or heard something significant," Bessie said.

"I have spoken to both of them, yes," John replied.

"What about Susan Haymarket?" Doona asked. "Or is she considered one of Elizabeth's friends about whom we don't know enough?"

"She and Elizabeth weren't friends," Bessie said. "I'm not sure where Elizabeth found her, but I believe she was paying Susan for her time and questionable expertise."

"Who else knew that her father was going to be at the party?" Doona asked.

"According to Susan, no one," John replied. "She'd told Elizabeth that she was bringing an Inspector Rhodes, but nothing more than that."

"Knowing Elizabeth, she told everyone," Bessie said, "but how could anyone have realised that he wasn't a police inspector at all?"

"Let's talk about motive, then," John suggested. "The things that Clara Rhodes told you were quite suggestive."

"Yes, and I didn't have trouble believing that the man was blackmailing people, either. He didn't seem like a very nice man," Bessie replied.

"So if we assume that he was blackmailing or attempting to black-mail one of the other party guests, we have a motive that could apply to just about any of the guests," Hugh said.

"I'm still not sure how they would have known that the man was going to be here," Bessie said.

"Perhaps he told someone he was coming," Doona suggested. "Maybe he rang someone to demand a payment and that person mentioned going away for the weekend. I would imagine Mr. Rhodes would have found it quite amusing to tell the person that he was going to be at the same party."

"And maybe they arranged to meet in the study while the lights were out," Hugh said. "Maybe Mr. Rhodes opened the door to whoever it was."

"Except he didn't have a key," John said. "There was only one key to the study door and it was in Elizabeth's pocket. We've checked and there's no way to open the door from the inside without the key."

"Jack is still looking for another way into the room," Bessie said.

"I'm really hoping he finds it," John told her. "Otherwise I'm not sure how the murderer got into the study."

"If there is a secret door, how would any of the party guests have known about it?" Hugh asked.

"We're trying to work out possible connections between the guests and the Pierce family, as well as to determine who might have had a chance to explore the house before the party. I've been told that no one was wandering around during the night, but that doesn't mean someone couldn't have accidentally tripped over the opening at some point before the murder," John said.

"Except if the door was that easy to find, surely Jack or the police would have found it by now," Bessie said.

"Maybe, or maybe someone tripped a switch entirely accidentally and discovered the hidden door," John said. "At this point, we're simply assuming that the door is there and accessible."

"Which takes us neatly to opportunity," Hugh said. "Since we don't know which guest Mr. Rhodes was blackmailing, we'll just have to assume it could have been any of them. Are there any guests who didn't have the opportunity to get through the secret door, though?"

"Jack said he could see Elizabeth and Andy while the lights were out, but they weren't on my list of possible suspects anyway," Bessie said. "Seeing as how we don't know how the killer got to Mr. Rhodes, though, I'm not sure we can talk about opportunity, can we?"

"When the lights first went out, I understand everyone was walking in a circle, saying his or her name periodically," John said.

"Yes, that's right. I can't even remember why now, but they were," Bessie replied.

"I don't suppose you were paying attention closely enough to have noticed if anyone suddenly went missing from the name calling?" he asked.

"I'm sorry, but I really wasn't paying attention," Bessie said. "It didn't seem to matter, and within a minute or two people started calling out each other's names and then completely random names. I don't know anyone's voices well enough to be sure who was shouting out and who'd gone quiet."

John nodded. "Presumably Vivian stopped shouting once she was meant to be dead?"

"I've no idea, but I still don't understand how that was meant to work. Elizabeth was supposed to be the killer, but she'd left the room before the lights went out. She shouldn't have been a suspect in the murder, as it happened while she was out of the room."

"Clearly Susan didn't know how to plan a murder," Doona said.

"Unless she was distracted because she was planning a real murder," Hugh suggested. "Maybe the murder mystery game was all just window dressing to distract from the real murder she was planning. Maybe she got it all badly wrong on purpose to make herself look incompetent, even while she planned the perfect crime."

"Why would she kill her father, though?" Doona asked.

"Money, probably," Hugh shrugged. "If she didn't know about her father's wife, she must have thought she was in line to inherit everything."

"Why didn't she know about Clara?" was Doona's next question. "It seems like something that should have come up in at least one conversation over the past three years."

"Clearly her father didn't want her to know," Bessie said. "From what Clara said, the relationship was volatile. Maybe he was waiting to see if they were going to stay together before he told his daughter about Clara."

"Where was Susan while the lights were out?" Doona asked.

"I believe she was in the corridor with Elizabeth," Bessie replied, "or in the doorway into the great room, anyway."

"Could Jack see her, then?" Hugh asked.

"He didn't mention her," Bessie said. "He could only see Elizabeth because she had a torch."

"Do you have some paper?" Doona asked. "I'd really like to see where everyone was. I'm having trouble visualizing it."

Bessie found a sheet of white paper and a pen. She drew the great room with the large dining table and the row of chairs.

"Mary and I were over here," she told Doona, adding herself and her friend to the sketch. "There was a bar here, but the man behind it left before the lights went out."

"So the party guests were walking in a circle around the chairs here?" Doona asked.

"It was more like a long oval than a circle, but yes. Here's the corridor and the study where Mr. Rhodes was waiting." Bessie added them to her drawing.

"The study and the great room do share a wall, then," Doona said. "If there is a hidden door in that wall, it would have been easy for someone to slip away."

"Yes, but no one has found it yet," John said.

"As far as I know, Susan was here somewhere," Bessie said, gesturing towards the door that led out of the great room, "and Elizabeth was in the corridor."

"And Andy joined her there?" Hugh asked.

"That's what Jack said," Bessie replied. "I didn't realise Andy had left the great room and I'm not sure how he found his way to the corridor without tripping over anything, though."

"From what I've heard, he's been spending a lot of time at Thie yn Traie," John said. "I gather he's learned his way around rather well. You didn't realise at the time that Andy had left the room?"

"I had no idea," Bessie sighed. "As I said, people were shouting all manner of things and I simply wasn't paying attention to them."

"I'm surprised he didn't trip over Vivian on his way back into the room," Hugh said.

"She was here," Bessie told him, putting an "X" on the drawing to mark the spot where Vivian had been lying when the lights had come back on.

"So not in the path of anyone coming or going from the circle," Hugh mused.

"No, she was out of the way. If anyone had tripped over her, though, they could have explained it away easily enough," Bessie pointed out.

"What about means?" Hugh asked. "I don't suppose the knife was something special?"

"It came from the kitchen at Thie yn Traie," John replied. "Mary is insisting that she's going to start locking up all the knives there."

"I don't blame her," Bessie said. This was the second time someone had taken a knife from the kitchen there and stabbed someone, after all.

"I think we're just talking in circles," Hugh said, "and making a lot of assumptions. I think you should take a closer look at Susan Haymarket."

"She was rather desperate to get off the island as soon as the body was found," Bessie said. "I have the impression that the police are still at Thie yn Traie mostly to make sure she doesn't leave."

"They're there for many reasons," John said. "Including keeping track of all of the guests."

"Did she tell you why she wanted to get away so badly?" Bessie asked.

"You know I can't repeat what she said in her interview," John replied.

"She said something to me that made me think she'd lied to Elizabeth. Maybe she was just worried about getting caught in her lies," Bessie speculated.

"From what you've said, I think it's pretty clear she lied to Elizabeth," Doona said.

"Yes, but maybe she lied about more than just her experience at party planning," Bessie replied.

"She's at the top of my list of suspects," Hugh declared. "I didn't like her at all."

"If she did kill her father, I think Clara should be worried," Doona said. "I can't imagine Susan was very happy when Clara turned up."

"No, she wasn't," Bessie agreed. "I was there and it wasn't pleasant."

"Where is Clara staying?" Doona asked John.

"Somewhere safe and secure," he replied. "She's agreed to stay for a few days in case any additional questions come up as the case unfolds."

"That was nice of her," Hugh said.

"I believe she sees it as a free holiday, rather than anything else," John said dryly.

"So where do we go from here? I don't know that we've ever had a less productive session than this one," Bessie said.

"As much as I hate to say it, I'm thinking about staging a reconstruction like we did for the New Year's Eve party," John said.

"That's probably a good idea," Bessie said.

"It will be a lot of work and it might not help, but it should give me a chance to see how the murder mystery evening functioned. Like Doona, I'm having trouble working out who was where, when," he replied.

"Can you find an excuse for me to be there?" Doona asked. "I hate that I missed all the excitement."

"We'll see. Maybe you can come as my assistant or something," John said. "But if you do, you'll have to work, not just sit around and watch."

"Of course I'll work," Doona said quickly, "and I'll pretend that I'm not just there because I'm nosy, too."

Bessie chuckled. "You could go in my place, if you'd like," she said. "I was just sitting quietly in the corner, anyway."

"Which means you were perfectly placed to observe everything," John said. "You managed to spot the one little thing that was the key to solving the New Year's Eve murder. I'm hoping you might do the same again for this one."

"That's hardly likely," Bessie said, "but you know I'll do my best."

The foursome chatted about the guests at Thie yn Traie for a while longer, but no one felt as if the conversation was actually useful. Eventually Hugh looked at the clock.

"It's later than I realised," he said, jumping to his feet. "I need to get home to Grace."

Bessie put some shortbread into a bag. "Take this home for your wife," she told him, "and don't think I won't mention it to her the next time I speak with her. You can't eat it on the way home."

Hugh looked so disappointed that Bessie cut another square of the sweet buttery treat for him to eat on his drive. While she was doing that, Doona and John cleared the table and got started on the washing-up.

"I can get that," Bessie told them after she'd let Hugh out.

"But you shouldn't have to," John said. "You were kind enough to open your home to us. The least we can do is clear up our mess."

"A few dishes and cups isn't a mess," Bessie said. "You brought dinner, as well."

While they were talking, John finished washing the last of the plates. He handed it to Doona, who dried it quickly and put it away.

"And we're done," John said. "It didn't take much time at all, anyway. You should see the mess at my house, or rather, you shouldn't. I don't know what the kids are doing all day, but it seems to dirty just about every plate, bowl, and glass I own."

"I did the washing-up last night when I was there," Doona said.

"Yeah, and Thomas used three bowls for breakfast this morning," John laughed. "I actually thanked Amy for only using two, when anyone sensible would use a single bowl. I don't know what they're thinking."

"They're thinking they can do what they please because someone else will take care of the mess," Bessie told him. "If they had to do the washing-up themselves, they'd quickly learn not to use so many things."

John sighed. "I know you're right, but they're meant to be on their summer holidays."

"Which means they have all the time in the world to wash a few bowls and glasses," Bessie said. "They're both more than old enough to have a few chores."

"Apparently their mother doesn't make them do anything. Harvey had a maid service that comes in twice a week," John said, his tone bitter.

"All the more reason for them to do chores here, then," Bessie suggested. "When they move out on their own they won't have a maid service. They need to know how to look after a home."

John nodded. "I just hate making them work on their holidays."

"I'm not suggesting you make them spend all day working around the house, but if they spend an hour each day doing chores, the house will be clean and they'll learn a lot. That still leaves them a great many hours of leisure and it means you don't have to clean and tidy after putting in a long day at work," Bessie told him.

"I told you that they're taking turns preparing dinner for all of us, didn't I?" John asked.

"You did. I'm sure they're using a lot of pots and pans while they're doing so, as well," Bessie replied.

"They seem to use every pot and pan I own, just to boil water," John said, shaking his head. "You're right. They should be doing the washing-up."

"Don't tell them that the idea came from me," Bessie said as she walked her friends to the door. "I don't want them angry at me."

"But it's okay if they're angry with me?" John asked.

Bessie grinned. "They'll be angry at you for lots of things over the next sixty or seventy years."

"I suppose that's true," John sighed. "Parenting is hard work. It's a good thing Hugh doesn't realise what he's in for."

"The species wouldn't survive if parents knew what they were in for," Bessie said. "I'm always amazed when people have more than one child, though."

"They're so cute and cuddly when they're babies," John said. "Thomas was just starting to toddle when Sue started talking about having a second one. I couldn't possibly have said no at that point."

"And now they're home alone, probably eating everything in the house," Bessie said. "Take them some shortbread from me." She handed the man a bag with the rest of the shortbread in it. "Do you want the ice cream, too?"

"We have ice cream," he replied. "In fact, we have a lot of ice cream and chocolate and biscuits, but not much real food. I need to go shopping tomorrow or else Amy will be making us ice cream sundaes for dinner."

"That sounds yummy," Doona said, "and I'm sure you'd be very popular with both children if you let her do it, too."

"It's more important that they be healthy than I be popular," John replied.

"Having ice cream for dinner once in a rare while won't hurt them," Doona suggested. "They'll feel as if they're getting away with something special, too. Don't you ever just have pudding for dinner?" she asked.

Bessie stared at her for a minute and then shook her head. "Pudding for dinner? Never."

"I'm with Bessie on this one," he said. "I might have done when I was younger, but I'd never admit to it now." He looked at Doona and winked.

"I have never had pudding for dinner," Bessie said firmly. "It simply isn't right."

"I think we should leave," Doona told John. "Before we get a lecture about healthy eating."

"Maybe we should stop for ice cream on the way home," John

suggested. "All this talk about pudding has made me hungry for something sweet."

"I don't know where we'd get ice cream at this hour," Doona said, looking at the clock.

"There's lots in my freezer," John told her. "Why don't you come over for a short while? I'm sure the kids would love to see you."

Bessie shut the door behind the pair, still shaking her head at the notion of having sweets instead of a proper meal. It was nice to see John and Doona spending time together, though. Bessie had hopes that their friendship might turn into more, but she wasn't about to say anything to either of her friends about it, at least not yet.

CHAPTER 11

*B*essie woke up the next morning eager to talk to Elizabeth. There was no point in ringing Thie yn Traie at six o'clock, however. The girl would still be in bed, probably for hours yet. Breakfast was porridge, something Bessie didn't really like but tried to make herself eat at least occasionally. She was feeling virtuous but grumpy when she put the box back in the cupboard. A little extra sugar in her tea helped improve her mood as she got ready to go for her morning walk.

The skies were overcast, but it was dry as Bessie headed towards the water. When she reached it, she turned and began a slow stroll down the beach. There was no one else outside, although Bessie saw a few people getting breakfast in the holiday cottages as she walked. While she felt as if she could walk for hours, she turned back towards Treoghe Bwaane not far past Thie yn Traie. As Bessie walked back, she noticed the young police constable at the bottom of the stairs was leaning against them and seemed to be asleep. Bessie was considering whether she should wake the man or not when she saw someone coming down the steps.

Elizabeth caught Bessie's eye from several feet above the beach. She looked at the constable and then laughed quietly. Bessie frowned as the girl sneaked around the man and leaped to the ground without disturbing him.

"Anyone could get up or down those stairs," Bessie said. "We need to wake him."

"He's fine," Elizabeth replied airily. "Everyone in the house is fast asleep, and Daddy hired extra security after that reporter tried to get in the other night. If anyone appears at the top of the stairs, they'll have a welcoming committee."

Bessie thought about arguing further, but Elizabeth took her arm and began walking down the beach towards Bessie's cottage. "We need to talk," she told Bessie. "I'm sure one of my friends must have killed that poor man and I don't know which one."

Inside Treoghe Bwaane Bessie put the kettle on. "Have you had breakfast?" she asked the girl.

"No, I didn't want anyone to know that I was up," Elizabeth replied. "I'd rather my friends didn't know I was speaking to you, you see."

"Why should they care if you want to visit me?"

"Daddy was telling them stories last night after dinner. We were all bored, so he started talking about the island and some of the things that have happened here since we've been here. Then he started telling them Aunt Bessie stories, all about all of the dead bodies you've found and how you've helped the police solve a dozen or more cases. At first no one seemed to believe him, but after the fifth or sixth story, they all started to come around."

Bessie sighed. "And now they'll all avoid me," she sighed.

"Probably, which is why I'm here. I thought if I told you everything that I know about each of them that you'd be able to work out which one is the killer."

"I doubt I can do that, but I'm happy to hear about them. I will have to repeat everything you tell me to John, though."

Elizabeth nodded. "I told him a little bit about them all, but, well, it felt odd talking to the police about my friends. I don't mind talking to you, though, even if you'll share what I've said with the police anyway."

Bessie didn't try to work out the logic in the girl's thinking. It seemed highly likely that there wasn't any.

"But you haven't had any breakfast. I have cereal, or I could make you some toast or something."

"A few slices of dry toast would be perfect. And coffee, if you have it."

Bessie set the coffee brewing and then made toast for her guest. When it and the coffee were both ready, she poured herself a cup as well, in spite of the just boiled kettle. Then she joined Elizabeth at the table.

"I thought about asking them all to come and talk to you, like we did the last time, but there are more of them this time and I wasn't sure I could come up with enough reasons to send them all here," Elizabeth said after a few bites.

"I hope it won't come to that," Bessie said. "Although John is talking about another reconstruction."

"Yes, he said something to Mum about that. She wasn't thrilled, but it was very effective last time."

"It was indeed," Bessie agreed.

"Anyway, that might be later today, so you need to know everything before it happens."

"Today? I didn't realise John was planning it that quickly."

"Maybe I misunderstood, but I know he isn't worrying about starting at the exact right time or any of that nonsense. He said something to Mum about fitting it in between lunch and dinner today so that no one has to worry about cooking anything for the reconstruction."

"That should make things easier for everyone."

"Anyway, who should we talk about first?"

"Vivian," Bessie suggested.

Elizabeth made a face. "She's not really my friend, she's more a friend of a friend, if you know what I mean. She has dozens of parties every year, so I thought she'd be a good person to invite. I'm hoping to start doing a few little things in London once in a while, you see. Vivian was my ticket into the London party scene."

"I hope she won't hold what happened against you," Bessie said.

"The murder won't bother her, but the badly planned murder mystery might. If she were going to have a party like that, she'd want it to be executed much more successfully. Having all of the guests wandering around the dark, shouting out their names? That wasn't at all appropriate."

"Maybe we should talk about Susan," Bessie suggested.

Elizabeth sighed deeply. "I got her name from another friend of a friend, someone I barely know. He said that she'd done a few parties for him, but when I rang him after Saturday and asked him for specifics, he went really vague on me. I suspect he and Susan had some sort of relationship and he lied for her to help her out."

"It was obvious on Saturday night that she didn't know what she was doing."

"Yes, I realise that. I should have insisted that we stop and simply have drinks and dancing or something rather than trying to carry on, but I kept thinking that things were going to get better."

"Except you were the killer in the pretend murder, right?"

"I was meant to be, but I told Susan that that didn't work, because I wasn't in the room when the victim died. She insisted it didn't matter and that the inspector would work it all out."

"Without bothering to mention that the inspector was her father," Bessie added.

"And not an actual police inspector. I feel I'm an idiot for believing anything that woman said."

"I hope you didn't pay her very much."

"I paid for her flights and also for her father's, but that was all. I was meant to pay her a great deal for running the party, but I tore up her cheque after the mess she made of everything."

"I'm sure she wasn't very happy about that."

"She wasn't happy, but she couldn't really argue. I suggested that if she wanted to discuss it further, I'd be happy to do some digging into her background, and she shut up about the money."

"Do you think she has a criminal record?"

"Probably. I can't help but wonder if she was planning to steal some things from the house before she left, but surely she'd know she couldn't get away with that."

"Do you think she had any motive for killing her father?"

"If she did, it was probably to do with money," Elizabeth said. "I know she was furious when her father's wife turned up at Thie yn Traie. She's still insisting that the woman isn't who she claims to be and that her father wasn't married when he died."

"I'm sure the police are investigating Clara's claims. It will be up to them and the solicitors to work out who inherits anything that Jerome Rhodes left behind."

"Susan said something about being glad she'd had the locks changed at her father's flat recently. I got the impression that he kept something valuable there, something Susan is worried that Clara might get her hands on."

"Clara told me some things that suggest that her husband might have been blackmailing people," Bessie told Elizabeth.

"That wouldn't surprise me. I didn't like him and I didn't like the way he kept staring at everyone all night long."

"Maybe he was just trying to stay in character."

"Or maybe he was hoping he'd see something that he could use to blackmail one or another of my guests."

"He was drinking very heavily, though."

"Yes, but I suspect he was used to doing so. He didn't seem all that drunk when I took him into the study. He managed to make a few rude suggestions to me as we went, anyway."

Bessie shook her head. "He wasn't a very nice man."

"No, he wasn't, and I can certainly see him as a blackmailer."

"Maybe he has a notebook at home with all the details about the people he's been blackmailing," Bessie suggested.

"If I were Susan, I wouldn't want any part of that. If we're right, something in that notebook may well have led to the man's murder."

Bessie nodded. "I wonder if John can have the flat searched? I shall have to ask him."

"If Clara knew what her husband was doing, she may be in danger, too."

"John has her somewhere safe."

"That's good. I didn't much like her, either, but I don't want anyone else to get murdered."

"Can you think of any reason why Vivian might be being blackmailed?"

"Vivian? I can't see her caring about anything enough. She jumps from man to man at an astonishing rate, really. The only reason she hasn't slept with both Richard and Sean while she's been here is because Richard isn't interested and Sean is too interested. I suspect she had a fling with Ernest years ago, because she hasn't paid him any attention and he's the only other single man around."

"There's Andy," Bessie pointed out.

"Yeah, she did try. He was polite but emphatic when he turned her down. I'm sure she'll keep trying if she gets more chances, but for right now I'm doing what I can to keep the two apart."

When Bessie looked surprised, Elizabeth laughed. "I do trust Andy completely, but I don't trust Vivian in the slightest. I'm simply trying to save Andy from having to fight her off."

"Perhaps someone should suggest to Sean that he stop chasing her and wait for her to chase him."

"I think it's too late for that. Vivian isn't big on second chances, and he was far too obvious from the start. As I understand it, he was mooning after her for months from a distance before they even met. By that time all of their friends knew how he felt."

"I'm starting to feel quite sorry for him."

"He's old enough to know better. He has a habit of falling for women who treat him like dirt. Most of them manage to get him to spend a fortune on them before they dump him. Vivian has enough of her own money that she couldn't be bothered to do that, at least. But give him a month or so and he'll be chasing after some other beautiful, spoiled, vain woman who will happily trample all over him until he runs out of money or she gets bored."

"My goodness, the poor man."

"The poor man is thirty-three and ignores every opportunity to spend time with nice, normal women who would be good for him," Elizabeth said tightly.

Bessie recognised bitter experience in the girl's tone. So she'd fallen for Sean at some point and been ignored. That was interesting.

"Can you think of anything that Mr. Rhodes might have been using to blackmail Sean?" she asked, changing the subject.

"It would have to be something to do with his job, I would think. He works in international banking. Maybe he's embezzling millions or something like that."

"I'm not sure how Mr. Rhodes would have been able to find out about such a thing," Bessie said thoughtfully.

"That's a good point. I doubt Mr. Rhodes knew anything about international banking."

"What about Richard Long?"

"He knows all about banking," Elizabeth began. Then she laughed. "You mean what about him a suspect, sorry. I don't know. He seems like a nice person, but he's, um, reserved. I've known him for maybe a year or more and I don't think we've ever done much more than exchange pleasantries."

"Do you think he's hiding something?"

"I didn't before, but now that you've mentioned it, maybe." She made a face. "No, I don't really think so, actually. I think he's just happy in the background. This party wasn't really typical of the sorts of places I usually see Richard. It's much smaller and more intimate than a typical night out in London. I'd never really noticed how reserved he is when we've been in larger crowds."

"Vivian seems interested in him."

"She's just chasing him because she's bored and because he so clearly isn't interested in her."

"He seems interested in Madison."

Elizabeth sighed. "I never should have invited that girl. I didn't want to, but Norma suggested her and I couldn't find a polite way to get out of it."

"She and Norma are good friends?"

"I don't really know, but I suppose they must be. I was telling Norma that I wanted to invite lots of people, especially the sort of people who might be interested in having the same sort of party, and she suggested Madison. Apparently Madison has been talking about having more parties in the next year or so, now that she's inherited some money."

"Is there a story behind that?"

"Not really. Her grandmother died when Madison was a child and left money in trust for all of her grandchildren. They weren't allowed to have the money until they finished university or turned thirty. Madison didn't bother with university, so she had to wait to get her inheritance until a few months ago when she finally turned thirty."

"And was it a lot of money?"

"I've no idea. From what I've heard, Madison didn't need the money, but she's happy to have it. As I said, Norma suggested that she'll be using the money to have parties, rather than to meet any expenses or anything like that."

Bessie shook her head. It was impossible for her to imagine frittering away large sums of money on parties, but Elizabeth's friends were quite unlike anyone that Bessie knew. "If she's that wealthy, I'm surprised she doesn't do more to look glamourous."

"She quite deliberate in her appearance. I think she likes standing out for looking plain and dowdy in the middle of a crowd of women in short skirts and tons of makeup. I know a number of men who've fallen for her, in spite of her appearance although her fortune may play a role in that."

"Do you think she's interested in Richard?"

"Not even the tiniest bit. Richard isn't old money, his father owned a chain of retail shops, and Richard worked for his dad for a while before he moved into banking. Madison is a snob."

"Poor Richard," Bessie sighed.

"I suspect he's only chasing her to get Vivian's attention. I don't think Vivian would be at all interested in him otherwise. She can be a bit of a snob, too."

"Can you think of any reason why any of them might be being blackmailed?"

"I'm sure Madison has secrets, probably lots of them, but I can't imagine how a man like Jerome Rhodes would have discovered them. As for Richard, I've no idea. He never talks about his family or his past, so there could be something there, I suppose."

"Who is left to discuss?"

"Norma and Ernest. They're an odd pair, really. I invited them because Norma has been talking for ages about coming to visit me. This seemed the perfect occasion to bring her over to see the island. I was also hoping she or her brother might be interested in having a similar party. They host a lot of parties, those two."

"They seem very close for siblings."

"Yeah, they're weirdly close, but maybe that's a twin thing and maybe it's to do with their upbringing. Their parents are somewhat unusual, and from some remarks I've heard over the years I suspect their childhood was difficult. They seem to have had to rely heavily on each other to get through it. Maybe that's just become habit."

"It must make relationships difficult," Bessie suggested.

"Ernest goes through women very quickly, but the endings are always civil and often incredibly friendly. Norma was in a relationship with another of my friends for about ten years, but it seems to have just fizzled out about a year ago."

"Any idea why either might be blackmailed?"

"None at all."

"What about Leonard and Liza?"

"I don't like him, but he and my father have common business interests."

"Why don't you like him?"

"He always looks at me as if he's taking off my clothes in his head," Elizabeth replied, shuddering. "He's never actually said or done anything inappropriate, but I just feel as if he would if he thought he could get away with it. I may be totally wrong about him, but I find him slightly creepy."

"And Liza?"

"She's arrogant and rude. She and Leonard both seem to think that money is the answer to everything, and I can't imagine they're overly bothered by morals or ethics." Elizabeth shook her head. "I'm probably being unfair, but I really don't like either of them. That doesn't mean I'm right, of course."

"It sounds as if you think either of them could have been being blackmailed."

"I suspect either or both of them have secrets they'd like to keep. It wouldn't surprise me to learn that Leonard cheats on Liza. I doubt she cheats on him, but that doesn't mean she doesn't have other secrets."

"I don't think we're getting anywhere," Bessie sighed. "Everything you've told me has been interesting, but none of it seems to give anyone a clear motive for murder. Let's talk about a hidden door between that study and the great room, instead."

"There isn't one," Elizabeth said.

"Are you certain?"

"I'm as certain as I can be. I've been living at Thie yn Traie for months and I've never stumbled across one. And now, after Saturday, everyone is looking for it. If it is there, it can't be that hard to find."

"Then how did someone get into the study to kill Mr. Rhodes?"

"They must have come into the corridor and opened the door somehow."

"But you were in the corridor with a torch."

"I was, well, a little distracted, at least for part of the time."

"Really?"

"Andy sneaked out to join me and we were, um, talking together for a while. I don't think anyone else came out of the great room, but they must have done."

"Where was Susan?"

"Who knows? She was standing in the doorway when the lights went out and she was there when they went back on, too, but I wasn't paying any attention to her while it was dark."

"It would have been easiest for her to get to the study," Bessie mused. "I don't know anything about locks. How do you think the killer got the door open?"

"Maybe he or she had a duplicate key from somewhere or maybe they were good at picking locks. I don't know, but I really don't think there's any other way into the study."

"You said everyone was trying to find a secret door?"

"The police didn't really want anyone in the great room at first, but they didn't actually say we couldn't use it. Every time I go in there, someone is standing there, tapping his or her way across the wall. There are a few shelves there as well, and everything on them has been taken off and moved around a dozen times or more."

"What about the other side, in the study?"

"The study is blocked off with police tape, so no one has been poking around in there, at least not yet. But if someone did get through a secret door into the study, he or she had to have gone in from the great room."

"And if the secret door is that hard to find, how did they manage to find it?"

"Exactly."

"Whose idea was it to put Mr. Rhodes in that room?" Bessie asked.

"Mine, or rather mine and my mother's. Once Susan explained how the party was going to work, and I realised that we'd need a place to stash the man while the lights were out, I talked to my mother and we agreed that the study was the best place. We were originally going to use the library, but, well, there are valuables in there. The study was mostly empty. Mum took the key to the library so that I had an excuse not to use it."

"So there was no way the killer could have known that Mr. Rhodes was going to be in that room in advance?"

"Susan and I discussed it. I suppose anyone could have overheard us, but I didn't notice anyone listening."

"The more we talk about this, the more confused I get," Bessie said. "If we accept that Mr. Rhodes was blackmailing someone, how did that someone know that he was going to be at the party? How did that someone know that he was going to be put into the study? And how did that someone know how to get into the study through a locked door?"

"Maybe the killer didn't know any of that stuff in advance. Maybe he or she just got lucky," Elizabeth suggested.

"I suppose that's possible, although it seems unlikely."

Elizabeth looked at the clock on the wall. "I should get back. Some of the others will probably be up by now. We were talking about going down to the Laxey Wheel or something today, just to get out of the house."

"I thought you said the reconstruction might happen later today."

"It might. The Laxey Wheel won't take long, though. We could all climb up and have a look around and still be home in time for lunch."

"Be careful," Bessie said seriously.

Elizabeth nodded. "It's odd to think that one of my friends is probably a murderer, but it seems as if that's the case. I mean, it isn't the first time, so I probably shouldn't be so surprised, but I am anyway. It would be hard to push someone off the Laxey Wheel, though, I think."

"Hard, but maybe not impossible. Perhaps you should visit a different site, one with fewer steps."

"Or maybe we'll just stay at home and watch telly or something. I feel as if that might be safer for everyone."

"How is your mother holding up?"

"She's okay," Elizabeth replied with a shrug. "Obviously she's not happy about being caught up in another murder investigation, but having been through it all before, at least we all know what to expect. I'm sure she'll feel better when the killer is behind bars and my friends are all allowed to leave, though."

"Tell her that I'm thinking of her," Bessie requested. "I may try to ring her later if it turns out that we aren't doing the reconstruction today."

"I'm sure she'd love to hear from you. She actually said something yesterday about sneaking away and staying with you until everything was all over, but she'd never leave Daddy like that. He needs her."

"She's welcome here, and so are you, for that matter."

"But not Daddy?" Elizabeth teased. She held up a hand before Bessie could reply. "I know, you like him, but there's no way his personality would squeeze into your spare room."

"If he needs or wants a place to stay, he's welcome as well. I'm fairly certain he'd be happier at a hotel, though."

"Oh, yeah, Daddy is all about luxury. Your cottage is cosy and wonderful, but it wouldn't suit him."

For which Bessie was grateful. "Well, you are more than welcome, as is your mother."

"I can't leave my friends and Mum can't leave Daddy, but I really appreciate the offer. Maybe once the murderer is behind bars and my friends have all gone, I'll come over and spend a night. Andy says your spare bedroom is his favourite place in the world."

"Andy stayed there quite a bit when he was younger. He didn't have a very happy childhood."

"He doesn't talk about it much, but it must have been difficult. Imagine being heir to a fortune and not knowing anything about it."

"He seems to have grown into a splendid young man anyway."

"He is rather splendid," Elizabeth said with a huge smile. "I know he'll eventually get tired of me, because I'm nowhere near smart enough for him, but I'm having a wonderful time with him at the moment."

Bessie bit her tongue. She was tempted to encourage the girl to go back to school, but she didn't want Elizabeth to think that that was the key to keeping Andy interested. Elizabeth would have to find her own way to do that.

"We didn't talk about Mona Kelly or her incredibly handsome companion," Elizabeth said suddenly.

"I believe they've both been eliminated as possible suspects."

"Really? I could totally see Michael Higgins as the killer."

"You could?"

"He was gorgeous, even though he's far too old for me. There was something mysterious about him. Ms. Kelly said that he worked for the government. I bet he was a spy. He reminded me of James Bond."

"He was very attractive, and he seemed very intelligent as well."

"Yeah, I could see him finding a way into the study without anyone noticing. Maybe he's a hired assassin. If that's the case, the police may never be able to link him with Mr. Rhodes."

"As I said, I believe the police have cleared him."

"Maybe he killed Mr. Rhodes for the government. Then the government told John Rockwell to stop investigating him. John wouldn't have a choice but to agree, right?"

"I've no idea, and it seems pointless to speculate. If Michael did kill Mr. Rhodes, I suppose he will get away with it."

"Ms. Kelly didn't do it, anyway," Elizabeth said firmly.

"Why not?"

"She simply wouldn't, not like that, anyway. If she wanted someone dead, she'd get someone like Michael Higgins to get rid of the person for her. I can't imagine Mona Kelly ever gets her hands dirty doing anything."

Bessie chuckled. "There is something almost too perfect about Mona, but I've known her for many years and I can promise you that she's quite capable of mucking in and doing hard work if it's needed. She's just been very fortunate in that she's never really had to do much."

"I'd love to know where all of her money comes from," Elizabeth said. "She lives incredibly lavishly, doesn't she?"

"She lives well, certainly, but I'm sure there are people who wonder where my money comes from as well."

Elizabeth blinked. "I've never thought about that. Didn't you inherit something from an old boyfriend or something?"

"It was something like that, anyway," Bessie told her, "and I was fortunate that my advocate invested my inheritance wisely on my behalf. Perhaps Mona was similarly lucky."

"Daddy said that she leads a charmed life, so maybe she was. Oh, goodness, I'd better go. I should have been home an hour ago." Elizabeth got to her feet and then pulled Bessie into a hug. "Thank you so much for everything."

Bessie wasn't sure what she'd done, but she nodded as she followed the girl to the door. Elizabeth dashed away, back down the beach, before Bessie could do anything further. As Bessie shut the door behind her guest, she tried to decide if Elizabeth had said anything that needed repeating to the police. As she wasn't sure, she rang the station.

"Laxey neighbourhood policing, this is Doona. How can I help you?"

"It's Bessie. Is John around?"

"He's not. He's up at Thie yn Traie. Is it urgent?"

"No, not at all. I just enjoyed a long chat with Elizabeth, that's all. I thought I would share what she'd told me with him, but none of it seems particularly important."

"I'm sure he'll still want to hear it all," Doona laughed. "I'll send him a text and let him know. Don't be surprised if he turns up on your doorstep."

"Do you know if the reconstruction is going to happen today?"

"I don't know yet, but I'm hoping for more information soon. That's one of the reasons why John went to Thie yn Traie."

"I'll just wait for someone to ring me, then," Bessie said.

"I have your mobile number. You don't have to sit around at home to wait."

"I know, but I probably will anyway. I didn't have any plans for today."

"If you're bored and you want to bake some brownies or something, I'd be happy to help you eat them later."

Bessie laughed. "I could make a tray of brownies. If I gave you the whole tray, you could share them with Thomas and Amy."

"Or I could eat them all myself," Doona said cheerfully, "but I'd probably share them with Thomas and Amy. I might even let John have one."

Bessie put the phone down and looked at the clock. It was too early to have lunch. She could read a book or bake. While both ideas were appealing, she didn't want to let Doona down, so she pulled out her cookbook and found the recipe for American-style brownies. It was one that she made regularly, so she only needed to double-check a few ingredients before she got started. The pan had just gone into the oven when someone knocked on Bessie's door.

CHAPTER 12

"I hope you don't mind my just appearing on your doorstep," John said as Bessie let him in. "Doona said you wanted to speak to me and I needed to speak to you as well. This seemed easier than ringing, since I was at Thie yn Traie."

"Elizabeth came over for a visit this morning," Bessie explained. "She gave me a little bit more background on her guests. I don't think any of it is relevant to anything, but I thought you should probably hear what she had to say."

"I definitely should."

Bessie put the kettle on. "How are the children?" she asked as she waited for it to boil.

"They're fine. They're enjoying spending time with their friends. I hadn't realised that they both made quite a few friends during the year they were here, and now they've made even more. They aren't looking forward to going back to Manchester, really."

Bessie swallowed a dozen questions as she made the tea. John and Sue would have to work everything out between themselves. This wasn't the place for other people to meddle.

"Let me tell you what Elizabeth had to say, then," Bessie said as she sat down opposite John after serving tea and biscuits.

He pulled out his notebook and smiled expectantly at her. "I hope this helps," he said softly.

When Bessie was finished, he sat back and drained his teacup. "Well, that was all very interesting," he said.

"But was it helpful?"

"Every bit of information is helpful. A case like this is like a giant jigsaw puzzle and every single piece is needed in order to see the whole picture. At this point, I don't know which little bits go where, but they all matter."

"But you said you needed to talk to me. Is something wrong?"

"Not at all. I just need to ask you to come to Thie yn Traie at two o'clock today. We're going to be holding the reconstruction at that time."

"I'll be there," Bessie promised. "Will it be like last time, where you want everyone to do everything exactly the same as the night of the murder?"

"I'm going to try to keep this a little less formal. I'm mostly interested in going through what happened after dinner, so we're going to start there and go through things very slowly. I've done several walk-throughs with a team of constables, but that hasn't achieved the results I want. I hope to do better with the actual people involved."

Bessie nodded. "You don't really need me, then," she suggested. "I was just sitting in a corner watching everything by that point."

"I'm hoping you might notice someone or something out of place," John replied. "You and Mary were best placed to spot something like that."

"I'll do my best," Bessie assured him.

"And now I need to get back to Thie yn Traie to make sure everything is ready for two. I'll be taking Mr. Rhodes's place in the reconstruction, by the way."

"That makes sense. Will we be sitting in the dark again?"

"There aren't any curtains on the great room windows, so no, you won't be in the dark. We are going to turn off the power again, just as it was done on Saturday night, but with all those windows, the great room should be quite bright. If we don't get any results from this attempt, we might try again after dark to recreate things more accurately, but I'm hoping we won't need a second try."

Bessie let the man out and then looked at the clock. It was time for lunch, but now she was full of tea and biscuits. Perhaps a short walk on the beach would stimulate her appetite, she thought. The beach, however, was crowded with families enjoying the day, which had turned sunny. After being nearly run into by a sobbing toddler, and then accidentally wandering into the centre of a spirited game of beach volleyball without a net or seemingly any rules, Bessie turned around and headed for home. She perched herself on the rock behind her cottage and enjoyed the sunshine herself for a short while before going back inside.

Tea and sandwiches were enough for lunch, and she ate them slowly while reading a book. By the time she'd finished the washing-up, it was time to leave for Thie yn Traie. Because of the crowds on the beach, Bessie decided to walk to the mansion along the road for a change. The large gates at the entrance were shut when she arrived.

"It's Bessie Cubbon," she said into the phone at the gate.

"I'll be right there," a voice replied.

Hugh Watterson strolled out of the house a moment later. "We're keeping the gates shut to keep out reporters," he told Bessie. "They all seem to have disappeared again, but they keep coming back."

"I didn't even think about that," Bessie replied. "The beach was crowded, so I thought this would be easier. I would have hated to get here and find reporters waiting, though."

"John was going to have me drive over and collect you, but when I rang to tell you, you'd already left."

"I left early to allow extra time for walking on the road," Bessie explained.

Hugh opened the gates and then locked them again behind her. "Everyone is assembling in the great room," he said, offering his arm.

Bessie took it and let Hugh lead her into the house. He remained at the door while she continued on into the great room. Mary rushed over to her as soon as she entered the room.

"I would have sent a car for you, but John said he was going to do so," she told Bessie.

"I left early to walk along the road, so I missed Hugh. You know I enjoy walking, though."

"Everyone is trickling in slowly," Mary told her, "and they're all obsessed with that wall."

Bessie grinned as she saw that most of Elizabeth's friends were standing together, tapping and knocking on the wall between the great room and the study. "No one has found a secret door yet, then?"

"No one has found anything," Mary sighed.

"I really would love a closer look myself," Bessie admitted. She crossed the room and smiled at the group that had gathered. "Nothing yet?"

"Nothing at all," Richard said from where he was stretched out on the floor. "I had this brilliant idea about there being something in the skirting boards, but if there is, I haven't found it."

"There aren't any cracks or anything that could be a door," Sean said.

"I don't think there's anything here," Madison whispered.

Bessie ran her hand along the wall. It was textured, which made it difficult to work out whether there might be a door there or not. Several shelves were affixed straight to the wall and Bessie found them all impossible to move in any way. The various items that had been on the shelves on Saturday night had all been removed. Before Bessie could get down on the floor to inspect the skirting boards, Elizabeth swept into the room.

"Does anyone know where Vivian has wandered off to?" she asked. "I told her to be here at two. She's not in her room."

"Maybe she went for a walk on the beach," Richard suggested. "She said something earlier about wanting a walk."

"Vivian was going to walk somewhere?" Elizabeth asked. "I don't believe it." Elizabeth's friends all laughed.

"She must be around here somewhere," Sean said. "Maybe she decided she didn't want to take part in all of this and is hiding in one of the wings."

Elizabeth frowned. "We don't have time to spend hours looking for her," she complained.

"She'll turn up," Richard said. "She's probably just waiting to make a dramatic entrance. Not everyone is here yet, anyway."

The words were barely out of his mouth when Ernest and Norma walked into the room.

"I hate to say this, but I'm pretty sure we're all wasting our time with this," Norma said.

"We aren't," Sean countered. "This time it will be lovely and bright in here and we'll all be able to see who sneaks away to kill Mr. Rhodes." Everyone laughed again.

"If the police think that's going to happen, they're deluded," Ernest said.

"We don't," John said coolly from the doorway. "But criminals make mistakes. Sometimes we can find a murderer simply because someone noticed a changed hairstyle. I can assure you that I don't expect the killer to sneak away from the party and break back into the study. He or she will, instead, be trying hard to pretend to have been here all along. That's not going to be as easy as he or she thinks it is."

Bessie looked around the room, hoping to spot someone looking nervous. From what she could see, though, mostly people looked bored.

"We're here," Leonard Hammersmith announced as he and Liza rushed into the room. "We were caught up in traffic. Sorry if we're late."

"You're right on time," John assured him.

"I hope that means we aren't late, either," Michael Higgins said as he escorted Mona into the room.

"Not at all. We're still waiting for a few more, actually," John replied.

"Andy is in the kitchen. I'm to get him when you're ready. He's just making some snacks for later, when this is all over," Elizabeth said.

"And George is in his office upstairs. I can ring him now if you're ready," Mary said.

"Susan isn't here yet," Elizabeth pointed out. "I reminded her before I came down."

"I can send someone to get her if you tell me where to find her," John said.

"No need. I'm here," Susan said from the doorway.

Bessie was surprised at the woman's appearance. She looked as if she hadn't slept since the last time Bessie had seen her. Susan walked to the nearest chair and slumped into it.

"It's just Vivian who is missing, then," John said. "Which room is she in?"

Elizabeth told him. "But she wasn't there when I came down. I'm not sure where she is."

John left the room. He was back a moment later. "While we locate Vivian, the rest of you can start to find your places, please. I want you to sit around the dining table in the same places you were in at the end of dinner."

Bessie trailed behind the others as they slowly made their way towards the table. She was more worried about Vivian than anyone else seemed to be. Hugh walked into the room as everyone began to settle into their seats.

"Ms. Walker isn't in her room," Hugh said. "I've checked with the constable on the beach and no one has come down those stairs today."

Bessie exchanged glances with Elizabeth. She hadn't mentioned the sleeping constable to John, but now she wondered if she should have.

"And you've been at the front door all day," John said. "She hasn't gone out that way, I assume."

"No, sir."

"Who saw her last?" John asked the group.

"She was at lunch," Elizabeth answered. "She left the room with Richard, I believe."

"We walked out together, anyway," Richard said. "She said something to me about wanting to go down to the beach. The idea didn't appeal to me, so I told her to have fun and went back to my room."

"Did anyone see her after that?" John asked.

When no one replied, he turned back to Hugh. "Have a constable check the beach, just in case she got past the man at the bottom of the stairs somehow." He turned to Mary. "Can you help organise a search of the house, please, Mrs. Quayle? You know it better than anyone."

Mary got to her feet and followed Hugh out of the room while John turned back to the group around the dining table.

"I'm going to have to ask you all to be patient with me for a short while. I'd rather not start with anyone missing, but if Vivian doesn't turn up in the next fifteen minutes or so, we'll do what we can without her."

Bessie smiled at Michael, who was sitting beside her. "I hope Vivian turns up soon."

"Yes, I'm a little bit worried about her," he replied, frowning.

"I wasn't sure if you'd be here or not. I thought you might be needed across." Bessie didn't want to ask any rude questions, but she was incredibly curious about the man's job.

He chuckled. "I'm mostly retired now and pretty much come and go as I please. Right now the island is considerably more interesting to me than London. I shall probably be here for another week or two at least." When he finished speaking, he glanced over at Mona Kelly.

What was it about Mona that so entranced men, Bessie wondered. "I hope you'll have a chance to see some of the island's historical sites while you're here," she said after a moment.

"We spent the afternoon at Peel Castle. It was charming."

"Bessie, do you think this reconstruction will actually solve the case?" Andy asked from Bessie's other side.

"I don't know that it will solve the case, but I'm hoping it will help."

"It's frustrating that Vivian decided to disappear now," he sighed.

"Do you have any idea where she might have gone?"

"None at all. She has a habit of wandering off when she gets bored, though. We were all going to play some cards this morning and she simply wandered off before we could get started."

"This was before lunch?"

"Yes. She was back for lunch."

"But you don't know where she was during the morning?"

"No, but she could have been anywhere. It's a big house and no one was looking for her. She could even have just been in her room, staying away from the rest of us. I wouldn't blame her. We're all getting rather tired of one another's company."

Bessie nodded. "But you haven't been staying here, have you?"

"No, not staying, but I've been here as much as I can be. I'm doing what I can to support Elizabeth. This has been difficult for her."

"I didn't realise you two had grown that close."

Andy flushed. "We're, well, we're trying it out, I suppose. She knows I'm leaving again soon, so we're trying to keep things casual, but, well, I'm pretty fond of her already. I just don't know if we can keep the relationship going while I'm away."

"I'll wish you luck, because I like you both very much, but long-distance relationships are very difficult. I hope you're both prepared if it doesn't work out."

"I keep telling myself that, but, well, we'll see. She's pretty amazing."

"She seems to be working very hard on her new business, as well."

"Yeah. She's been hoping she might get a few jobs in London starting in the autumn, so she can be closer to me, but there's a lot more competition in London for party planners."

Before Bessie could reply, John walked back into the room. "I appreciate everyone's patience," he said. "We've just about completed a search of the house, and so far Vivian is proving elusive. Does anyone have any idea where she might have gone?"

"Did you try the beach?" Richard asked.

"Yes, she's certainly not anywhere within an easy walking distance of the house," John replied.

"Maybe she caught a taxi into Ramsey or Douglas," Elizabeth suggested.

"Even if the constable on the front door didn't stop her from leaving, which he should have done, he would have noted that she'd gone," John replied.

"Unless he let her go and now he's afraid he'll be in trouble for it, so he's lying about it," Sean said.

John frowned. "It's a thought," he said softly.

Bessie knew that Hugh would never have let the girl leave Thie yn Traie, and that he'd never lie to John, either, but she bit her tongue. Next to her, Michael suddenly rose to his feet.

"Inspector, if I could have a word," he said.

Everyone in the great room watched as the man walked over to John. They talked in low voices for a moment and then left the room together. There was some commotion in the corridor and then John was back.

"Just give us a few more minutes, please," he said. "If everyone could simply wait in here, I'd appreciate it."

Michael hadn't returned. Bessie thought about trying to talk to Andy, but it seemed as if everyone in the room was trying to listen to whatever was happening in the corridor. After several minutes, Elizabeth jumped up.

"I can't take it anymore. I have to know what's going on." She walked across the room and disappeared out the door. Only a moment later she was back, her face pale.

Andy jumped up and crossed to her side. "Are you okay?" he asked, putting his arm around her.

Elizabeth shook her head and then buried it in his chest. As she began to cry, John walked into the room behind her.

"So as not to keep you all in suspense any longer, Ms. Walker has been located. She was found in the study and appears to have a head injury. She's being taken to Noble's now," he announced.

As he left the room, everyone began to talk excitedly about what he'd said. As Bessie had no one sitting on either side of her, she sat back and tried to listen to the conversations around her.

"...police seal still in place..."

"...must have seen something..."

"...doing in the study?"

If the police seal was still intact on the study door, then Vivian must have found another way into the room, Bessie mused. Had the killer spotted her opening the secret door and hit her over the head to stop her telling anyone about it? That was one possibility, but there were many others. Before Bessie could make much of a list of them, though, John was back again.

"Again, I appreciate your patience," he said with a sigh. "Before we can begin the reconstruction, however, we're going to need to take statements from everyone about this latest incident. I'm going to ask you all to stop talking amongst yourselves until after I've spoken with everyone. I'd like to start with Bessie Cubbon, please."

Bessie was startled, but she got to her feet and followed John out of the room without a word. He led her to the same room that he'd used the night of the murder. "I haven't seen Vivian all day," she said as she dropped into a chair.

"I know that. I was just wondering if you had any thoughts on what might have happened to the girl," John told her.

"I can only assume that she stumbled upon the hidden doorway and that the killer found out and hit her over the head," Bessie said.

"That's certainly one possibility," John replied. "Can you think of any reason why anyone else would have wanted to hurt her?"

"Not off the top of my head, although I didn't find her particularly likable. But the fact that she was found in the study in spite of the police seal has to be a factor, surely."

"It certainly seems to confirm that there's another way into that room. We're pretty sure the killer knew about the alternate entrance. What we don't know is who else might."

"A bunch of Elizabeth's friends were looking for the entrance when I arrived," Bessie told him. "None of them seemed to know where it was."

"Which would be easy to pretend, even if you did," John sighed.

"I would have thought Vivian would have told everyone if she'd found it," Bessie said.

"Unless she told the killer first and he or she bashed her on the head to keep her quiet."

"Is she going to be okay?"

"I certainly hope so. I suspect she might be able to solve the case if she recovers."

"If?"

John hesitated and then sighed. "It's going to be touch and go for a while, I understand. They took her to Noble's with sirens blaring."

"So even if she's okay eventually, she might not remember what happened," Bessie sighed.

"Exactly. Which is why we're still going to go ahead with the reconstruction. We can't count on Vivian handing us the solution."

"Is there anything else I can do?"

"For right now, just keep an eye on everyone," John requested. "I suspect our killer is getting pretty nervous. I'm going to send people back into the great room after I've spoken to them. Maybe you could chat with them as they return." He shook his head. "I don't really like you talking to suspects, but in this case, I'm making an exception."

Bessie grinned. "As we're all stuck here waiting for the reconstruction anyway, I've nothing to do but talk to suspects. I doubt I'll learn anything, but I'll try."

"Thank you," John said. He escorted Bessie back into the great room and led her to a small group of couches on the opposite side of the room from the dining table and row of chairs still in place from the party. "I'll leave you here," he said. "And send the others to join you after I've spoken to them. Mary should be in soon. I've already spoken with her."

"What now?" George asked as John approached the dining table.

"I'm going to talk to each of you in turn," John explained. "It shouldn't take long as we only need to discuss a short period of time, but I'm hoping to work out what happened to Vivian as quickly as possible. She may well be recovered enough to answer questions in another hour or so, anyway."

Bessie tried not to look surprised at John's words. No doubt he was trying to put extra pressure on the killer by suggesting that Vivian wasn't badly injured.

"After I've spoken to each of you, I'd like to ask you to join Miss Cubbon on the other side of the room. I'll ask you to remain silent while you are waiting to see me, but once we're finished you're welcome to talk quietly amongst yourselves. I think that's everything. Mr. Quayle, if you'd like to come with me, please?"

George followed John out of the room. A moment later Mary walked in and joined Bessie.

"I'm not staying, as I'm trying to reach Vivian's parents and deal with a dozen other things, but I thought I should check on you and make sure you're okay," she told Bessie.

"I'm fine, aside from being worried about Vivian."

"Yes, she didn't look good when she was taken out of here, but you mustn't repeat that. I believe Inspector Rockwell is trying to give the impression that she'll soon be telling the police exactly what happened to her."

Bessie nodded. "That seems a smart strategy. No doubt it will worry whoever hurt her."

Jonathan Hooper appeared in the doorway. "Mrs. Quayle? Telephone."

Mary quickly got up and followed the man out of the room, giving Bessie a nervous smile as she went. Bessie settled back in her seat and tried to study the men and women on the other side of the room. The silence only served to increase the tension in the room, and from that distance Bessie decided that everyone looked nervous and worried. She was grateful when Hugh walked in a few minutes later.

"Mr. Rice, if you could come with me, please?" he asked.

Sean was back only a short while later. He glanced around the room as he walked into it and then crossed it and sat down next to Bessie. "This is ridiculous," he mumbled as Hugh asked Richard Long to come with him.

"I just hope poor Vivian is okay," Bessie said.

"The inspector seems to think that she'll be fine. No doubt she'll be able to answer his questions later today, which makes questioning all of us pointless," he replied.

"It may take her a day or two to remember everything that happened. Obviously, the police don't want to wait to work out what happened to her."

"Except she was probably attacked by the same person who killed Jerome Rhodes. Questioning all of us is a waste of time. The killer isn't going to admit to seeing Vivian after lunch."

"Perhaps not, but he or she is bound to make a mistake at some point," Bessie said.

Sean shrugged. "Let's just hope it's soon. I'd really like to get out of here."

Richard joined them a moment later as Madison left the room with Hugh. "I wish I understood the order in which we're being questioned," he said as he dropped into a chair.

"He's just choosing people at random," Sean said.

"Maybe. I wish we'd been able to see Vivian before she went. I'm worried about her," Richard remarked.

"You've been avoiding her since you arrived," Sean retorted. "Surely you're happy she's gone?"

"I'm happy she won't be here, stirring up trouble anymore, but that doesn't mean I'm not worried about her. I didn't really like her, but I didn't want her to get hurt any more than I wanted that other man to get murdered," Richard replied.

"As I understand it, she's expected to make a full recovery. She may even be back here in the next day or two," Bessie said, not entirely truthfully.

"Back at tiny-ntay?" Richard asked. "I didn't realise that."

"It's Thie yn Traie," Bessie corrected him. "It's Manx for Beach House."

"Is it? I didn't realise," he said with a shrug.

"And yes, I believe that's what the inspector said. I might have misunderstood, of course," Bessie replied.

"I'm not being horrible, but I'd much rather she didn't come back here," Richard sighed.

Madison wandered over as Norma McCormick was led away. "This is awful," she said in a low voice as she joined Richard on his couch.

"We'll get through it," he told her, taking her hand and giving it a squeeze.

"Oh, Richard, do you think so?" she asked breathlessly.

"Of course we will," he replied firmly. "The police will have to let us go soon. We've all been incredibly cooperative."

"I don't want to do this reconstruction thing," Madison sighed. "It's going to bring back all manner of awful memories."

"I'm sure you'll be fine," Bessie said. "We all have to do what we can to help solve Mr. Rhodes's murder and also help work out what happened to Vivian."

"She probably hit herself over the head, just to cause drama," Madison suggested.

Bessie sat back and listened as the trio discussed ways in which someone could hit themselves on the head hard enough to cause serious injury. Something was nagging at her, but she couldn't quite work out what it was. Norma joined them a short while later and her brother quickly followed her.

"This is growing tedious," Ernest said as he joined the group. "I can't help but think that if the police haven't solved the case by now they simply aren't going to manage it."

"I don't think Inspector Rockwell will be giving up," Bessie told him.

"Perhaps not, but he will have to let us all go soon. He can't keep us here forever," Ernest replied.

"Perhaps the reconstruction will help," Bessie said. "It should be interesting going back through everything that happened that night."

"I still don't see how anyone managed to get away from the party, kill someone, and get back in the dark. It was incredibly dark," Richard said.

"That's for the police to work out," Norma said, "and it's probably what the inspector is hoping the reconstruction will show."

"But what if the reconstruction shows that it isn't possible?" Sean asked. "Maybe they should check again. Maybe Mr. Rhodes stabbed himself."

Elizabeth's friends laughed as if that was the funniest thing they'd heard in a long time. Bessie played with the idea in her head, but she had confidence that John and the coroner knew what they were doing. They'd decided that it was murder.

Susan was the next to join the group, sliding into a chair and then folding her arms and staring straight out at the sea, ignoring everyone.

"Are you okay?" Bessie asked her.

Susan glanced over at her and then rolled her eyes and went back to staring out the window. Her mood seemed to be contagious as the rest of the group lapsed into silence. While Bessie was trying to work out an appropriate way to restart the conversation, John walked back into the room with Andy and Elizabeth.

"I've spoken to everyone who was here before Vivian's disappearance," he said from the doorway. "Did anyone who arrived later in the day see Vivian at all?"

Liza and Leonard exchanged glances and shrugged. Mona was silent. After a moment John continued.

"In that case, I think it's time we start working on that reconstruction. I'd like to do things a little bit differently than the original plan, however. I would appreciate it if you could all take seats around the dining table where you were at the very start of the evening, please."

There was a good deal of muttered grumbling as everyone got back to their feet, and some arguments back at the table as people tried to remember where they'd been sitting for the first course of the dinner party.

Bessie took her seat next to George, who'd dropped into his chair at the head of the table almost before John had finished speaking. She wasn't sure where he'd been while the questioning had been going on, but she was pretty sure she could smell whisky on his breath as he greeted her.

When everyone was seated, John sat down next to Bessie in the seat that Mr. Rhodes had occupied on the night of his death. Hugh flushed as he sat down between Sean and Michael in Vivian's place.

CHAPTER 13

"I'd like you all to chat together, trying to remember what you talked about the night of the party," John said. "We're only going to do this for a few minutes, but I'm hoping it might jog memories."

"Jog them in what way?" Sean demanded.

"I want you all to be thinking about how the people around you were behaving on the night of the party," John told him. "Did anyone seem particularly nervous or upset? Did anyone say anything about Mr. Rhodes or about the party's theme? Did you feel as if anyone was avoiding Mr. Rhodes or seeking him out? Go back over your conversations that night in light of subsequent events. And yes, I'm asking you to think of every other person here as a possible murderer. I won't apologise for that, because someone in this room murdered Jerome Rhodes."

A few people gasped at the words. Bessie could only hope that they'd be effective. Someone in the group had probably heard or seen something that would help solve the case; it was just a matter of working out what that something was. Bessie couldn't help but feel as if she'd missed a hint somewhere along the line, but she simply couldn't work out where.

"Susan, where were you during dinner?" John asked.

The woman had been standing near the door; now she walked towards the table. "I walked around, mostly," she said. "I had to explain how everything was meant to work, you see."

"Right, so can you please repeat your introductory remarks? You don't have to be exact, but I'd like to hear what you said," John said.

"I just explained that after each course the gentlemen would all move two places to the right," Susan said in a dull voice. "And I reminded everyone to stay in character and to share the background information that they'd been given."

"I have copies of all of the character cards that were handed out that night, don't I?" John asked.

"You do, although why you wanted them I don't understand," Susan replied.

"Investigations are all about gathering information," John replied. "What happened after you were done with the introductions?"

"The soup was served," Susan replied.

John nodded at Jonathan, who was standing in the doorway. He disappeared, and a moment later several waiters came in, carrying empty trays. While they mimed delivering soup bowls to everyone, Bessie turned to George. "I believe we said a few words to one another," she said.

"Yes, I think I told you about my part in the story," George agreed, "and then told you about my new company in the south of the island, didn't I?"

"Yes, I believe you did."

George chuckled. "I'm very proud of my latest acquisition, really. Mary tells me that I've bored everyone I know with it."

"And then I asked after your children and grandchildren," Bessie remembered.

"Which is Mary's concern, not mine," George shrugged, "and then you started talking to Mr. Rhodes, didn't you?"

"I believe I did," Bessie agreed. She turned and smiled at John. "The soup was very good, but Mr. Rhodes didn't like soup."

"Is that all he said?" John asked.

"He said something about Vivian not remembering her part at all and that that was fairly typical with these sorts of parties."

"Which suggests that he'd been to at least one or two before."

"Or that he wanted me to think that he had."

"Yes, there is that," John mused.

"That was about all that was said, really. The soup course didn't take long."

"Did he seem very drunk?"

Bessie thought for a minute. "He didn't, really, even though I'd seen him drinking quite a lot. He wasn't slurring his speech, and when the men got up to move around, he didn't stumble or have difficulty walking."

John nodded and then looked around the table. Most people were sitting quietly, not speaking. He looked over at Susan. "I assume the waiters cleared the bowls before the men moved around the table."

Susan shrugged. "I don't remember."

"They did," Bessie told him, "and then Susan told the men to take their drinks and move around the table."

"Susan, if you could," John said.

The girl frowned and then sighed deeply. "Yeah, well, guys, grab your drinks and shift two places to the right, please."

A moment later Ernest slid into the seat George had just vacated. "Good evening," he said. "I'm meant to be some sort of disreputable rogue, I believe."

Bessie nodded. "That's exactly what you said on Saturday."

"It's what I said to everyone," he told her. "I didn't realise it at the time, but it's certainly made tonight a lot easier for me."

"And then we talked about the price of property on the island for a bit."

"We did. I'm sure you can understand why Norma and I have agreed that the island isn't for us."

"Yes, I suppose you haven't had a very pleasant visit."

"No, we're both eager to get home and, well, forget all about this week, I'm afraid."

"I don't really blame you, considering the circumstances. But now I must speak to Richard."

Ernest nodded and began to chat with Elizabeth while Bessie turned to the man on her left.

"Good evening," she said.

"Good evening. I'm sure I must have introduced myself as one of Elizabeth's friends."

"Yes, I'm sure you did. And then we talked about the island and how nice it is to be able to see the sea."

"I believe that was about the extent of our chat," he said. "I must say that, at the time, I didn't think I'd be seeing you again."

"Things haven't exactly gone as planned, have they?" Bessie asked.

"No, not at all," he replied.

At John's prompting, Susan sent the men on their way again. As Leonard sank into the chair next to Bessie's, he sighed deeply.

"This was incredibly dull the first time, but the food was excellent. Doing it all again with imaginary food is just tedious," he said.

"But if it helps the police with their enquires, it will be worth it," Bessie said.

"Yes, well, that's a very big if, I must say."

"But what did we talk about?"

"My restaurants. And then the food came, and it was delicious, and I stopped talking so that I could enjoy it properly."

Bessie nodded. That was how she remembered it as well. Sean was on the other side of her, yawning.

"My goodness, it's only the middle of the afternoon," she said.

"I haven't been sleeping well," he told her. "I really hope the police get things sorted quickly. I don't know that I'll sleep until the killer is behind bars. What happened to Vivian is incredibly worrying."

"It is, I know, but we're meant to be recreating our conversation from Saturday. You said something about your father and his third wife."

"Fourth wife," Sean corrected her.

"And then I told you that Liza was thinking of having one of these parties," Leonard announced. "We won't now, of course, not after everything that happened this time, but we were thinking about it before."

"I believe we talked for a short while about Mr. Rhodes," Bessie said, "and about how much he'd been drinking."

"Did we? I don't recall," Leonard said. He turned and said something to Elizabeth as Sean touched Bessie's arm.

"This may have been when I started babbling about Vivian," he said, blushing. "I was quite, that is, I was hoping, I mean, she's really beautiful."

"Yes, she is," Bessie agreed, glancing at Hugh who was sitting where Vivian had been on Saturday. He caught her eye and winked at her.

"And then we talked about some of the women from my past and you were kind enough not to point out that I have terrible taste in women and deserve to be treated badly."

"I don't think anyone deserves to be treated badly," Bessie told him.

"Maybe not, but I really should learn from my mistakes, shouldn't I? I keep falling for the same type of woman, over and over again, and it always ends badly. I'm sure if I could just get Vivian's attention, I would do things right this time."

"Perhaps you should start looking for a different type of woman, rather than try to change your behaviour with the women you like."

"But I can't help being attracted to certain types of women," Sean argued. "I mean, Madison is sweet and all, but I'm not at all attracted to her. No, Vivian is the woman for me, I just need her to see it that way."

"After everything that has happened this week, you might be better off looking for another woman," Bessie said dryly.

Sean sighed. "Maybe getting hit on the head will make her realise how perfect I am for her. It could happen, couldn't it?"

Bessie stared at the man for a minute, unable to work out how to reply. She felt fortunate when Susan interrupted.

"Time for the sweet course," the woman said unenthusiastically. "Gentlemen, you need to move for the last time, please."

"And what a delicious sweet course it was," Bessie told Andy as he sat down next to her. "I wish you'd done that again for us tonight."

Andy shrugged. "I offered to do some food, even just snacks and finger foods, but the inspector didn't want to complicate things. I believe we're all going to have access to soft drinks after the dinner portion of the reconstruction is over, at least."

"I could do with a drink," Bessie murmured.

"Yeah, me too, and not a soft one," Andy told her.

Bessie turned to Michael Higgins. "And how are you finding the reconstruction?" she asked the man.

"It's always interesting to watch a professional at work," he said, nodding towards John.

"Do you think all of this will actually accomplish anything?"

"It's surprising how often these things do. People who are trying to hide something make mistakes all the time. It wouldn't surprise me if someone noticed something today that helped crack the case. It may take a day or two for that person to realize it and let John know, but I am expecting some result from today."

"I hope it isn't too much later," Bessie told him. "The attack on Vivian is worrying."

"Yes, it is," Michael agreed.

"And that's the end of that," Susan announced.

The waiters all moved in and began to pretend to remove plates from the table under Jonathan's watchful eye. When they'd finished, Susan waved a hand. "Time to move into the sitting area, I believe."

Bessie pushed back her chair and stood up. Mary was already making her way towards the couches where she and Bessie had sat for the rest of the evening. John caught Bessie's arm as she walked towards Mary.

"I'd like you and Mary to sit a little bit closer today," he said in her ear. "Just in case."

He walked away before Bessie could ask what he'd meant by his words. Presumably he was hoping she'd hear or see something that she'd missed from her seat on the other side of the room. She crossed to Mary.

"John wants us to sit closer today," she told her friend.

"Oh, dear, I was hoping to stay out of the way," Mary sighed. "I'm still waiting for several people to ring me back. Vivian's mother was trying to arrange a flight over and her father suggested that he might send his private physician to oversee her treatment. I'd hate to disrupt the reconstruction, but I'll have to answer if either of them ring."

"I'm sure everyone will understand," Bessie said. "Let's move over towards the centre of the room. That should be close enough for John, but still out of the way."

Bessie and Mary settled into chairs not far from the others. Almost as soon as they'd sat down, Jonathan crossed to them.

"I'm sorry, Mrs. Quayle, but Mr. Walker is on the phone for you," he said.

Mary nodded and then followed Jonathan out of the room. She stopped to say something to John on her way past. He nodded and then looked over at Bessie. The others were still wandering around the room as John joined Bessie.

"I don't really want to carry on until Mary is back," he told Bessie in a low voice. "The longer they take to organise themselves, the better, really."

"I'm sure no one can remember exactly who was where," Bessie replied. "It didn't seem important at the time."

John shrugged. "I don't know if it's important now," he said, "but I do think you and Mary are the most likely to spot any anomalies."

"We'll do our best," Bessie said.

"Right, everyone stop," John said, getting up and walking over to the others, most of whom seemed to be simply wandering around. "You seem to be having difficultly working out who was where," he said.

"Liza and I were here," Leonard said from his seat on one of the couches. "We sat here as soon as we left the table and we didn't move until we were told to walk in pointless circles around the row of chairs."

"I'm sure I was on this couch," Richard said firmly. "And Madison was sitting beside me."

"I thought I was in a chair," Madison sighed. "But if you say so, I'll sit on the couch." She plopped down next to Richard and stared down at the floor.

"Ernest was at the bar," Norma said.

"Was I? I suppose you're right," Ernest replied. He crossed to the bar and leaned against it.

"Andy and I were at the bar, too," Elizabeth said, pulling Andy with her across the room.

"I was chatting with Vivian," Norma told John. "I think we were standing about here." She walked to a random place and stopped. Hugh, still taking Vivian's place, moved to join her.

"Sean was standing behind Vivian, staring at her," Norma added. "It made me uncomfortable, so after a short while I walked over to the bar."

"Don't do that yet," John said.

"I was with George," Mona said. "We were waiting for Michael to get us some drinks." She walked between the couches and took up a position near the windows. George joined her while Michael looked at John.

"I went to the bar, got a round of drinks, and then joined George and Mona," he explained.

"Just stand near the bar for a minute, please," John told him. "Where was Mr. Rhodes?"

As everyone looked at John blankly, Bessie shut her eyes and tried to remember.

"I think he was in a chair a short distance away," Susan said after a moment. "I was standing out of the way, watching while everyone chatted."

"I don't even remember seeing him after dinner," Sean said. "Maybe he'd already gone into the study by the time we settled over here."

"No, he was here until we lined up the chairs," Elizabeth interjected. "I took him off to the study once everyone else was sitting in the row of chairs."

"So where was he?" John asked.

"Maybe next to Richard?" Sean suggested. "There was a chair next to you, wasn't there, Richard?"

The man shrugged. "Maybe. I wasn't really paying attention."

One of the waiters helped John moved a chair over next to the couch where Richard and Madison were sitting. "About here?" he asked.

Sean shrugged. "Yeah, I think it was about there."

No one else said anything, so John slid into the seat. Susan was pacing back and forth near the dining table. Bessie studied the scene in front of her. As far as she could remember, it was close, if not exactly right.

"Mr. Rhodes moved his chair closer to Richard," Mary said as she walked back into the room. "I remember seeing him sliding it closer and wondering why he'd done so."

John shuffled the chair along a bit. "Better?"

"Maybe even more," Mary suggested as she sat down next to Bessie. "It may have been the angle I was sitting at that made it seem so close, as well. Anyway, he didn't sit there for long. As soon as Susan started setting things up for the pretend murder, he said something to Richard, and then went to the bar."

"What did he say to you?" John asked Richard.

Richard shrugged. "Probably 'I need a drink' or something like that. It wasn't anything important."

"Okay, so Mr. Rhodes is sitting here. Michael gets drinks and then takes them to Mona and George." John nodded, and Michael left the bar and joined Mona and George near the windows.

"And then I walked over to the bar to get away from Sean," Norma said.

"Thanks," Sean said under his breath.

"And Susan told us all about the rules for the murder game," Elizabeth said. "We were meant to pretend that there was a horrible storm outside."

"Leonard told us all to get drinks, and then Susan told us to get comfortable. Then she said only the killer would be moving around after the lights went out," Sean said.

"Except we all quickly realized that that would never work," Norma interjected. "There was no way the pretend killer could move around safely in the dark, even if he or she knew exactly where his or her victim was sitting."

"So Susan came up with another plan," Elizabeth said. "That was when we arranged the chairs in the row."

"Okay, who helped arrange them?" John asked, getting to his feet.

"Not Mr. Rhodes, that's for sure," Sean laughed.

"It was just staff and me," Elizabeth said. "We arranged the chairs and then Susan told everyone to move into them."

"Okay, then, can you all please take seats in the row, in the same place you were on Saturday?" John asked.

It quickly became apparent that no one remembered where he or she had been on Saturday. Bessie exchanged glances with Mary. "I don't really remember who was where," she whispered.

"I don't, either, except I noticed that George was on the end. I was afraid he might try to sneak away when the lights went out because I knew he was getting fed up with the whole thing. That was before Susan had everyone start walking in circles, of course," Mary replied.

"I was on the end," George announced loudly before walking over and sitting down. "And Mona was next to me."

Mona joined George. Whatever she said to him as she slid into her seat made him laugh.

"And I was next to Mona," Michael said, joining her.

"Now we're getting somewhere," Bessie whispered.

But for a moment it seemed as if things were back to a standstill as Elizabeth's friends began to argue amongst themselves as to who was next to Michael. After a minute, John held up a hand.

"Michael, do you recall who was sitting next to you?" he asked.

"Madison," the man replied quickly.

"That's what I said," Sean shouted.

"I didn't remember it that way," Madison said defensively as she crossed the room. "If you are sure, I'll sit here anyway." She dropped onto the seat and folded her arms, frowning as she stared at the floor.

"Michael is right," Mary whispered. "She was next to him."

"Now that she's sitting there, it does look right," Bessie agreed.

"I was next to Madison," Richard said, "and Vivian was next to me."

He and Hugh took their seats. After a bit more debate, all of the others fell into place as well. Bessie and Mary exchanged glances.

"I believe that's right," Bessie said.

John was standing near Susan and Elizabeth. "Neither of you sat down?" he asked.

"No, I was still trying to keep the party running, and Elizabeth was in charge of locking away my father," Susan told him.

"Is that what happened next, then?" John asked.

"After we worked out the logistics," Sean said. "Susan made us all walk around the chairs so that it wouldn't be obvious who the killer was, or something like that."

"Explain to me exactly what you were meant to do," John requested.

"Everyone was meant to walk around the chairs slowly. When you reached the first chair in the row, you were meant to call out your name," Susan said.

"Why?" John asked.

"To help the killer find the victim," Susan explained. "The killer was meant to step out of the line and wait for the victim to come past. Then he or she was supposed to tell the victim to play dead."

"Except Elizabeth was the killer, right?" John asked.

"Yes, that's right," Susan replied.

"And Elizabeth wasn't even in the room while all of this was happening, correct?" was John's next question.

Susan flushed. "I may not have planned things exactly right," she said.

"Elizabeth, how did you let Vivian know she was meant to be the victim?" John asked.

"I just whispered in her ear when we crossed paths right after dinner," Elizabeth explained.

John made a note. "Did you give her specific instructions on where to go or what to do when she was meant to be dead?"

"I told her to fall out of her chair onto the floor," Elizabeth said. "At that point I still thought that everyone was going to be sitting in seats while the lights were out."

"If that was the case, why did everyone have to walk around?" John wondered. "If Elizabeth was the killer and she'd already told Vivian to play dead, surely you could have just switched off the lights, no one would have had to move except for Vivian when she fell to the floor, and then the lights could have come back on?"

"If I would have thought of that, that's what we would have done," Susan sighed. "I wanted it to be realistic, though. Elizabeth wasn't meant to tell Vivian anything before the lights went out. She was supposed to come back in and tell Vivian to play dead while it was dark."

"She would have struggled to get across the room and back in the dark," John suggested.

"She had a torch," Susan told him.

"But surely everyone would have noticed if she came in with her torch in her hand," John said.

"She left it on the table in the corridor. It gave a little bit of light, to the doorway and into the room. She would have been fine," Susan said.

John looked at Elizabeth, who shrugged. "I might have managed it. I know the room really well, anyway, but I'd already asked Andy to join me in the corridor so we could chat during the lights out. I set the torch on the table to help him find his way out of the great room."

"Did anyone notice Andy leaving?" John asked.

"I thought I saw someone walking away from our little circle at one point," Norma said, "but I didn't pay any attention. The killer was meant to step out and so was the victim, after all."

"So Andy walked away from the circle and used the light coming in by the doorway to navigate his way across the room," John said with a sigh. "Presumably the killer could easily have done the same thing."

"That still doesn't explain how the killer got into the study," Sean said.

John nodded. "Before I address that, I'd just like to point out to everyone that all of this information should have been given to me when I first spoke to you about the murder."

"Sorry," Elizabeth said softly. "I wasn't thinking all that clearly that night."

"Or any night since," Mary whispered to Bessie. "I'm going to have to have a word with that girl."

"I didn't really notice the light in the corridor," Bessie said.

"No, I didn't either, but I don't think I was paying much attention to what was happening," Mary sighed. "I was just wishing they would get on with things."

Bessie nodded. "I felt as if I could see the shapes of people moving around the chairs, but I don't remember seeing anyone walking away."

"And we know Andy walked away from the group, and so did the murderer," Mary said. "And Elizabeth's torch probably gave the murderer enough light to do so," she added with a sigh.

"No one can possibly blame Elizabeth for any of this," Bessie said stoutly.

"She's the one who planned the whole thing, brought Susan and her father to the island, and lit a path to the corridor for the killer," Mary said.

"None of which makes her responsible in any way for what happened. If she hadn't put her torch on the table, the killer would simply have found another way. You know that."

Mary nodded. "I don't mean to sound as if I'm blaming Elizabeth. Mostly I'm blaming myself for allowing the party to happen in the first place. The whole idea worried me, but I let Elizabeth talk me into it anyway."

"You were trying to be supportive of her and her career. You shouldn't regret that."

"Okay, so everyone was sitting in the chairs when Elizabeth left with Mr. Rhodes?" John asked, calling everyone's attention back to him.

"Yes, that's right," Elizabeth said. "We went out into the corridor and I unlocked the study and ushered him inside. I waited until he was sitting down to shut the door. I didn't want him falling over anything when the lights went out."

"Did he seem very drunk to you?" was John's next question.

Elizabeth shrugged. "He made some rude suggestions to me as we left the room, but I don't think he'd have needed to be drunk to do that. He didn't stumble over anything and he managed to walk in a fairly straight line from this room to the study."

John nodded and then made a note. "Okay, let's walk through that part while everyone else just waits."

The pair were only gone for a few minutes. When they came back, John left Elizabeth in the doorway and rejoined the others.

"What happened in here once Mr. Rhodes and Elizabeth were gone?" he asked.

"Everyone got up and began to walk in a slow circle around the chairs." Susan said.

"Show me," John requested.

There was a bit of grumbling as everyone got to their feet and began to walk around the chairs. They began calling out their names as they passed the first chair again, as well. John made another note before he held up a hand. "And then the lights went out?"

"Elizabeth went and turned them off," Susan replied.

"Elizabeth, can you go and turn them off again, please?" John asked.

Elizabeth disappeared through the door. A moment later the room went noticeably darker. There was still a considerable amount of light flooding in from the windows, however, unlike Saturday evening.

"And for how long were the lights out?" John asked.

"About fifteen minutes," Susan said. "Elizabeth was meant to be timing it."

"I was timing it," Elizabeth said as she walked back into the room.

"Where were you standing?" John wanted to know.

Elizabeth led him back into the corridor. After a minute, Bessie could see that he'd switched on a torch, presumably having Elizabeth place it where it had been on Saturday.

"This is when I snuck out," Andy called.

John stuck his head back into the room. "Sneak out again, then, very slowly," he said.

Andy reached the first chair in the row and called out his name, then began to walk very slowly towards the corridor. He was sliding his feet along the carpeting, so when he came to the low step just before the door, he managed to navigate it without tripping.

"That was clever," Mary whispered. "He knew he had a clear walk to the door, aside from that one step."

"Yes, and so did the killer," Bessie sighed.

"I'm sure I didn't notice him sneaking away on Saturday," Mary said, "but there was so much commotion going on right in front of us, that's hardly surprising."

"And we were further away from the group and also from the light in the corridor. It's possible we simply couldn't see it from where we were sitting," Bessie suggested.

The group walking in circles had started to get bored. One of the girls shouted out "Richard" and everyone laughed again. That started everyone off with calling out random names. John stood in the doorway and watched as they continued for what felt like a long time.

"And then I asked when we were going to have lights again," Sean said.

"And someone bumped into Vivian and she shouted," Ernest added.

"And then I gave up," Richard said. "I told everyone that I was going to sit down and warned them not to trip over me." He stopped walking and sat down on the closest chair.

"And we all thought that was a good idea, so we all sat down," Norma said.

John watched as everyone slid into seats along the row. "How much later did the lights come back on?"

"It felt like hours," Sean said.

"I believe it was about five minutes," Bessie called.

"And then I switched the lights back on," Elizabeth said.

"Please do so," John told her.

When Elizabeth came back in a minute later, Hugh was just

stretching himself out on the floor, roughly where Vivian had been lying.

"I announced that Vivian had been murdered and Elizabeth rushed away to ring for Inspector Rhodes," Susan said.

"And Vivian wanted a drink," Norma added.

"We all wanted a drink," Richard said.

"Yeah, that's true," Ernest agreed.

"And then Elizabeth went and unlocked the study door and found the body," John said. "I don't want to reenact that part, though. The study is still off limits."

"Oh, sorry about that," Jonathan Hooper said. He shrugged. "I didn't realise."

Bessie's jaw dropped. The man was standing in a doorway that hadn't been there a moment earlier. One that connected the great room to the study. Jonathan had found the secret door.

CHAPTER 14

The entire room erupted into shouts as people rushed towards Jonathan. Hugh and John leapt in front of everyone and herded them backwards.

"No one is meant to be in the study," John said firmly. "I'd appreciate it if you'd all take your seats again."

There was a good deal of muttering as people returned to their seats, but everyone complied.

"I am really sorry," Jonathan said again, "but I knew there had to be a secret door somewhere and now I've found it."

John and Hugh joined the man in the doorway. For several minutes they inspected the opening before stepping back.

"Can you shut the door?" John asked.

"I can try," Jonathan told him. He took a step backwards. A moment later the door slid back into place. Once it was completely closed, Bessie couldn't be sure where it had been.

"It's very well done," Mary said.

"I wonder why the Pierce family wanted a secret door between the study and the great room," Bessie replied.

"It isn't the only one. We've found a few others and I'm sure there are more. I don't know if Mr. Pierce wanted them included or if his children had a say in the construction, but we're slowly learning Thie yn Traie has lots of secrets," Mary told her in a low voice.

John knocked on the wall and a moment later the door slid open again.

"It's really very clever," Jonathan said. "It was easier to work out how to open from this side, but there must be a way from the great room as well."

"Show me how you do it on that side," John requested.

The pair disappeared through the door. A moment later it slid shut and then open again. When John walked out, he spoke to Hugh briefly and then turned to the people still sitting in their row. As he walked towards them, the door slid shut again and Hugh began tapping and pressing on the wall.

"We'll leave Constable Watterson to work out how to open the door from this side," John said. "Knowing that the door is there is what matters now. Whoever killed Jerome Rhodes knew about that door and used it to his or her advantage. I just have to work out which one of you knew about it."

"I certainly didn't," Sean said. "But I wish I had. Now I wonder if there are any more secret doors around the place."

"You'll have to talk to Mrs. Quayle or her daughter about that," John said. "For now, I'd like to go back to the very beginning. Let's walk through what happened when you all arrived at Thie yn Traie."

Someone groaned and Michael held up his hand. "Does that mean you won't be needing Mona or myself any longer?" he asked.

John frowned. "If you don't mind, I'd be grateful to you if you could stay for another half hour or so. I'd like to think we're getting closer to a solution."

Michael nodded. "I believe you are. We can certainly stay if we won't be in the way."

"Which of your friends arrived first?" John asked Elizabeth as he flipped back through his notebook.

"Everyone arrived on Friday evening," Elizabeth replied, "in some order or another. They came in two groups. I'm pretty sure that

Vivian arrived in the first group. Ernest, was she with you and Norma?"

"Yes, we arrived first and then the others came on a later flight," Ernest confirmed.

"How much later?" John asked.

"Oh, maybe an hour?" Ernest made the reply a question. "I wasn't really paying attention, but we were having dinner when they arrived."

"And who was in that group?" was John's next question.

"Richard, Madison, and me," Sean told him. "We were all on the same flight, although I don't think neither Richard nor I knew that Madison was going to be there."

"Elizabeth arranged my flight for me," Madison said in her whispery voice. "She told me that everyone else was flying over earlier. I was surprised to see Sean and Richard at the gate."

"We were meant to be taking the earlier flight," Sean said, "but I got held up at the office and Richard was kind enough to wait for me."

"And you were about an hour behind the others?" John checked.

"About that, I suppose. If it had been much more than that, I probably would have looked at chartering something or waiting until morning," Sean replied. "I didn't want to turn up here at midnight or later."

"If the others were at dinner when you arrived, what did you do?" John asked.

"We went in and joined them," Sean told him. "It was just a big buffet, and there was plenty of food."

John looked down at his notes. "And after dinner, what happened?"

"We all came in here and had a few drinks," Elizabeth replied. "Susan hadn't arrived yet, so we didn't talk about the murder mystery evening at all."

"And after a few drinks you all went to bed?" was John's next question.

"Yes. I think we headed up to our rooms around midnight, or not much after," Elizabeth said.

"Can you remember in what order everyone left the great room?" John wondered.

Elizabeth laughed and then shook her head. "I wasn't paying any attention. Norma left first because she had a headache. No one really lingered after that, though."

"You don't know who the last person out of the room was?" John asked.

"I was, of course," Elizabeth said. "I was the hostess, after all."

"If I could please have a word with you privately," John said.

Elizabeth shrugged and the walked over to him. They exited the room together. With nothing else to do, Bessie watched Hugh. He was on his hands and knees, pushing and tapping along the skirting boards. John and Elizabeth were back a moment later.

"I'm going to need to speak of each of you individually," John announced.

"If you're expecting one of us to confess to stumbling across the secret door, you're wasting your time," Sean said. "That would be tantamount to confessing to murder."

"Not necessarily," John replied. "Maybe one of you found the sliding door and happened to mention it to someone else. Anyway, I'm not looking for confessions, I'm just trying to work out where everyone was on Friday evening and Saturday morning."

As John left the room with Sean, Bessie went back to watching Hugh. He was starting to look quite frustrated. After another minute, he knocked on the wall and the panel slid open again.

"You can't find it?" Jonathan asked from inside the study.

"I can't, but I know it's here," Hugh replied.

"Do you want to switch places?" Jonathan offered. "Maybe I'll have better luck, having found the trick on this side."

"Maybe you should give it a try, anyway," Hugh said, getting to his feet. "We can always get back into the study through the regular door if necessary."

Jonathan walked out of the study and began running his hand over the wall next to the opening. Hugh did the same on the other side.

John and Sean returned and John left with Richard while everyone watched the two men who were trying to find the secret to the sliding door.

"Maybe it only opens from the study side," Elizabeth suggested.

"Unlikely," Jonathan told her. "All of the other hidden doors in the house open from either side."

"So there are more," Ernest exclaimed. "Where are they?"

Jonathan shook his head. "You'd have to discuss that with Mr. Quayle or Miss Elizabeth," he replied.

"Elizabeth, where are they?" Ernest demanded.

"One is in my father's office and another is in my bedroom," Elizabeth told him. "They both simply open into corridors and I can't imagine why the Pierce family bothered to have them."

"What about trap doors or tunnels or things like that?" Ernest asked. "What other secrets are there at tiny tray?"

"It's Thie yn Traie," Elizabeth told him.

Bessie frowned. Someone else had mispronounced the name of the house earlier. Who had it been?

"You look as if you're thinking very hard," Mary said a moment later.

"Eureka!" Jonathan shouted as the hidden door slid back into place. He glanced around and then blushed. "I've always wanted to say that," he said in an apologetic tone.

"Can you open it again?" Hugh asked.

"I certainly hope so," Jonathan replied. He bent down and did something to the skirting boards and the door slid open again.

"And that's that," he said with satisfaction. "It isn't even that complicated, once you know what you're doing."

Hugh had the man demonstrate and then shook his head. "I should have worked that out," he said. "You're right, it isn't that difficult."

"It's just tricky enough that you wouldn't discover it by mistake, though," Jonathan suggested.

"I was actively looking for it and I didn't discover it," Hugh replied.

Bessie sat back in her chair. When Mary looked at her a moment later, Bessie sat up. "Richard mispronounced Thie yn Traie earlier," she said.

"As he's not from the island, that's hardly surprising," Mary replied.

"But on Saturday evening he said it correctly," Bessie told her. "I didn't really notice at the time, but I should have."

"Maybe Elizabeth told him how to say it and then he forgot," Mary suggested.

"Maybe, but everyone else keeps calling it 'tiny tray' and he called it 'tiny-ntray.' It seems odd to me."

"Do you think he's been here before?" Mary asked. "I know he hasn't been while we've owned the house, but maybe he knows the Pierce family."

"He told me hadn't ever been to the island before," Bessie replied, "but that doesn't mean he doesn't know the Pierces."

"You're suggesting that one of them told him about the secret door?" Mary asked.

Bessie shrugged. "That's one possibility. I don't know, but I'm going to talk to John, that's for sure."

A moment later, John walked back into the room with Richard. As Richard returned to his seat, Hugh showed John how to access the secret door from the great room.

"It's very cleverly done," John said. "I'm not sure how anyone could have discovered it by accident."

"It's easier to open from the other side," Jonathan said. "Perhaps Mr. Rhodes opened the door himself."

"That's a possibility," John said thoughtfully. "If he did, he let someone in and then went back and sat down in the chair."

Bessie got to her feet and crossed the room. "Can I have a moment of your time?" she asked John.

He looked surprised and then nodded. "Of course you can," he said. "I'll be right back," he told everyone else before he led Bessie to the door. They walked a short way down the corridor before John stopped.

"What's wrong?" he asked.

"At the party, when I spoke with Richard, he pronounced Thie yn Traie correctly," Bessie told him, "but today he pronounced it wrong."

John raised an eyebrow. "I see."

Bessie flushed. "I know it doesn't seem like a big deal, but it was odd on Saturday that he knew how to pronounce it, and it's odd today that he seems to have forgotten."

"So maybe he's been here before," John mused, "but he's trying to hide that fact by deliberately mispronouncing the name."

"Maybe. He definitely told me that he'd never been to the island before when we spoke on Saturday," Bessie said.

John nodded. "I'll talk to him again, after I've spoken to everyone else. There may be a simple explanation, but it's certainly worth following up on."

John escorted Bessie back into the great room and then took Madison out for questioning. Now that the secret door had been found, Hugh was simply standing in front of it. Jonathan was nowhere to be seen.

"This is boring," Liza said loudly.

"I'm sorry, but Inspector Rockwell is doing his best to talk to everyone as quickly as possible," Hugh told her.

"You told me that you're here all the time," Richard said to Liza. "Did you know about the secret door?"

Liza laughed. "I'm here occasionally for dinner. My husband has business interests with George. Our visits include cocktails and a delicious meal. They do not include a tour of the house or an opportunity for me to poke around at the skirting boards."

Bessie studied the woman. Jonathan had told her something similar: that Liza and Leonard were at Thie yn Traie fairly regularly. Was it possible that one or the other of them had discovered the secret door? While she was mulling that over, John came back in and took Susan away.

"Perhaps everyone would like some refreshments," Mary said after a short while. "Inspector Rockwell won't mind, will he?" she asked Hugh.

"I can check," Hugh offered. He walked out of the room and was back only a moment later. "Inspector Rockwell doesn't mind," he told Mary.

Mary nodded and then picked up a telephone that was on one of the tables. A few minutes later several members of her staff came into the room. Five minutes after that a table full of food was laid out in one corner of the room. From where Bessie was sitting, the offerings looked quite substantial.

"Everyone help themselves," Mary said. "Someone will be behind the bar momentarily."

Bessie sat still and watched as Elizabeth and her friends filled plates and got drinks. Michael and Mona also took advantage of the offerings, talking and laughing together as they did so. When they'd returned to their seats, Liza and Leonard walked to the bar and got drinks. When Susan walked back into the room a moment later, she headed straight for the bar.

"Mr. and Mrs. Hammersmith, if I could have a few minutes of your time, please?" John said from the doorway.

"Good thing we didn't get food," Leonard muttered as he put his drink down. Liza carried hers with her as she followed the men out of the room.

"Get something to eat," Mary urged Bessie. Bessie walked over to the table and filled a plate for herself. Everything looked delicious. When she sat back down, she looked over at Mary.

"Who prepared all of this?" she asked her friend.

"Our chef has been cooking all day, since we have so many guests to feed. I just asked her to turn everything into finger foods and pile things onto plates, that's all," Mary replied.

"Well, she's done a good job," Bessie told her. "Everything is very tasty."

"Good. I believe she's trying to outdo Andy when she gets the chance."

Bessie shrugged. "It isn't that good."

Mary smiled. "I didn't think it would be."

By the time everyone had eaten, John had finished his latest round of questioning. Bessie watched anxiously to see what he was going to do next as he rejoined the group in the sitting room.

"I'm sorry to have kept you all for so long," he began. "I'm hugely grateful to Mrs. Quayle for providing you with refreshments while you waited. We've walked through the entire evening now, and then we were interrupted by the discovery of the secret door. What I was going to ask before that happened was whether anyone noticed anything in our reconstruction that was different to the actual party evening."

Bessie looked around the room. No one spoke for several minutes.

"I find it hard to believe that no one tripped on any of the chairs or ran into the person in front of them or anything like that," John said.

"We were all sort of shuffling up against one another," Madison said. "I kept my hand on the person in front of me the whole time."

"Did you now?" John asked, "and did the person behind you keep his hand on you?"

"I don't remember," Madison told him.

"I'd appreciate it if everyone could go back and sit on the chairs for a moment," John said.

There was a great deal of grumbling as people put down their plates and made their way back towards the chairs. As they went, John spoke again.

"Richard? What's the name of this house?" he asked in a casual tone.

Richard stopped and stared at John for a minute. "I'm sorry, but I'm not sure I understand the question."

"What's the name of this house?" John repeated himself.

"This house? Its name? This is some sort of trick, isn't it?" Richard said sharply.

"Not at all," John said in a calm voice. "Maybe you'd rather we talk about this away from the others."

"Away? Why would I... You're trying to set me up for something, that's what this is!" Richard all but shouted.

"Not at all," John assured him. "I'd just like to talk to you for a minute."

"About the name of the house? That doesn't make sense. Ask Elizabeth; she knows how to say the name. It's nothing to do with me. I'm not saying another word without my solicitor present."

John raised an eyebrow. "That seems a rather extreme reaction to a simple question," he said mildly.

"It isn't a simple question, though, is it? You're trying to trick me in some way. I'm not sure how, but that's what you're doing," Richard said loudly.

"Let's go back to the station and talk there," John suggested. "You can ring your solicitor if you'd prefer, once we get there."

"Oh, I'll ring him. And I won't say another word until he arrives," Richard said firmly.

"In that case, I suggest we leave the reconstruction there for tonight," John said. "Hugh, can you please make note of exactly where everyone was sitting when they were in their row, before they began walking around? Once you've done that, everyone is free to go."

"Richard, are you okay?" Madison asked.

"I'll be fine," Richard replied. "Once the inspector gets over the ridiculous notion that I had anything to do with that horrible man's death."

"That's my father you're talking about," Susan snapped.

"I'm sorry, but he was a horrible man," Richard told her. "He was sneaky and manipulative and he was a blackmailer."

Bessie glanced at John. As far as she knew, that particular fact wasn't common knowledge.

"If you'd like to come with me, please," John said to Richard.

"Can you arrest him for saying such horrible things about my father?" Susan demanded.

"Not since they're all true," Richard laughed bitterly.

Hugh took a step closer to the man, placing himself between Richard and Susan.

Undeterred, Susan took a step to the right and shouted at Richard. "You seem to know a lot about my father, considering you only met him the night he died. Or did you know him before you got here? Have you neglected to mention that little fact to the police?"

"I didn't know him," Richard said quickly, his face red. "I didn't know him or anything about him. But I've heard plenty since he died."

"Really?" Sean interjected. "Because I haven't heard anything at all."

Richard looked over at him and then sighed. "It's all just a conspiracy," he said loudly. "You've all gone together and decided to accuse me of murder, that's what's happening here. Next you'll be lying about my being in the line while the lights were out."

"I don't remember your hand on my back for the entire time," Madison said softly.

"Of course you don't, because you're part of the conspiracy," Richard shouted. "Everyone can say what they like. I know what really happened that night."

"Maybe you should tell me all about it," John suggested. "Down at the station," he added quickly.

"I can tell you now," Richard said. "The lights went out and I started in the circle with the others. Somehow I got confused and wandered away from the group. Before I knew what was happening, Mr. Rhodes grabbed my arm and dragged me into the study. He started threatening me and waving a knife around. He was desperately drunk, of course, and before I could think what to do, he suddenly fell over. When he hit the floor, he landed on the knife that was still in his hand."

John nodded. "Let's go down to the station. You can tell me the whole story there."

Richard shook his head. "You aren't going to believe me, are you? You'll make out like I killed the man, but it wasn't like that at all."

"I'm prepared to hear your story and then compare it to the evidence," John told him, "but this isn't the place for this discussion."

Hugh took another step closer to the man. Richard looked around the room, a desperate look in his eyes. As Hugh moved closer again, he started shaking his head. "No, I won't," he said firmly.

As Hugh's hand closed over Richard's arm, Richard twisted away. He raced across the room and ran out the door with both Hugh and John right behind him. Mary was on her feet, starting after them, but George stopped her.

"Let the police handle it," he said softly as he pulled Mary into a hug.

Bessie felt a tear slide down her face as she watched Mary bury her face in George's chest. Elizabeth was crying on Andy's shoulder and many of the others looked shaken and upset. Susan had dropped into a chair and was sobbing into her hands.

Picking up a tissue box, Bessie crossed to the girl and put her hand on Susan's back. After a moment, Susan lifted her head and took a tissue. Before she spoke, John walked back into the room.

"We've had to ring for an ambulance," he said in his senior policeman's voice. "I'll need additional statements from everyone."

No one complained this time. Instead, everyone waited in silence as John spoke with Michael and Mona first. Hugh walked back into the great room a short time later. Bessie knew him well enough to be able to tell that he'd been shaken by what had happened as well. She gave him an encouraging smile, which he acknowledged with a nod.

"I've sent Mr. Higgins and Ms. Kelly home," John announced when he walked back in a short while later. "If I could speak to Mr. and Mrs. Hammersmith next, they'll be able to leave when we're done as well. Then I'll work my way through those of you who are staying here."

Bessie wasn't sure where that left her, but she didn't say anything. If John wanted to leave her for last, that was his business.

"Is it okay if people have more food?" Mary asked.

"Yes, that's fine," John said in a tired voice.

"You should take a plate back to the interview room with you," Mary suggested. "Young Constable Watterson should eat as well."

"The constable is welcome to have something," John said, nodding at Hugh. "I may get something later. Right now I'd rather get through these interviews."

Liza and Leonard followed John out of the room while Hugh put a few things onto a plate. Bessie frowned when she noticed how little he'd taken. Hugh must be very upset if he wasn't eating. The room was oddly silent as people moved around, getting drinks or more food. No one looked at anyone else or spoke. Eventually Bessie couldn't take it any more.

She got up and crossed to Hugh. "Are you okay?" she asked.

He looked surprised and then nodded. "I'm fine," he assured her. "It was all just a bit of a shock."

Bessie wanted to ask him what had happened to Richard, but she knew he couldn't tell her, especially not in front of the others. Instead, she gave him a hug and then crossed to the bar where Susan was slowly sipping a drink.

"Are you okay?" she asked the girl.

"I don't know," Susan replied. "I think I'm in shock, really. I knew that my father had been murdered, but, well, I hadn't really thought about what that meant. I hadn't really considered the idea that someone killed him, someone in this house. I can't imagine why Richard did it. I can't believe that he knew my father."

"That's for the police to work out," Bessie said. "First they'll have to establish his guilt, though."

"I don't think there's any doubt that he's guilty of something," Susan said. "The police will have to work out exactly what, of course."

Bessie got herself a glass of water and then walked over to the food table. Elizabeth and Andy were standing together, staring at the display.

"It isn't as good as yours, but it's all quite edible," Bessie told them.

Andy smiled at her. "I'm not really hungry," he said.

"I don't think I'll ever want to eat again," Elizabeth said with a dramatic sigh. She glanced at Andy and then flushed. "I mean, that was just horrible to witness," she said in a low voice.

"It was, indeed," Bessie agreed.

"Mr. Caine, I can talk to you next if you're anxious to get away," John said from the doorway.

"I do want to get away," Andy said. Elizabeth frowned. "Will you let me take Elizabeth with me when I go?" he asked.

"Certainly, why don't you both come and talk to me together," John said. "Once we're finished, you'll be free to go."

Elizabeth walked over and had a word with her mother before she and Andy walked out of the room. Bessie filled a plate, more for something to do than because she was hungry, and then rejoined Mary on the couch.

"I've told Elizabeth that she can stay with Andy tonight," Mary said softly. "She knows I'd rather have her here when she has guests, but after everything that happened, I think it might be better if she had a break from them."

"Perhaps John will let them go as well," Bessie suggested, "and maybe there will be room on tonight's late flight to London."

"If Inspector Rockwell is willing to let them leave, I'll charter them a plane back," Mary said.

Bessie hid a smile. Clearly Mary was tired of playing host to Elizabeth's friends.

Ernest was the first of Elizabeth's friends to talk with John. When he walked back into the room, he was smiling. "The inspector has given me permission to leave," he told everyone. "He's said you'll all be free to leave after he speaks with you as well. I'm going to ring the airport and see about flights back to London."

"Make sure you get me a seat," Norma said as she left the room for her conversation with John.

By the time Norma, Sean, and Madison had finished with John, Ernest had a plane chartered for early the next morning.

"I'm off to pack," Ernest said after he'd shared the news. "We need to be at the airport at six, so everyone should have an early night. Susan, do you want to come with us? There's plenty of room on the plane."

Susan, who was just getting up for her session with John, shook her head. "I really appreciate the offer, but I think I'm going to stay here for another day or two. I want to find out everything I can about what happened to my father." She glanced at Mary. "Don't worry, though, I'll be moving into a hotel tonight, if I can. I may even look up the woman who claims to be my stepmother. We probably have a lot to talk about."

A short while later John walked back into the great room. He looked exhausted as he glanced around the room. "Mr. and Mrs. Quayle, I haven't taken your statements yet," he said.

"Why don't you do it in here, while having something eat," Mary suggested. "We can talk in the corner, away from Bessie, if you prefer."

"That would probably be for the best," John said. At Mary's urging, John put a few things on a plate and then he and Mary and George settled into the corner to have their chat. Bessie felt rather alone as she waited for them to finish. After a few minutes, though, Jonathan joined her.

"He's saving the best for last," he said, nodding towards John as he sat down.

Bessie smiled. "I suppose he's left me for last because he doesn't think I'll be able to contribute anything."

"Are you okay?"

"Me, I'm fine," Bessie said firmly. "Since you're here, tell me how you found the secret door."

"After the ambulance took Vivian away, I had a word with the inspector. They'd had the study under lock and key since the murder, but after Vivian's attack, any evidence that might have been in there was probably gone or contaminated. At least that was the argument I gave the inspector. Fortunately for me, he agreed and told me I could have a try at finding the secret door from inside the study."

"And you managed it," Bessie said. "Congratulations."

"Thanks. I've found quite a few secrets at Thie yn Traie since I've been here, actually."

"One day you'll have to share them all with me," Bessie told him.

"First I should probably share them with Mr. and Mrs. Quayle," the man laughed.

Across the room, John was getting to his feet. His voice carried to Bessie as he spoke. "Thank you for your time. I will probably be in touch again soon."

He walked over to Bessie and offered his arm. "Why don't we go back to your cottage for our conversation?" he asked.

CHAPTER 15

"Tea?" Bessie asked as she and John walked into her cottage a few minutes later.

"No, Mary insisted that I have something to eat and drink. I'm fine," John replied.

"Can you tell me what happened to Richard?"

"He ran off and used another secret door to get outside. We had a man stationed behind the house, though. When Richard saw the constable outside, he, well, he jumped off the cliff."

Bessie shuddered. "You said you needed an ambulance. Please tell me he survived the fall."

"He did, but he's in pretty bad shape. He's been taken to Noble's. The last update was critical but stable."

"What about Vivian?"

"She's in serious condition, but expected to survive. It may be some time before we can ascertain whether any serious damage has been done to her."

"And you're convinced that Richard killed Jerome Rhodes?"

"He certainly showed that he had insider knowledge of Thie yn Traie," John replied.

"I wonder how he acquired that."

"I suspect we'll find that out when we investigate his past further. Now that we only have one suspect to consider, things should move fairly quickly."

"And everyone else can go home," Bessie sighed.

"I wasn't going to be able to keep them much longer anyway. Several of Elizabeth's friends had solicitors ringing up to demand that they be allowed to leave. I believe the chief constable would have insisted on letting them go tomorrow regardless."

The pair talked through the evening, with John taking notes while Bessie recounted her version of events. "You were there, of course," she concluded.

"Yes, but I need to be sure that everyone's account is in agreement, especially since Richard is critically injured."

"It will be interesting to hear what you find out," Bessie said as she walked the man to the door. She hoped that the subtle hint would be enough to get him to visit again once the investigation was complete.

A few days later, as Bessie returned from her morning walk, she saw John's car parked outside Treoghe Bwaane. She picked up her pace and met the man as he climbed out from behind the steering wheel.

"Moghrey mie," she said brightly.

"Moghrey mie," he replied.

"I can make tea or coffee," Bessie offered as she let them into the cottage.

"I don't really have time for either," John said apologetically. "I just wanted to share a few things with you that will be in the local paper later today."

"Sit down," Bessie suggested.

John took a chair at the kitchen table. "I suppose I could manage a cuppa," he said.

Bessie put the kettle on and then piled biscuits onto a plate. By the time she'd put them on the table, the kettle had boiled.

"Okay, what's the skeet?" she asked once the tea was made and she'd sat down across from the man.

"Richard is going to make it, but he may be paralyzed from the waist down," John said sadly. "He broke his back when he fell."

"How awful!" Bessie exclaimed.

"It's terribly sad, especially considering that he may well be spending the rest of his life in prison."

"He did kill Mr. Rhodes, then?"

"Yes, he's confessed to that and to the attack on Vivian."

"Was he being blackmailed?"

"He was," John sighed. "Not that that justifies his killing the man, but all things considered, I do have some sympathy for him. Less so for the attack on Vivian, of course."

"Do you know why he was being blackmailed?"

"Apparently Richard used the pub that Mr. Rhodes frequented as a meeting place. He used to meet unsuitable women there, but also met a drug dealer there on occasion."

"My goodness, he seemed like such a nice young man," Bessie said.

"From what he's said, I believe he was under a great deal of pressure at work and that he's rather shy. I think he had trouble meeting women and found that, um, paid companions were simply easier. He also found that drugs made coping with the pressure easier, although I don't believe he was using regularly."

"And then Mr. Rhodes started blackmailing him?"

"When Mr. Rhodes met everyone on Saturday evening, he recognised Richard. When he had a chance to speak to him, apparently Mr. Rhodes suggested that he might just tell everyone what he knew unless Richard wanted to buy his silence. He and Richard were going to talk after the party."

"But instead, Richard killed him."

"Richard knew the Pierce family. Apparently when he was younger he used to spend time with the two boys, Daniel and Donald. They told him all about Thie yn Traie and its secret doors, passages, and tunnels."

"There are tunnels?" Bessie gasped.

John chuckled. "I'm going to have to talk to Mr. and Mrs. Quayle. I don't think they have any idea."

"So when the lights went out, he found his way to the secret door and let himself into the study?"

"Yes. He took a torch with him and switched it on once he was in the room. He claims he just went in to talk to the man and that Mr. Rhodes was passed out in the chair when he found him."

"So he stabbed him? How horrible."

"Richard claims he tried to talk to the man, but he couldn't get anything sensible out of him. He says he was worried that once Mr. Rhodes rejoined the party he'd start talking about everything because he was so drunk. Richard also insists that the knife was on the desk in the study. He suggested that Mr. Rhodes brought it with him for protection or something."

Bessie shivered. "And then he needed it, but it was used against him."

John nodded. "The solicitors are going to have a tough time working all of this out, but that's their job. I've done my part."

"What about the attack on Vivian?"

"Vivian actually accidentally tripped into the skirting boards and opened the secret door. Richard happened to be behind her and saw it happen. He was convinced that once the secret door was found, we would know he was guilty, so he hit her over the head to keep her quiet. He insists that he didn't mean to hurt her, but I'm not sure I believe that."

"How is she?"

"Making a slow recovery. She doesn't remember the attack or anything about that day, but otherwise she seems to be doing well. Her parents have had her transferred to a specialist clinic in London now."

Bessie nodded. "It's all incredibly sad."

"Yes, it is. There are times when I question my career choice."

Bessie patted his arm. "You're an excellent police inspector and the island is a much safer place with you here doing your job. I hope you aren't seriously considering doing something else?"

"Not really, but cases like this are difficult."

"I'm sorry," Bessie said.

"Anyway, I can't quit now, not when Andrew Cheatham is coming to visit next month. I'm looking forward to sharing a few cold cases with him."

"Andrew Cheatham? The man we met at Lakeview Holiday Park? He's coming to the island?"

John frowned. "I assumed you knew. Oh, dear, maybe he was planning to surprise you."

"Maybe he was hoping to avoid me," Bessie countered.

"Oh, no, I'm sure that's not the case. He rang me to check on where you lived and to get the number for the holiday cottages. He specifically said he was looking forward to seeing you again."

Bessie sat back in her chair, not sure what she was feeling. She'd enjoyed getting to know Andrew when they'd been on holiday, but the thought of seeing him again made her feel slightly ill. Or maybe she was just a little bit excited.

"I'm sorry if I've spoiled the surprise," John said.

"I'm glad you have," Bessie replied.

GLOSSARY OF TERMS

Manx to English

- **moghrey mie** - good morning

House Names – Manx to English

- **Thie yn Traie** - Beach House
- **Treoghe Bwaane** - Widow's Cottage

English to American Terms

- **advocate** - Manx title for a lawyer (solicitor)
- **aye** - yes
- **bin** - garbage can
- **biscuits** - cookies
- **bonnet (car)** - hood

- **boot (car)** - trunk
- **car park** - parking lot
- **chemist** - pharmacist
- **chips** - french fries
- **cuddly toys** - stuffed animals
- **cuppa** - cup of tea (informally)
- **dear** - expensive
- **dosh** - money
- **estate agent** - real estate agent (realtor)
- **fairy cakes** - cupcakes
- **fancy dress** - costume
- **fizzy drink** - soda (pop)
- **ginger (hair)** - red
- **holiday** - vacation
- **jumper** - sweater
- **lie in** - sleep late
- **midday** - noon
- **pavement** - sidewalk
- **plait (hair)** - braid
- **primary school** - elementary school
- **pudding** - dessert
- **skeet** - gossip
- **skirting boards** - baseboards
- **starters** - appetizers
- **supply teacher** - substitute teacher
- **telly** - television
- **torch** - flashlight
- **trolley** - shopping cart
- **windscreen** - windshield

OTHER NOTES

The emergency number in the UK and the Isle of Man is 999, not 911.

CID is the Criminal Investigation Department of the Isle of Man Constabulary (Police Force).

When talking about time, the English say, for example, "half seven" to mean "seven-thirty."

With regard to Bessie's age: UK (and IOM) residents get a free bus pass at the age of 60. Bessie is somewhere between that age and the age at which she will get a birthday card from the Queen. British citizens used to receive telegrams from the ruling monarch on the occasion of their one-hundredth birthday. Cards replaced the telegrams in 1982, but the special greeting is still widely referred to as a telegram.

When island residents talk about someone being from "across," they mean that the person is from somewhere in the United Kingdom (across the water).

Someone who is "sleeping rough" is generally living outdoors (and homeless).

Your "local" is the pub you visit frequently, usually close to your home.

I often get asked for Bessie's shortbread recipe, so I thought I should include it in a book. I hope you all enjoy!

Bessie's Favourite Shortbread

Shortbread is actually really easy to make, which is why it's one of Bessie's favourite treats. Here's my recipe, given to me by a friend, and a few hints...

1 1/4 cups of flour (all-purpose in the US or plain flour in the UK)
   3 Tablespoons of granulated sugar
   4 ounces of butter (Use real butter, it tastes much better.)

Cut the butter into small cubes, but keep it cold until you are ready to use it.
   Mix the flour and sugar together and then cut in the butter until the mixture resembles fine crumbs. Knead it together, and the heat from your hands will start to melt the butter until it all comes together in a smooth ball.

You can shape it into a circle and then cut it into traditional wedges or you can roll or pat it into whatever shape you like. At Christmas, I double the recipe and add a bit of extra butter (to soften the dough slightly) and then put it through a cookie press.

Bake at 325 F or 165 C for about 25 to 30 minutes if in a circle or just about 12 minutes for small pressed cookies. You can sprinkle the tops with sugar if you prefer. Caster sugar is ideal (a fine sugar that is readily available in the UK, but hard to find in the US), but I do use colored sugar at Christmas time.

Bessie adds a little bit of pure vanilla extract to her shortbread, but you can add whatever flavorings you like. Try a bit of lemon or orange zest or some cinnamon and nutmeg (added to the dry ingredients before you add the butter).

I sometimes like to add mini chocolate chips or butterscotch chips after the dough has been kneaded, although the dough can be a bit crumbly, which makes it harder to incorporate additions. (It still tastes wonderful, though! Looks aren't everything!)

ACKNOWLEDGMENTS

Thanks to my editor, Denise, for her continued hard work.

To Kevin, who takes the wonderful photos on the covers of my books.

To my beta readers, who help polish every text.

And to my readers, who are the reason why I keep doing this!

AUNT BESSIE SOLVES

RELEASE DATE: OCTOBER 19, 2018

Aunt Bessie solves murders with alarming regularity.

Elizabeth Cubbon, known as Bessie to nearly everyone, has been caught up in far too many murder investigations lately. When a friend from the UK, police inspector Andrew Cheatham, comes to visit, she can't help but take an interest in a cold case he mentions, however.

Aunt Bessie solves his case, or at least presents him with an intriguing new avenue to investigate.

Andrew is excited about the possible solution to the thirty-year-old case, but he's also eager to spend some time working on a cold case that is puzzling Inspector John Rockwell.

Can Aunt Bessie solve both cases and still find time to show Andrew around the island she loves?

ALSO BY DIANA XARISSA

Aunt Bessie Assumes

Aunt Bessie Believes

Aunt Bessie Considers

Aunt Bessie Decides

Aunt Bessie Enjoys

Aunt Bessie Finds

Aunt Bessie Goes

Aunt Bessie's Holiday

Aunt Bessie Invites

Aunt Bessie Joins

Aunt Bessie Knows

Aunt Bessie Likes

Aunt Bessie Meets

Aunt Bessie Needs

Aunt Bessie Observes

Aunt Bessie Provides

Aunt Bessie Questions

Aunt Bessie Remembers

Aunt Bessie Questions

Aunt Bessie Solves

The Isle of Man Ghostly Cozy Mysteries

Arrivals and Arrests

Boats and Bad Guys

Cars and Cold Cases

Dogs and Danger

Encounters and Enemies

Friends and Frauds

Guests and Guilt

Hop-tu-Naa and Homicide

The Markham Sisters Cozy Mystery Novellas

The Appleton Case

The Bennett Case

The Chalmers Case

The Donaldson Case

The Ellsworth Case

The Fenton Case

The Green Case

The Hampton Case

The Irwin Case

The Jackson Case

The Kingston Case

The Lawley Case

The Moody Case

The Norman Case

The Isle of Man Romance Series

Island Escape

Island Inheritance

Island Heritage

Island Christmas

ABOUT THE AUTHOR

Diana grew up in Northwestern Pennsylvania and moved to Washington, DC after college. There she met a wonderful Englishman who was visiting the city. After a whirlwind romance, they got married and Diana moved to the Chesterfield area of Derbyshire to begin a new life with her husband. A short time later, they relocated to the Isle of Man.

After over ten years on the island, it was time for a change. With their two children in tow, Diana and her husband moved to suburbs of Buffalo, New York. Diana now spends her days writing about the island she loves.

She also writes mystery/thrillers set in the not-too-distant future as Diana X. Dunn and middle grade and Young Adult books as D.X. Dunn.

Diana is always happy to hear from readers. You can write to her at:

Diana Xarissa Dunn
PO Box 72
Clarence, NY 14031.
Find Diana at: DianaXarissa.com
E-mail: Diana@dianaxarissa.com